Bethany Riehl

Facebook.com/BDRiehl

Cover Design by : Blue Azalea Design
(http://www.blueazaleadesign.com)

Scripture taken from the NEW AMERICAN STANDARD BIBLE(R), Copyright (C) 1960,1962,1963,1968,1971,1972,1973,1975,1977,1995 by The Lockman Foundation. Used by permission.

ISBN: n/a (ebook)

ISBN-13: 978-1545480212

ISBN-10: 1545480214

Dedication

For my Mama. If I could, I would give you both of my lungs. But for now, I'll give you the shells of all my peanuts. I love you.

"The mind of a man plans his way,

But the LORD directs his steps."

Proverbs 16:9

Chapter One

I cannot believe I let Lucy talk me into this.

Amelia Howard slanted an annoyed look at her sister. Five years her junior and the baby of the family, Lucy read the familiar glance and flashed an impish grin. She looped her arm with Amelia's.

"Oh, come on. You love me," Lucy purred.

A snort. "Right. Like a stubbed toe I love you. Remind me again why I need to be here?" Amelia asked quietly as they shuffled forward in line. Half a dozen couples stretched two-by-two in front of them, staggered up the flight of narrow wooden stairs. She kept her eyes fixed on the spiked heels of the woman in front of them.

If I don't make eye contact with anyone, maybe I can get out of here with my dignity intact.

Lucy sighed. "Because, dear sister, this reunion will be good for you; you need to remember your youth. You were a rock star in high school. And, let's be honest: lately you've become…how do you say? An old lady."

"Saying something mean in a French accent doesn't make it cute, Lucy."

The couple in front of them turned their heads inward toward each other ever so slightly, no doubt trying to catch a glimpse of the rock-star-turned-old-lady-student from their high school days.

Nope, there went her dignity.

Amelia blushed and gripped Lucy's arm. "I was by no means any kind of star in high school. And you mean Old Maid," Amelia added dryly, her voice low.

"No, I mean old lady. You are the only one who thinks in terms of marriage all the time. This is good for you, trust me."

Amelia rolled her eyes toward the ceiling at Lucy's exaggerated sing-song tone.

The early summer evening would have been better enjoyed outside at a nearby restaurant in Amelia's opinion. Instead, they waited on creaky stairs leading to an event center above her favorite pizza place in Downtown Boise. The aroma of spicy sausage, garlic, and tomatoes made her stomach cramp.

I bet they have tables available on their patio. Maybe I could talk Lucy into sister night with a lovely plate of cheesy carbs instead of making small talk with people I haven't cared to be in contact with for the last ten years.

Scratch that. There was *one* person Amelia wished she could see.

Who am I kidding? He would never come to something like this.

Still…it was a possibility. Her mouth turned to cotton at the thought. At the memory of the last time she saw him.

The couple in front of them stepped forward and the sisters were finally able to move off of the stairway. The wide hallway before the ballroom was decorated with a blue and silver balloon arch. A long table covered with linen stood like a soldier before the door, daring anyone to cross without first checking in. Lucy pulled Amelia close to scan the name tags scattered across the surface. Two women that looked vaguely familiar were seated behind the table and watched them expectantly. Amelia quietly gave her name.

She looked over the names, wondering how many of her former classmates would actually come for the ten-year reunion. The number of remaining nametags gave no indication of who could be inside. She fleetingly looked for his name, but didn't see it. Not that that meant anything.

Stop it, Amelia. Why do you want to see that jerk, anyway?

Her mind flashed to a hot summer day. To air weighted with tension. The feel of cold water, warm lips and—

Seriously, stop it.

"Oh my goodness! Amelia Howard?" one of the women squealed, her voice rising an octave higher with each word, drawing the attention of anyone within a city block.

Amelia peered closer at her face, but the name of the woman evaded her.

Sure, I can remember the names of every one my students for the last five years, but this woman that I graduated with?

Amelia narrowed her eyes. *Nope. Nothing.*

She forced a wide smile and attempted a nonchalant glance at the plastic nametag clipped to the woman's rhinestone studded blouse.

"Sarah?" The fog around her memory cleared. "Sarah Hansen? Wow, you're so…sparkly," Amelia commented lamely. Flashbacks of a jumpy, bubbly, talkative brunette with braces assaulted her. And glitter eyeshadow. She remembered that those brown eyes had often been all aglow during the glitter eyeshadow trend.

That's right. Sarah Hansen. Nice girl. Loud, but nice. And—well—sparkly.

"Oh, it's Brown now. I married Kirk. Remember him? Kirk Brown? Class that graduated before us? Well, he and I are married." She extended her left hand and wiggled all five fingers to flash a large diamond ring as proof. "Five kids in six years. So I never sleep, you know what I mean? The doctor said we're so fertile that if I want to sleep anytime soon we should get fixed, but I'm just not sure that's the step we should take." Her words came out in a rush, tumbling over one another in their race to overshare.

Lucy squeezed Amelia's arm to pull her down the table.

"Sis, I found your nametag." Her voice garbled with barely contained laughter.

"Well, Sarah, it's, um, good to see you. And, uh, good luck with that sleeping-or-getting-fixed thing." She offered a lame little wave and turned to her sister. Lucy pinched her arm, avoiding eye contact. Amelia swallowed a yelp and followed Lucy into the event center.

The Gathering was a quaint reception hall and catering company located in the heart of Downtown. Walls of red brick, high ceilings, exposed pipes and beams made for a charming urban setting. There were twenty or more tall round tables staggered along one side of the room, encouraging guests to circle up for conversation. Bistro lights were strung in a zig zag pattern across the top half of the room, their muted glow enchanting. Long tables decorated with linens of their school colors lined the wall adjacent to the tables, adorned with salads, fruit and cheese platters, crackers and petite sandwiches. Large glass beverage dispensers lined the end of the table, small chalkboard signs labeling each: lemonade, iced tea, and mint infused water. A DJ was nestled behind a table in the corner, cranking out songs that were popular in their high school days. A waiter walked by them with a tray of shrimp skewers and Amelia reached for one.

"Amelia, what are you doing? You're allergic to shellfish."

"Yes, I know. But if I choke just one of these puppies down, you will have no choice but to rush me to the ER. Trust me, it's worth it if it means I won't have to go through any more conversations like that one," she pointed the skewer in the direction of the fertile Sarah-Hansen-Now-Brown.

Lucy gingerly took the skewer away from her sister and tossed it in a nearby garbage can.

"Come on, let's get some lemonade and say hello to people you actually spent time with. It will be good. You'll see," she said, tugging on her arm.

Amelia groaned, but obliged. There was truly no arguing with Lucy once she set her mind to something. The youngest of four children born to their parents, Lucy had entered her world commanding it. She was sunshine and joy, and she knew it. Amelia's position as the oldest often left her rolling her eyes at what Lucy had been able to get away with, but even she was more lenient and agreeable to Lucy than their brothers between them.

However, after twenty minutes of uncomfortable small talk with older versions of people she had barely known ten years before, Amelia was not feeling so agreeable. When another classmate was finished showing off pictures of her family on her phone, Amelia excused herself to go to the bathroom. She dragged Lucy with her and punched her in the arm once they were in the privacy of the small room.

"Ow," Lucy protested, rubbing the offended extremity. "What was that for?"

"Lucy, do you know why I don't like reunions? Because if I wanted to see these people, I could! None of us have moved away," she waved her arm toward the door. "The only person I really hung out with would never come to one of these. And it's not like we would pick right up where we left off. But them? They all get together still. With their families," her voice caught on the last word and she turned to the sink, pretending to check her make-up. "How many more private jokes and weekend get together stories do we have to hear, anyway?"

"I'm sorry, Sis. I really thought *someone* would be single and you would see that you're not the only one." Lucy winced, realizing how un-helpful her comment was.

Amelia took a deep breath. "I don't know what's wrong with me. I love my job, I love my life…" her voice trailed, wondering if she was telling the truth. "But, good golly, the people in my class sure went on to procreate, didn't they?"

"And they are *proud of it*," Lucy muttered. She scrunched her nose. "I'm sorry, Amelia. This was a bad idea. We can sneak out. I'll even treat you to Chinese on the way home."

"Now you're talkin'," Amelia said, straightening.

They exited the bathroom and turned to leave the hall. Before they rounded the corner, Amelia ran into a hard chest. A *very* hard chest. Strong hands reached out to steady her and Amelia's eyes traveled up tanned forearms, broad shoulders, past a chiseled jaw, gleaming smile and into a familiar pair of dark brown eyes flecked with gold.

"Creed?" she breathed.

Chapter Two

"Amelia?" His eyes crinkled at the corners, melting her insides with their familiarity. She stepped back from his hold, embarrassed. Her arms tingled with memory of the last time they saw each other.

Be cool.

"Wow, Creed. I haven't seen you in forever. It's a relief to run into you here amongst all of these proud parents," she giggled, then cleared her throat. She smoothed her hands over her skirt, and laughed again.

Nailed it.

"Yeah, you, too." He eyed her warily before asking, "So what are you up to these days?"

"Uh, I'm a teacher. Elementary. First grade." Her heart raced. She grinned like an idiot.

Sheesh, Amelia. Did you forget how to speak in full sentences?

But this was *Creed Williams*. How could she stay calm and speak like a composed adult with her heart racing, her throat dry, her knees shaking? He had been her best friend all through high school. Her one and only true crush, although he never knew it. Well, at least not before that one day. No hiding her feelings in that kiss.

Many Taylor Swift country songs had been belted out in her car with Creed as the object of her affection. But to Creed, she was just his friend, his fellow cheesy horror movie fan, and just about the only girl in high school he never dated. Joy bubbled up inside her, remembering how much fun they'd had as teens. She hoped the giddy feeling didn't leak onto her face.

Oh, who are you kidding? You're acting like Olé when he thinks you're taking him on a walk, she thought, picturing the exuberant joy of her golden retriever when she put on her shoes in the morning.

She forced herself to remember that after high school, *after* Creed gave her the best kiss of her life, he went to college, promising her that he would keep in touch. He hadn't. After five unanswered letters, Amelia took the hint and stopped writing. There. That calmed her down.

Almost.

If only she hadn't been reliving that kiss for the last ten years.

"Wow, that's great. My daughter is going into first grade this year," he said, jolting her back to the present.

Daughter? An image of her dog's tail drooping in disappointment flashed through her mind.

"A daughter? Wow, Creed. You procreated." Amelia just about open palmed her forehead when Lucy finally stepped forward to rescue her.

"Creed! It's so good to see you," she said, slicing a worried look at Amelia.

"Whoa, little Lucy?" Creed gave her a side hug and stepped back to look her over. "Last time I saw you was...well, I can't even remember."

"At my graduation."

All of them turned toward a much taller, younger version of Creed. He stepped from behind them into the small circle, his eyes locked on Lucy.

"Chad?" Lucy breathed before he enveloped her in a bear hug.

Amelia shook her head. "I can't believe Chad is all grown up!"

She remembered Creed's younger brother was the same age as Lucy, although she had no recollection of their siblings knowing one another. She did vividly remember that Chad had often followed her and Creed around, driving them crazy.

As Lucy and Chad excitedly talked over one another, she glanced wide-eyed at Creed, "Whoa, I had no idea these two were even friends."

Lucy elbowed Chad in the stomach. "We hung out at camp every summer—"

"And then she went off to college and forgot all about me," Chad interrupted.

Lucy blushed. Amelia knew there was much more to Lucy's story than that.

"Hmmm, that sounds familiar," Amelia commented, slanting a look at Creed, shifting the spotlight from Lucy.

A wave of emotion passed over his face, but Amelia couldn't read it. It seemed Lucy wasn't the only one with painful secrets.

After an awkward stretch of silence, Creed lightly hit the back of his hand against Chad's chest.

"We'd better get back to work."

"Work?" Amelia and Lucy questioned in unison.

"Did you really think I would be here willingly? I'm a photographer and videographer. I was hired to document this magical evening." Creed stretched out his arms and winked as he backed away.

Amelia's cheeks flush with heat. She glanced at Lucy, ready to proclaim that she wasn't exactly enthusiastic about her presence there, either.

9

"I'm his assistant," Chad added before Amelia could say anything.

He cupped one hand against his mouth and whispered dramatically, "And by assistant, I mean that I'm here to protect him from crazy ex-girlfriends-turned-soccer-moms armed with pictures of their many, many children."

Amelia and Lucy laughed as he backed away, then fell into silence, both lost in their own thoughts and memories. Suddenly neither woman was interested in leaving early. They found a table just as the DJ announced that the organizer of the event had an announcement. Fertile Sarah-Was-Walker-Now-Brown took the mic and ran through a list of people to thank for helping her to put the evening together. She held up a stack of envelopes secured together with a rubber band and smiled.

"I don't know if you remember this, but as our Class President, I asked you all to write down where you saw yourself in ten years, put it in a sealed envelope and give it to me at graduation. I tucked away your letters all those years ago and have them here for you tonight."

The room erupted in groans and cat calls and gales of laughter.

Amelia brightened slightly. She leaned over to whisper to Lucy, "Aww, that's a fun surprise. I don't even remember doing that."

Lucy didn't answer. Amelia turned to find her little sister gazing across the room at Chad. She nearly elbowed her with a snide remark, but noticed Chad was gazing right back. A small smile crept across Lucy's lips and Amelia turned back to the front of the room.

Sarah called out their names one by one and Amelia eagerly accepted her letter when it was time. The envelope felt full. Senior year had been wrought with decisions that had shaped Amelia's life and she couldn't wait to see how much of who she was now would be reflected in those pages.

* * *

Every cell in his body hummed as Creed walked away— once again—from Amelia Howard. And again, he knew that he really didn't have a choice.

One of many regrets in his life was losing contact with the best friend he'd ever had. In fact, it ran a close second to the biggest regret: missing his daughter's first few months of life. Not that he had had any choice in that one.

Lord, You knew she would be here. And somewhere in the back of my mind, I hoped she would be…is this a chance to finally make things right? You know the regret I have carried.

Lost in thought and memories, Creed plucked the camera from a large leather satchel stashed behind a fern in the corner of the room and looped the strap around his neck. He held it up to his face and scanned the room, adjusting the lens to zoom in when he located Amelia and Lucy taking seats at a table on the opposite side of the room. Amelia took a sip of water, her hazel eyes widened in a comical expression as she peered over the rim of the glass at her sister.

He watched her openly with the camera as his cover, admiring the way she'd styled her long auburn hair in waves down her back. A silver bracelet around her thin wrist sparkled beneath the twinkle lights as she slipped a small pink tube out of her purse and applied a light layer of gloss across her full lips. A strange sensation clutched at his chest when Amelia pressed her shimmering lips together, her brow furrowed. He remembered those lips. Far too well. She was even more beautiful than he remembered. The camera gave a soft "click" as he captured her laughing at something Lucy said.

"What'cha lookin' at?" Chad's warm breath tickled his ear. Creed jumped and dropped the camera to his chest.

He slugged his kid brother in the arm. "Not cool, man."

Chad gave a cheeky grin and checked on the video camera they had pointed at the makeshift stage at the front of the room. Satisfied with the placement, he stepped back and crossed his arms over his chest.

"So, how long has it been since you've seen Amelia?"

Creed let out a puff of air. "Not since I left for college."

Chad whistled low.

"Does she know about—"

The DJ stepped onto the stage, cutting Chad short. Creed took the opportunity to focus on work and try to shake Amelia from his mind. He took a series of shots of Sarah on stage as well some of his former classmates accepting their letters.

He took five of Amelia receiving hers. So much for keeping her out of his head. Now she filled his SD card.

When Creed's name was called, he was surprised. Taking the time to write a letter to his future self and give it to Sarah certainly wasn't something he thought his eighteen-year-old self would have done. He folded the thin envelope and shoved it in his back pocket, then moved around the room, squatting, bending, twisting to get the just the right shot of everyone peeking into their past. Friends swapped letters, laughing; couples sat quietly with their heads together, sharing old dreams.

Creed couldn't help it—he made his way to Amelia who sat alone hunched over a small stack of papers. He glanced around the room and found Lucy and Chad deep in conversation near the video camera. Turning back to Amelia, he lifted the camera and framed her in the shot.

Her teeth pulled at her bottom lip while her long fingers gripped the sides of the letter as if her life depended on it. The shutter of the camera startled Amelia and she glanced up, eyes shimmering in the muted glow from the bistro lights. Creed felt his lips curl up in the corners. What a poised, beautiful woman Amelia had grown into. A thought came to him and he glanced his eyes off of her left hand— no ring.

Doesn't mean she's not taken, Williams.

He cleared his throat and gestured to the papers. "So, did all of your dreams come true?"

A shadow passed over her face before she quickly folded and stuffed them back in the envelope. Her hands trembled slightly.

"Yup. Teacher—check. Independent—check. Close to my family—check," she sniffed.

Creed couldn't turn away from the sadness welling in her eyes. He immediately felt compelled to fix it somehow.

"Look, Amelia, I—"

"Sorry, here I am. I didn't mean to abandon you. We can go now," Lucy interrupted, her face flushed.

Amelia stood quickly. "Great." Her eyes avoided his, but as she walked by, she squeezed his arm gently.

"It was really good to see you, Creed. I hope your daughter enjoys first grade," her lips curled upward around the words but something shifted in her glance. Seeing her pain, though not comprehending it, Creed stepped back to let her pass.

"It was really good to see you, too," he answered, but she didn't seem hear him.

Why are you just standing there, dummy? Go ask for her number.

He took one step before a hand reached out to curl around his arm.

"Creed, did you get a shot of Emily Scarsdale and her husband?" Sarah asked, stepping beside him. "Her prediction for her life came true to a 'T'—down to her husband's job and gender order of their children. Come on," she tugged his arm.

Creed allowed himself to be pulled away, once again, from Amelia Howard.

It wasn't until the reunion came to a close that Creed remembered the envelope in his back pocket. He packed everything in his trunk and bid Chad goodnight before he sat in the front seat of his car and read the single sentence by the glow of the streetlight above him.

He looked up, eyes unfocused. Fifteen words scratched out a decade ago pierced him.

"You're an idiot," he muttered to himself before he started the car and drove to his sister's house to pick up his daughter.

Chapter Three

"Oh my goodness, you have to calm down!" Lucy gingerly lifted two steaming mugs of peppermint tea from Amelia's kitchen counter and walked them two steps into the living room.

Amelia sat on her worn microfiber couch, a hand-me-down from when their parents upgraded their living room, legs tucked under her with the letter in her hands.

"But, Lucy, everything about my life is so pathetic compared to this letter!" Amelia cried. "It's all here: my hopes and dreams to travel the world and do exciting things. I wanted to be a missionary in the rainforest somewhere. Instead, every choice I have made—from my career to where I live to where I go to church—*everything* about my life is because of *him*."

"Who? Creed? Because *that* is who we should be talking about." Lucy perched on the edge of the couch and set both mugs on the coffee table.

"No, because of C.B.," she muttered.

If Lucy's curled upper lip hadn't spoken of her disgust, the low pitch of the, "Oh," she muttered in response certainly did. It was no secret that Amelia's family was not fond of her almost-husband from college.

The clock above Amelia's kitchen sink echoed into the silence.

"I thought you were over all that." Lucy said.

Amelia stood without a word and walked slowly to her bookshelf, running slender fingers along the spines of almost a dozen books before stopping to pluck out a blush pink journal.

"I thought so, too," she admitted as she reclaimed her seat on the couch. She thumbed through a few pages, her eyes skimming the loopy handwriting before she found what she was looking for.

"I have verses quoted in there, excerpts from books I read on dating and not dating. I started this after C.B. broke things off and since then I have held every decision I make up to the ideas I documented here."

She cleared her throat and read aloud, " '*So perhaps one question you should ask yourself is if the writer of Proverbs 31 intended for us to live our lives honoring our spouse* now, *even before we've met them? What better way to love our future husbands than to enter into that promise with no regrets?*' "

Lucy titled her head at her sister and lifted one shoulder. "Okay, so what's so weird about that? She's talking about purity, right? You and I both know what an important thing it is to save ourselves for marriage."

"Yes, but I took it further than that. I took that to mean that I should keep my future husband in mind with *every* decision I make as a single woman. That essentially I should live as if I'm already married to him. I planned my life around this non-existent man. All because things with my college boyfriend didn't work out and his mom said some mean stuff. I'm such an idiot!"

"Oh, I doubt that's true, Amelia. I remember that C.B.'s family was a little…stiff. And that when you were talking engagement you changed your major because they encouraged you to. That doesn't mean your whole life is pathetic. It worked out in the end, didn't it?"

"No, Lucy. You don't get it." Amelia let her sister take the journal and, needing something to hold, she wrapped her fingers around the warm mug and sipped the tea. The mint soothed her senses slightly, but not enough.

16

"My other journals?"—she swept a hand toward the full bookshelves— "Full of letters to my future spouse. C.B. said that being a missionary wasn't practical, that it was the worst choice I could make for my future marriage. I became a teacher to make life with a family easier; so I could have the same schedule as my kids. I have lived minimally in this teeny apartment and saved most of my paycheck for all of these years so that if we wanted a house right away we would have a healthy nest egg. I have avoided friendships with men because I didn't want to dishonor my husband. Don't ask me how I planned to meet him that way, though," Amelia added dryly. She rolled her eyes at herself and Lucy suppressed a giggle.

"Let's see, what else? I love cats but never got one because I know most men don't like cats. Because *C.B.* didn't like cats."

"But you're forgetting that C.B. was a cold, emotionless idiot. And you have Olé who is ten times better than any cat," Lucy interjected.

Olé, hearing his name, lifted his chin from his front paws and tilted his head at Lucy, tail thumping against the floor.

Amelia leaned down to where he lay next to her feet and scratched his head. "That's true. But, Lucy, I've done all of my living in anticipation of getting married. What if I never do? What if I don't actually want to be a teacher? What if I want to buy a house on my own? What if I want to splurge for once and go on vacation to Europe or Hawaii?"

"I'll go with you." Lucy grinned and wiggled her eyebrows up and down.

Amelia gave a small laugh, then buried her face in her free hand, defeated. "Seriously, Lucy. My whole life feels like one pathetic lie." She took the journal back and glowered at it, miserable.

She opened it again. "All because of these verses: 'An excellent wife, who can find…the heart of her husband trusts in her…she does him good and not evil all the days of her life.' I underlined the last part because C.B.'s mom quoted it to me often. Now I see that maybe that just meant honor him with thoughts and purity. Not every single decision I make until I meet the guy."

Lucy reached out and took the journal away. She snatched up the letter from the coffee table and placed it in Amelia's lap.

"Sis, I know I'm just your kid sister, but hear me out. Maybe this is a good thing. An opportunity. You now see why you've made the choices you have. And they are not bad choices. But if you don't like your life, change it."

Amelia rubbed her nose. "And do what?"

"Whatever the Lord leads you to do. Just listen to Him. Wait for direction. Maybe you've simply been working to honor the wrong person. And, honestly, you are not even thirty yet! You have the rest of your life to do everything in this letter. Or write a new one. Then take it back to your twentieth reunion and show them all."

Amelia snorted. "Right. I'm not going back to that place. Those people are nuts!"

Lucy stayed another hour, talking Amelia down from her ledge of panic before she let herself out. Amelia sat in the quiet, choking up when Olé, sensing her mood, climbed gingerly onto the couch next to her and settled his head in her lap. She stroked his smooth red coat, staring blankly at her bookshelves.

At last she rose, striding purposefully across the room. In no time she found a spiral notebook that was mostly empty and penned the date at the top in sharp letters.

Determined, she wrote a new plan—with no thought of marriage or a family. Just her and the Lord. She moved on from planning and simply poured out her heart: her hopes, her frustrations, and her disappointments. By midnight, Amelia was determined to be different. Do differently, plan differently. She re-read the letter she wrote in high school, drawing inspiration from the young girl that was so full of hope.

Unbidden, thoughts of C.B. and his disdain for her near the end of their relationship tried to interrupt her plans, but she shook them off.

Harder to ignore were images of Creed and his handsome face. She had to rid herself of any thoughts of him. She would most likely never see him again. And, besides, he had a family. She would have to forget about their friendship, their history…the one blissful kiss that she had obviously worked up in her imagination over the years.

The one that sent her spiraling down the boring path she'd found herself on.

She ignored the sharp clench in her chest and wrote on.

Chapter Four

Creed tried to find Amelia on Facebook that night, but without success. Either she didn't have an account or used a fake name.

Other than that, he wasn't sure how to locate her. He contemplated contacting the organizers of the reunion the next day for her information, but was fairly certain that they would not give it to him. Not to mention that such an inquiry would fire up their high school rumor mill. Not that it mattered to him, but it might matter to Amelia.

He woke early the day after the reunion to spend time in the Word as he strived to every day. He struggled to concentrate and after he reread the same page twice without remembering the passage, he shut his Bible and went to the kitchen for another cup of coffee.

He filled his mug—a colorful, clunky, chipped number that had his daughter's handprint painted on one side—and leaned against the counter to sip the dark brew slowly, his thoughts and prayers tangling.

The house was quiet and dark. Moonlight peeked through the slats in the kitchen window blinds, streaking the floor in slits of silver. Soon the chaos of single parenting would carry the rest of the day away at an alarming rate. But before dawn? The house popped with static silence, fresh coffee permeated the air, and if he could only reign his thoughts in, his soul would drink slowly of the truth found in God's holy word.

Lord, I can't concentrate today. Seeing Amelia was...wonderful. But for all I know she has a man in her life or has no interest in hearing from me after the way I ignored her when I went to college.

He palmed the back of his neck, remembering a series of bad decisions in that season of his life. One mistake rolled into another, until he was deliberately living a life that he knew was not honoring to the Lord; and one that he knew would be incredibly disappointing to Amelia.

Creed continued to pray on his way back to the recliner in the corner of his living room. *God, I really blew it. I wouldn't give up Izzie for anything, but I am still ashamed of the actions that conceived her. Seeing Amelia last night brought it all back; the shame and regret.*

Creed opened his Bible again and was finally able to concentrate. He thanked the Lord again for his redemption. For second chances.

"Daddy?" a little voice croaked from the bottom of the stairs, and Creed turned to find a sleepy, messy-haired Izzie squinting into the lamp light.

"Hey, Kiddo. Good morning," Creed smiled. He set his coffee and Bible on the table next to him before opening his arms to her.

Izzie eagerly came forward and climbed onto his lap.

Creed thought back on his life when he first learned that he had a daughter. By the time he was halfway through his college years, he had dated numerous women—none for very long.

Hailey was a woman he had dated briefly his sophomore year, but she had switched schools after summer break. He didn't see her until nearly a year later when she arrived unannounced at his apartment one day with a small baby an infant car seat. He had welcomed her inside, curious about what she wanted. Curiosity escalated into panicked skepticism when Hailey gestured toward the infant and said, "Creed, meet your daughter, Izzie."

A loud, incessant buzzing took over his thoughts, barely masking the frantic crescendo of his heartbeat. His knees buckled and he sat down hard on the couch in his living room, just staring at the sleeping baby. Hailey plunked a large diaper bag down next to him, jolting him from his stupor.

"I can't do this anymore, Creed. I can't afford to do anything or go anywhere. I miss going out with my friends. I miss sleeping. I miss…everything. I'm tired of people telling me what a terrible mother I am. I don't want to do this anymore," Hailey repeated, no emotion registering on her face.

Creed had rolled on waves of emotion through that conversation; disbelief, anger, fear, and confusion, before he crashed back on the shore of disbelief.

"How do you know this kid is even mine?"

"I just do, Creed. Anyway, look at her."

Creed forced himself to look at the baby. He couldn't ignore the strawberry blond hair that matched her brows and soft lashes, or the dusting of freckles across her cheeks and closed lids. Hailey had a point. But even if the baby was his…

"Then why didn't you tell me when you found out you were pregnant? I mean, how old is this baby? Two months? Three?"

"She's three months old."

Hailey ran her fingers back through long, tangled hair. "And I didn't tell you before because I didn't know if I wanted to go through with it, and I knew you were raised in church. I had no idea if you would suddenly get all preachy on me. I know friends that had their boyfriends turn that way once things got too real. I wanted to make my own decision about what happened to my body." Hailey regarded him, then the baby.

"Maybe I made the wrong choice," she said, barely loud enough for him to catch it.

22

Her words made Creed sick.

In the end, Hailey had walked out, leaving Creed to wonder what kind of a mother would leave her child with a stranger. Even more concerning—what did he do now?

Over the course of the next few weeks, Creed's parents traveled across two states to help him figure out what to do. He was able obtain a paternity test which confirmed the child, Izzie, was his. He dropped out of college, moved home with his parents, and had his heart turned inside out by his daughter. Through late nights of Izzie screaming while she adjusted to the right formula—and to him—Creed prayed as he never had before. Over and over the new father found himself on his knees, begging the God he had long ago abandoned for direction.

Izzie's presence changed Creed immediately. He was her father; she needed him. He clung tightly to the Lord, knowing he could never do it on his own.

Almost seven years later, Creed and Izzie lived a simple but full life. His photography business allowed him the flexibility to be home most of the time that she was. His days had morphed into a steady predictability that would have made his younger self squirm.

Seeing Amelia had jolted him from the comfortably stale routine.

"I'm hungry, Daddy," Izzie yawned.

Pulled back to the present, Creed kissed her on top of the head and stood, holding her firmly in his arms. "You are? What do you want me to do about it?" he teased.

"I want Mo Joe's," she declared.

"Oh you do, do you? Hmmm, well are you sure you don't just want cereal from the pantry instead?"

"No way." Izzie scrambled to be free of his hold so that she could jump up and down on the chair. "Mo Joe's! Mo Joe's!" she cheered, though not demandingly.

Her mood—and impish grin—was infectious. He had to admit that breakfast out with his girl sounded like a great start to the weekend. Not to mention Mo Joe's signature donut pancakes dripping with coffee infused syrup.

Dang. Did she know his weakness or what?

He schooled his features into a serious frown and scratched his chin. "Well, I don't know. You might need to sing for a breakfast like that. You know, earn your keep."

Since she was old enough to talk, Izzie and Creed had enjoyed singing a variety of songs together, mostly jazzy classics. He periodically set up his camera equipment to capture the duets, editing them to send to his family. It was a fun hobby, one that he knew he would cherish for years to come. Izzie's range of ability made him one proud Papa.

She twisted her lips and looked up toward the ceiling, thinking. In a far too grown up move that Creed found endearing, Izzie snapped her fingers with an "Aha!"

She began to sing an Ella Fitzgerald song, raising her brows at him when he joined her, knowing he couldn't resist her charming ways. A few lines in and she kissed him on the cheek before running down the hall to change.

Creed chuckled. Yup. He was wrapped around her finger for sure.

Chapter Five

Weeks passed and, though Amelia hadn't made any grand moves toward a new, independent self, she felt lighter, happier. Somehow letting go of her carefully laid plans made her feel in control of her life for the first time in a long while.

She began to dream again.

Her new dreams made her realize how much she had changed over the years. Maybe she wasn't quite ready to be a missionary, but she researched various mission groups and chose a few to support on a monthly basis. She prayed often about how best to serve the Lord with the flexibility being single offered her.

Most of all her thoughts kept circling around the idea of owning her own home. She'd never considered buying one herself, but hadn't she been scrimping all of her years of teaching for a healthy down payment?

When she called the apple orchard to arrange her yearly field trip, the proprietors—Bev and Marty Forrester— told her surprising news: they were selling their old farmhouse. They had recently built a new house on the opposite side of the orchard, but in order to add the new barn they dreamt of, they needed to sell their little house.

"When Marty and I first talked about selling, you came to mind. We always thought it would be there for our kids to enjoy when they came to visit, but it really made more sense to just add a guest suite in our new house. The land surrounding it is about two acres. The house and land have been fenced off and have their own gravel drive next to our private road. I know that's a lot of land…"

Amelia's heart quickened as they talked, imaging Olé having all that land to roam free. She pictured the white farmhouse that sat just back from the entrance of the orchard. She'd always admired its front porch, stone chimney, and white picket fence that surrounded a long ago abandoned garden. Sure, the paint was crumbling and maybe the inside would need work—

"We recently renovated the inside," Bev Forrester was saying. Amelia sat forward. *Focus, girl.* "One of our sons wanted to try his hand at house flipping, so we agreed to split the cost with him. You're welcome to come look at it. We remembered that you always say how much you love our home whenever you're here with your students. Both of us felt compelled to ask you."

Amelia made arrangements to take her father out to the home with her that week, working hard to stamp down the flutters of hope that dawned in her spirit. Bev met them at the house and walked them through, offering a running commentary that Amelia barely heard.

Yes, the porch needed work, but would hold out until the following spring. The fireplace needed to be inspected and cleaned, but her Dad had a friend at church that would be willing to help. The paint was peeling, but that only got Amelia excited to research paint schemes. All of her Pinterest dreaming was going to finally have a place to come to life in this house!

Inside, the home truly was updated. There were a few rooms she would repaint as soon as she could. Yellow kitchens were pretty, but this one was too bright. A soft gray would more adequately tie in the white cabinets and cream quartz countertops. She ran her hand along the cool slab of the long island, amazed at the quality of the kitchen remodel. The white apron sink beneath the large window made her drool.

"This room used to be closed off from the rest of the house," Bev said. "Our son knocked down a few walls to make it open. I guess that's how folk like it nowadays.

Personally, I like having my kitchen tucked out of sight—that way no one who drops in sees my dirty dishes."

Amelia smiled, taking in the open room. It was perfect. The walls were lined with windows, the summer sunshine streaming through the west side and warming patches on the wood floors. The downstairs was small; just the kitchen, the living room, a mud room off of the kitchen, and an area between the kitchen and living room for a table.

A large farm table with benches would go perfect right here.

A narrow set of stairs ran along the back wall and ended in the kitchen near the mudroom.

"I love that the stairs are so open," Amelia commented. She could sand and stain the spindles white to create a more clean, updated look.

"It used to be walled in so you only saw the stairs once you were in front of them. Another thing my son did. I love that change—it makes the room much bigger. And look," Bev opened a door tucked under the place where the stairs met the second floor. "He even converted this closet to a small guest bathroom."

They checked out the upstairs with two modest rooms and a master suite. The bathroom would need updating eventually, but it was by no means urgent.

"Thank you for showing me the house, Bev." She glanced at her Dad who had remained quiet for most of the tour, quietly knocking on walls and turning on faucets. "I'll have an inspector out here if you don't mind and get back to you. The price we discussed seems very fair to me. I'll be in touch."

Bev accepted Amelia's offered handshake. "We're not in a rush, dear. I would rather you have it than some stranger."

The inspection came back with only a few minor fixes and Amelia's dad encouraged her that it would be a great investment. She applied for a loan at her bank and, based on her down payment, was quickly approved.

It had all moved so fast. There was very little planning involved and that was completely out of character for Amelia. Lucy kept reminding her that she had spent enough of her life planning.

"It seems to me, with everything moving as smoothly as it is, that this is the Lord working. Trust Him, Sis. I know you love the Lord, but you told me that you've habitually taken the reigns instead of following His lead. Now's your chance. Don't think about it so much."

Her words rang in Amelia's ears when she signed the papers just before the start of the school year. They pushed up closing when after Amelia confirmed that her landlord—and budget—would be allow her to live in her small apartment until some things could be fixed before moving in.

In all the excitement, her mind buzzed with possibilities for her future. There was virtually no room in her busy life to think about Creed or his daughter or the way her heart ached ever so slightly every time he came to mind.

Virtually.

* * *

"Okay, you can't be mad," Creed's sister Kate said on a Monday morning one week into the school year.

Creed had just settled Izzie in the backseat when he answered the phone.

"Kate, we had a long weekend and I'm just getting ready to drive Izzie to the bus," he answered as he lowered himself into the car.

"Ok, you already sound grumpy and that's not going to help me. I just said you can't be mad," she said in that breathless you-are-gonna-kill-me-but-it-was-totally-not-my-fault tone that she had used since they were kids.

He narrowed his eyes and held the keys in his lap. Maybe he shouldn't be driving for this one. He listened without comment while Kate explained that she had taken a video that he and Izzie had made years ago and entered it into a national contest.

"It's called, *This is You, America*, and the winner gets fifty thousand dollars. *Fifty thousand*, Creed."

"Okaaaay..." he drew out. He glanced at the clock. Shoot. He didn't have time for this. He slid the key into the ignition. "Kate—"

"So the contest folks called me today and told me you're one of the top ten finalists."

Creed stopped short, leaving his keys hanging there. He whistled low.

"Okay, so why would I be mad about that?"

"Well...they told me that your video is currently the most popular of them all, and number one in the 'trending' category on all social media sites."

"What does that mean?"

"It means every gentle-comedy-loving person in our nation and beyond is tweeting, liking, and sharing this to their friends that tweet, like, and share," her voice squeaked out high and airy. Creed could imagine her squinting one eye shut, her face scrunched as if waiting for a blow.

Awareness dawned. "What? You didn't give them my name, did you?"

She exhaled loudly into the mouthpiece. "Of course I did, Creed. I want you to win that money! You've worked so hard for so long to take care of Izzie and raise her by yourself. I'm proud of you. I thought you could start her college fund and then take her to Disneyland or something."

"And what, have you and your family join us?"

Kate hesitated. "Well, I wouldn't have said no."

Creed chuckled in spite of himself, then sobered, rubbing a hand down one side of his face. "Oh, Kate. What have you done?"

"Sorry, Creed," she said, her voice breathy. "I really was trying to do a good thing. And that video of you two is so sweet. I'm not at all surprised that people are sharing it all over."

Creed explained that he needed to hang up so that he could drive Izzie to the bus stop and wait until it arrived. Creed's parents had insisted on paying for Izzie to go to a private Christian school starting that year. While it humbled him to accept such a gift, Creed knew what an incredible opportunity they were providing for his daughter. The clincher, though, had been the fact that the one bus that ran on his side of town picked up just a few blocks away from their townhouse. He could drive Izzie and wait until the bus arrived without having to scramble to get to his downtown studio to open for the day.

Kate apologized again and he shrugged.

"Nothing you can do about it now, I guess. I'll see you at the church picnic on Friday."

"Okay. Hey," she called before he could hang up.

"Yeah?"

30

"Where exactly did we land on you taking us to Disneyland when you win?"

Creed snorted. "Jury's still out. See you later."

Creed hung up and backed his car out of their spot and let himself daydream about winning the grand prize for just a moment. Although he was able to rent a two-story townhome in a nice community with a pool and playground, Creed wished that he could afford a real home for Izzie. One with a large yard. Big enough for a dog.

Every kid needs a dog, he often thought to himself. *A nice Golden Retriever.*

Chapter Six

"Okay, class, line up at the door. Quietly!" Amelia added quickly as the room of first graders burst to life.

What a day, she thought, pausing just a moment to rub away the beginning of a headache at her temples. The other first grade teacher's nephew had moved into their area unexpectedly, and she insisted on switching one of her students to Amelia's class to make room. The teacher was married to the principal, ensuring she got her way no matter what Amelia thought. Thankfully the young girl had made the switch easily.

But no matter how smooth it had been for the new student, the change had been enough to rattle the class and disrupt their daily routine. Amelia couldn't wait to get home and retreat to a warm bubble bath, a new novel, and a cup of hot chocolate.

"Miss Howard? I can't get my bag untangled," a young boy called out, breaking through the fog. She shook her head and forced a smile. *Only a few hours more. Just get these kids home and get this room back in order. Then you can go home and settle in with your book.*

Pep talk on board, Amelia quickly helped the students find their backpacks and lunch pails, before she led the chattering bunch through the hall and out to the buses and waiting parents. She released the students one by one; each was given the choice of a high-five or quick hug from their teacher. Most of the girls shyly accepted the hug while the boys tried to out-do one another for the hardest high-five. Amelia shook out her hand after the last student, smiling as she watched mothers hug their children close to ask about their day. A familiar sadness clenched her heart.

So many years spent—and wasted—planning for her own family.

Amelia lingered outside of the door, watching to be sure each of her students found their way to the right place. Over her years of teaching she had spent many late afternoons with panicked students that had either missed the bus or been forgotten by a parent. When she first became a teacher, Amelia imagined that one day her own child would wait in her classroom while she finished her work day. It was the perfect set-up for a mom and the sole reason she had chosen to be a teacher. Maybe if she had—

"Amelia! I have been trying to find you all day!"

Thankful to be pulled from the sadness rushing in, she turned with a grin toward her boisterous friend. Chloe— loud, spunky, wonderful Chloe—taught third grade just down the hall from Amelia. The women had been hired together years ago, both fresh out of college. They became fast friends the summer before their first year when both spent countless hours prepping their new classrooms. Over the years, they had quietly shared their frustrations with the rigid rules set in place by the private school.

"All day? I guess I've been hiding away in unexpected places. Like my classroom," Amelia said dryly, a thumb hooked over her shoulder in the direction of their shared hall.

Chloe marched toward her, a flowy calf length skirt billowing around her legs. Her blond hair was styled in a pixie cut, accented by dangly apple shaped earrings and a red beaded necklace. Amelia couldn't help but admire her petite friend's style. She was known among the students for her colorful jewelry and matching personality.

"Bye Mrs. Whinery, Bye Miss Howard," two students called, as they walked by, arm in arm.

Amelia and Chloe turned similar smiles and waves to the girls, then stood shoulder to shoulder, turning their faces inward slightly to talk covertly while students funneled around them.

Chloe shook a finger in the air. "No, Ma'am, every time I tried to peek in your door, you were reading to the students or helping someone at your desk or—"

"Oh, no. Don't tell me I was caught doing my job. Not again," Amelia interrupted, her hand clasped at the base of her throat, eyes rounded in horror.

Chloe, not to be put off, kept right on talking, "And then at lunch, I looked for you everywhere. I even tried to text you."

Amelia shrugged. "Sorry, I had to sneak to the dentist on my break. I left my phone in my desk all day. My class has music right after lunch this year, so I can get a lot more done on my lunch hour, isn't that nice?"

Chloe narrowed her eyes.

Amelia's lips twitched and she placed a hand on her friend's shoulder.

"Chloe? Will you ever forgive me for choosing the dentist over your delightful company? And may I ask what had you in such hot pursuit of me today?"

Chloe snapped her fingers at two rough-housing boys, flattening her lips at them before she planted a hand on her hip and leaned closer to Amelia.

"So. Did you see it?" she half whispered.

"See what?" Amelia waved to a student calling her name. The young boy blushed and waved again before he jumped into a waiting van.

"What do you mean, 'what'? *It*. The only thing every woman was talking about this weekend and today. I sent you the link last night!" Chloe's voice rose an octave, but her volume stayed even.

Amelia crossed her arms and slanted a baffled glance at her friend. "Sorry, I haven't checked my email today."

An exasperated puff of air fluffed out Chloe's side-swept bangs, "Ugh. Amelia, I keep forgetting you don't have a smartphone. You need one. You miss everything."

Amelia held one finger in the air, brows raised. "Exactly. That's why I don't have one. I check into Facebook once a day on my computer, but don't get caught up in the mundane details. I get to miss out on minute-by-minute rants about coffee shop lines, groans about husbands, cheesy pictures of everyone's dinner. I like to have *real* relationships with people—"

Amelia's anti-social media diatribe was cut short when Chloe grasped her arm in a vice-like grip.

"No way," she gasped. "There he is! One of my friends recognized him and said his daughter started here this year. Oh my goodness, I can't believe that's him!"

"Who? Chloe, seriously, what is going on?"

Amelia took in Chloe's clenched lips and wide-eyes, then followed her gaze to her new student, Izzie Williams. Izzie was an animated, adorable six-year-old with a gap-toothed grin and wild red hair. She was talking fast, waving her hands in the air to a man crouched down in front of her, his back to Amelia.

In some ways the little girl reminded Amelia of Junie B. Jones. She spoke her mind and had seasoned the day with humorous comments and observations. Chloe's grip tightened and Amelia almost grabbed her right back when Izzie pointed in her direction and her father stood and turned to see where Izzie was pointing.

He was strikingly handsome. Broad-shouldered, ruddy; a charming smile. His eyes locked on Amelia's and the smile flattened in shock.

Oh my goodness.

It had been almost two months since she had reconnected with Creed at the reunion. Not that there was any actual connection that had taken place beyond the short catch-up. Not like Lucy and Chad who had been nearly inseparable ever since that night. But as for Creed and Amelia, neither had tried to connect with one another. She had thought of looking him up on Facebook, but stopped short. What if there was a way for someone to see any inquiries on their page? The thought mortified her. What if he was married? And what if he wasn't and had tried to find her? For the first time ever Amelia regretted using a fake name for her social media accounts.

Who am I kidding? Creed cut me off years ago. He obviously moved on and made a life for himself. Get a grip, Amelia.

Still, how could she have not connected that Izzie was his daughter? He had said she was going into first grade, but they had never discussed what school. Now that she knew of the relation, the resemblance between Creed and his daughter was uncanny. They shared the same subtle smattering of freckles across their faces, the same rust-colored hair. The same...

He flashed a smile at his daughter. Chloe whimpered.

"Seriously, Chloe," Amelia repeated. "You are a married woman. What on earth is going on with you?"

Before Chloe could answer, Izzie and Creed linked hands and made their way over to them. Annoyingly, Amelia's stomach did a little flip as he drew near. Father and daughter's matching grins were almost her undoing. Creed was a father. Creed was a *father!*

Chloe stood frozen, squeezing the life out of Amelia's arm.

"Hi, Izzie," Amelia forced out in an even tone. No easy feat considering the moisture had been sucked from her mouth.

"Hiya, Miss H," Izzie called. "I want my dad to meet ya."

Creed stepped forward, eyes sparkling, and stretched out a hand. "Miss H., huh?"

"Yup. That's me." *Obviously, Amelia.*

She nonchalantly tugged her numb arm from Chloe's grip to shake the offered hand.

His eyes began to crinkle in the corners, but dimmed as he took in Chloe's still-wide eyes and Amelia's faltering voice. His demeanor swiftly changed as he straightened his shoulders and placed a hand on Izzie's shoulder.

"Well, Izzie just wanted me to meet you. I guess we switched things up today?"

Amelia just stared at him. Chloe nudged her in the ribs with a pointy elbow.

"Um, y-yeah. I, uh, I'm sorry about that. I thought Mrs. McClary would have talked with you about that beforehand."

Creed glanced down at Izzie with a smile. "Well, I got an email Friday afternoon. I planned to be here this morning to help Izzie with the switch, but she insisted she would be okay. I know we're just in first grade here, but I thought it was important to let her do it alone if she felt ready."

Amelia thought it was sweet that he had planned to be there, but then backed off to let his girl be independent. She loved parents that took ownership of their children's education alongside them, as well as those that let their kids learn some things by experience.

She also loved brown eyes flecked with gold…

Amelia mentally shook herself, taking note of his serious tone, his cold demeanor. His girlfriends in high school were all the jealous types; maybe his wife was the same. They wouldn't want Izzie to take home an awkward report to Mommy.

If this guy has a kid in your class, there is a Mama somewhere that's attached to him. Knock off the drooling, she chided herself. But then again, single dads were certainly not unheard of…

She tried to nonchalantly check his finger for a ring, but he had his left hand in his pocket, the right settled on Izzie's shoulder.

"Well, it's nice to, uh, touch base with you. Izzie is delightful. I'm happy to have her as part of our class." Amelia bit her lip when Chloe surreptitiously pinched her on the elbow.

Creed nodded curtly and led Izzie away, leaning over as they walked so that he could take in her animated chatter. The buses had departed, and most of the students had cleared off the sidewalk. Amelia blinked at the long line of cars inching out of the school lot.

I can't believe that just happened.

Chloe let out a small squeal and clasped her hands beneath her chin like a schoolgirl. "Girl, the chemistry between you was magnetic!"

Amelia, finally free to rub her still numb arm and stinging elbow, turned on her friend. "What is going on with you? And how did you know that I was friends with him in high school?"

Chloe's jaw came unhinged. *"You were?"*

A handful of female teachers rushed over, all talking at once.

"I can't believe she is in your class!" one gushed.

"I mean the way they go through the whole routine, you know they must sing together all the time," another elbowed the first in agreement.

"And the way he talks to her and looks at her!" A third woman fanned herself dramatically.

Amelia planted fists on her hips, arching a brow at Chloe.

Chloe held up her hands. "Okay, ladies. okay. Amelia hasn't seen it yet."

"How is that even possible?"

"She doesn't have a smartphone and only checks Facebook once a week—."

"I check it every day—"

"Whatever," Chloe fluttered her hand in the air as if shooing away the unnecessary comment.

"Oh, that's right."

"You need to fix that."

"I can't believe she has no idea!"

The teachers clucked around her like a flock of chickens pecking over the last morsel of food. They led Amelia back to Chloe's classroom and sat her at the desk. Chloe pulled a phone out of her purse and swiped her fingers across the surface. After a few moments, a grin broke through and she handed the phone to Amelia.

"Just watch."

A stilled video of Creed and a much younger Izzie filled the palm-sized screen. Chloe pressed the play icon as soon as the phone was in Amelia's hand. Izzie's hair was sticking up all over as if she had just woken up, and she was seated on what looked like a child's bed. Her flannel pink and purple snowman pajamas were at least one size too big. The room behind her was lilac purple, the bedspread she sat on was pink with white polka dots. Creed appeared to be kneeling behind Izzie on the floor, his elbows propped on the edge of the bed. A purple ukulele decorated with white flowers looked fragile and unnervingly adorable in his strong hands. The women around her began to talk, but Chloe shushed them all.

"Amelia hasn't seen it," she reminded them.

Izzie's mouth moved and Chloe pushed a button on the side of the phone to turn up the volume. The small voice was an octave higher than Amelia heard that day from the spunky girl.

"Daddy, will Santa heaw us if we sing loud?"

The little girl kept her eyes toward the camera, as if she could see herself in the reflection. There was an unnatural light illuminating them both and the picture was so sharp that Amelia guessed Creed had set up all of his videography equipment to capture the moment. Before she could melt into a puddle over that insight, Creed stopped strumming to look at Izzie.

Tender eyes fixed on his daughter, he responded, "You know, I don't think Santa is in our state quite yet, but if he is, I bet he'll hear us."

Izzie's eyes widened and she folded her legs in front of her, grabbing her bare toes. "But Daddy! Then Santa won't come. If he heaws us, he'll leave." She rocked back and forth, still holding onto her feet.

Creed strummed the instrument softly. "No, baby, he won't," he assured her. His soft tone rippled pleasantly through Amelia.

Izzie eyed him before turning back to the camera to watch herself talk.

"Okay, Daddy, but if I say, 'Hush,' that means Santa is hewe and we have to be quiet, okay?"

Amelia grinned at her apple red cheeks and pouty little lips. She guessed Izzie must have been four when the video was made.

"Okay, kiddo," Creed grinned and began to play a tune. Amelia smiled, too, entranced when Izzie joined in, her voice sweet, clear, and only slightly off–key as she sang the opening chorus of Nat King Cole's *L-O-V-E*.

Just as Creed joined in with his even baritone, Izzie hushed him, her eyes roaming back and forth across the room, her head still, hands raised expectantly. Creed obediently paused with her, listening as well, his eyes twinkling at her reflection in the camera.

"Do you heaw that, Daddy? I heaw him," Izzie whispered loudly.

"Nah," Creed's fingers continued to pluck at the strings, but his eyes never left Izzie's face, "that's just the neighbors coming home."

Izzie's eyes continued their comical back and forth dance, but she joined in with Creed when he picked the song back up. Without missing a word or key change, Izzie and Creed performed the entire song, Izzie stopping him once or twice to tell him how she wanted him to sing the melody or harmony. He waited patiently as she ordered him about, and changed with ease to accommodate her wishes. They both pressed their lips together and imitated the trumpet solo in the song. From the way they shifted in and out of harmonizing and changing their roles, it was obvious that Creed and his daughter sang together often.

Amelia felt a stir in her heart, watching him watch Izzie. The stir gave way to an uncomfortable ache and Amelia suddenly wished she wasn't watching this private family moment. Her eyes stung and she blinked rapidly to stop tears from forming.

Why on earth am I crying? But she knew the answer. It was the way Creed looked at Izzie. It was remembering how much it hurt when Creed didn't write back all those years ago. It was the dreams that had tortured her nights since the reunion. Dreams of being friends with Creed again, laughing with him, watching a movie with him, hugging him tight. The memory of his warm lips on hers.

All Amelia wanted to do was hide in her home and find this video on YouTube to watch over and over again. But she knew she needed to forget this sweet video, put on her teacher face for the rest of the year and move on.

One detail of the video stood out, crushing her resolve: the hand Creed moved expertly on the neck of the ukulele—his left one—was glaringly void of a wedding ring. Not even so much as a dent or tan line to hint at the existence of one.

The song ended, and the women, including Amelia, laughed as Izzie gave out one final, "Hush!" and Creed twisted his face into a comical, exaggerated listening pose before the screen froze.

Chloe turned off her phone and stuffed it back in her purse. The clucking teachers bombarded Amelia with questions, wanting to know her reaction to the video that was apparently a "trending topic".

Chloe's voice rose above the rest, "Oh, ladies, Izzie being her student isn't even the best part."

Everyone quieted down and looked at Chloe questioningly. Amelia shook her head, "No," but Chloe opened her big mouth anyway.

"Amelia knows her father. They were friends in high school."

Amelia wanted to sink into her chair as half a dozen pairs of eyes turned on her like a flock of hungry vultures.

Chapter Seven

Creed tried to focus in on Izzie's excited chatter. He usually loved this part of the day, but after the day he'd had, it was all he could do to plaster a smile on his face and ignore a raging headache. Besides that, his heart was still pounding with the realization that Amelia was Izzie's teacher. And that once again, he had walked away from her.

All because of that stupid video.

The email from the principal explaining that Izzie would switch to Miss Howard's class had frustrated him. He hadn't paid much attention to the new teacher's name. When Izzie revealed that her best friend was in the new class, Creed's irritation eased.

Izzie usually rode the bus to the high school campus for pick up since it was closer to their home, but with the change, Creed rearranged a meeting with a client to surprise her at school. He found Izzie and asked her to point him toward the new teacher. Shock coursed through him when he turned to see Amelia standing where Izzie pointed. Then she just stood staring at him, her face white, her friend's eyes fixed on him like a piece of candy, and he knew—they had seen the video. The realization was humiliating and reminded him of his hectic morning.

I still can't believe Kate did this, Creed thought, resisting the urge to pound the steering wheel in frustration.

"Daddy?" Izzie spoke from the back seat.

"Yeah, Kiddo?"

"Why are you mad at Aunt Kate?"

He winced, realizing that she'd listened to his side of the conversation that morning.

"I'm not really. She shared something of mine that I wished she hadn't of, that's all."

"Miss Howard said today that sharing is good, but I'm with you, Dad. It's the pits," Izzie stated blandly before turning her attention back to digging in her backpack.

Creed's ears burned when Izzie spoke of her teacher.

"What did Miss Howard say about sharing?" he turned down the volume on the radio.

"Miss Howard said we're going apple picking next week, and we should share the apples with our families," she said, voice muffled by the depths of her backpack. "I'm okay sharing with you, Dad, but she also said we should share with our friends and today that girl Thea told me that I had to share my favorite pencil 'cause Miss Howard said so. I told her that didn't count."

"Well, I hope you were nice. Apple picking sounds fun," he added, trying to change the topic back to Miss Howard—Amelia.

"Yeah, we need volunteers," Izzie said, waving a sheet of paper, presumably a permission slip, in the air. Her Rs were only slightly off these days, and Creed smiled, remembering Izzie's slight speech impediment from her toddler years.

Izzie suddenly perked up from the back seat.

"Hey, Daddy-O, did you know that some kids saw that video we gave Aunt Kate of our Christmas song?"

"Did they?" Creed asked, listening carefully to see if she was embarrassed or had been harassed in any way. If so, Kate was going to be in more trouble with him then she realized. Thankfully Izzie gushed about the attention she received from school. She giggled, recalling how her classmates all wanted to pretend to be her when they played at recess.

"I'm a famous first grader, Daddy. *Famous.*"

"Whoa," he responded, not ready to tell her just how famous she was.

Chapter Eight

"Explain again how seeing Creed was a test?" Lucy asked, flipping the turn signal on and glancing over her shoulder before merging onto the freeway. She had invited Amelia to join her and friends at the park for a picnic and volleyball game at the end of the week. Amelia hadn't seen Creed again, but dealing with the emotions that raged through her at having his adorable daughter in her class had been draining. She was looking forward to a relaxing evening at the park.

Amelia hesitated. No one, not even Lucy, knew about the kiss Creed had planted on her before he left. No one knew how she had played with the idea of following him to his college and throwing out the entire idea of not dating until she met her husband. For weeks she agonized, missing her friend. She'd written him, sharing her feelings at long last and…nothing. No answer. She couldn't tell all that to Lucy.

Amelia adjusted her sunglasses as the car turned toward the glaring late afternoon sun. Weighing her words carefully, she answered. "When you left after the reunion, I took out my old journals and confirmed all of the ways that I've been living my life for some possible 'future husband'," Amelia held her hands up, pantomiming quotation marks in the air. "At first I went through and wrote out all of my dreams for myself instead of what I thought would make a man happy."

"And?" Lucy asked.

"And then I realized that that wasn't the right direction either. It hit me really hard that I've let my thoughts all of these years focus on my future husband and not on the Lord. Not once have I truly asked what He wants for my life. And then everything with the house happened and you reminded me of that. It's been so amazing to just follow His lead on this. Leaning on Him instead of having some husband be the end goal. Now I find myself asking what I can do for His kingdom, instead of when He's going to do something for me, you know?"

Lucy dipped her chin and said in a low, dramatic voice, "Ask not what His kingdom can do for you; ask what you—" she cut off at Amelia's crinkled forehead. "Sorry," she mumbled. "Bad Kennedy impression. Go on."

"Anyway, you see before you a new Amelia," she sat up, straightening her shoulders. "One who takes chances, lives for the Lord by His grace, and has no desire to get married."

Lucy snorted. "Right. You? You've been ready for marriage since you were sixteen."

"Exactly," Amelia held up one finger. "And years of living as if I am already married is over. It's pathetic, really. I am embracing my freedom as a single woman and taking charge of my life in a new way. Starting with talking my sister into helping me paint my new kitchen tomorrow." She leaned over and wiggled her eyebrows at Lucy.

Lucy ignored her. "So what does all that have to do with seeing Creed again?"

"It was a test because Creed is the only man in a long time that has been attractive to me. And even though he's obviously unavailable—"

"Actually, Sis, Chad told me a little bit about Creed's story. He's not married. Izzie's mom isn't even in the picture."

"Oh, that's sad for Izzie."

Amelia let that sink in for a moment. Her mind wandered slightly before she reeled it back in. She shook her head, determined. "Still, it's a possibility dangling in front of me to see if I'm truly ready to live a normal life. I can't go right back to what I was just because a handsome face shows up."

Lucy opened her mouth to respond, then closed it again. She turned onto a side street and steered the car through a round-about before entering the large city park. She parked in front of a covered picnic area. Amelia could see some of Lucy's friends gathered there already, as well as a handful of other people that she didn't recognize. The crowd was much larger and more diverse than Lucy had led her to believe it would be. Why would a casual BBQ between friends have a band playing at the small band shell and a bouncy house? It looked more like a company picnic. She arched a questioning brow at her sister.

Lucy shrugged, her hand on the door handle. She licked her lips nervously, "Well, Sis, it's good that you feel strong in your conviction because, uh, the Williams family is here, too, and that most likely means—"

"The Williamses are here?"

"Yeah, so like was saying—"

A man standing near the outside of the grouping of picnic tables turned toward the car. He wore faded jeans that hung just right on his hips and a soft blue t-shirt that accentuated his muscular build. Though a baseball cap had been pulled low over his eyes, a familiar smile split his face. His daughter jumped up and down beside him in excitement.

"Creed's here."

Amelia and Lucy stated the obvious simultaneously.

Amelia swirled with emotion. Shock. Elation. Sadness. Confusion. Annoyance that her sister hadn't thought to warn her of Creed's presence. If Amelia had known she would see him, she would have done more than change into jeans and a baseball t-shirt. She would have at least grabbed a hat to hide under. She raised a hand and wiggled her fingers at Izzie.

"Why is Creed here, Lucy?" she questioned through a tight smile.

"This is a church picnic and, uh, he and Chad go to the same one," Lucy answered. "I tried their church last week and really liked it; a lot of my friends go there. If I would have known Chad went there as well, I would have tried it years ago. But that's not the point, is it?"

Lucy's babbling stuttered to a halt under Amelia's withering glare.

Lucy swallowed hard. "Well anyway, I thought you could stand to try something new, too. You definitely aren't going to meet anyone going to Mom and Dad's church and hiding in the nursery every Sunday."

"Lucy! I just said that I don't want to meet anyone!" Amelia said, hoping no one would notice that she gripped the sides of the front seat as if the car could somehow anchor the world that had suddenly begun to spin.

Lucy smiled mischievously.

"Well, technically you don't have to *meet* anyone…" she tilted her head in Creed's direction a few quick times. "You already know that guy."

Amelia narrowed her eyes at Lucy. "You are in so much trouble."

Her sister responded by giggling before she slammed her car door.

Amelia sighed loudly. She exited the car on shaky legs. Creed and Izzie were kneeling in front of the bouncy house, both working to remove Izzie's sneakers. Amelia walked around the edge of the crowd in the opposite direction, avoiding Creed. For the next few minutes, she caught up with some of Lucy's friends that she recognized. Out of small talk, her heart still pounding with the nearness of Creed, she sat at an empty table and watched the volleyball game hoping to collect her thoughts.

Amelia smiled when Izzie shouted, "Hiya Miss Howard!" from the entrance of the bouncy house before she dove in with the other kids.

"Yes, hiya, Miss Howard," a deep voice echoed behind her, causing a tingle to spread from her cheeks to her fingers and all the way down to her toes. She resisted the urge to roll her eyes at her reaction. *Note to self: bring emotions in line with your convictions.*

Amelia turned to face Creed, one brow arched. "Well, hello, *Mr. Williams*," she replied, hoping he didn't hear the slight tremble in her voice. Honestly? That baseball cap? How old was that thing, anyway? And did he have any idea how attractive he was?

"Hey now, no need to be snarky," Creed held up his hands and sat next to her on the bench.

Amelia placed a hand over her heart. "*I'm* snarky? You're the one who was acting so strange at school on Monday."

Creed winced. "Sorry about that. Your friend was giving me weird looks and I was beyond shocked to see you. Izzie usually rides the bus and I had no idea you were going to be her teacher," he said with a shrug. "She seems to be doing great, though. She comes home much more animated than she did with that other teacher."

"I'm glad. She's a great kid and a wonderful addition to our class. But I'll save all that for when you and your wife come to the parent/teacher conference next month." Amelia inwardly cringed. Lucy had *just* told her that there was no Mrs. Williams, but somehow she needed to hear it from him.

Creed looked straight into her eyes. "I'm not married, Amelia."

A warmth spread through her at the tenderness in his gaze. An image of the video of him and Izzie flashed through her mind and she could have melted into a puddle right there. Without thinking she admitted, "I saw a very interesting video this week, Creed."

His ruddy face flushed and he buried it in his hands with a groan. "Ugh, that video."

She laughed. "Well if you didn't want people to see it, why on earth did you submit it to that contest?"

He raised his head, pulling his hands down his cheeks. "One word: Kate."

Amelia remembered his older, slightly over-bearing sister. "Ah."

"I sent that to our family years ago, and I guess she thought that gave her the right to share it," he explained further. He watched Izzie jump in the bouncy house, pensive.

Amelia elbowed him lightly in the ribs. "I thought it was sweet. I forgot what a crooner you are," she said with a wink.

Only, that wasn't necessarily true. Before she could stop herself, she tumbled into a long forgotten memory...

> Amelia lay sprawled on the floor of Creed's bedroom, textbooks spread out before her, the end of a pen in her mouth. Creed perched on the edge of his bed and strummed his guitar gently.
>
> "Amelia, how can you study right now? It's Saturday. The sun is out. Let's go hiking or something."

She rolled up onto a hip, one hand cupping her waist, her head propped in the other. "Creed, The SATs are coming up. How can you *not* be studying right now?"

He smiled and lifted his eyebrows at her. He went back to his guitar without answering. Amelia rolled her eyes and rotated back onto her stomach. Creed began to strum the chords to *Black Horse and a Cherry Tree* and suddenly his creamy baritone filled the room with a new verse:

"Woohoo, whoohoo

Now my best friend studies all day long,

So I'm gonna get her out today

Woohoo, Woohoo.

I found a trail I can't wait to show her,

So she's gonna come with me today."

Amelia laughed and sat up, picking up the tune. "But she says, 'No, no, no, no, no, no, no, no. No, that's not the thing for me'."

Creed stopped strumming and set the guitar aside. "Seriously, Amelia. We can't sit inside all day. Let's go hiking."

She twisted her lips to the side thoughtfully. "Why don't we study first, then go hiking later as a reward?" She patted the floor next to her.

"Can't later. I have a date."

Amelia swallowed her disappointment. Creed just broke up with Vanessa and he already had another date? The guy had more relationships in one week than she had had in their entire high school career. She worked to school her features.

"That's not my problem, Creed. I have to study. If you want to go hiking maybe you should take your date."

"I don't think Sarah is that kind of girl," Creed said, stretching out on his bed above her, tossing a football into the air and catching it again.

"Sarah? Don't tell me you're going out with Sarah Daniels?" Amelia curled her lip in disgust.

Creed sat up and wiggled his brows at her. "What's wrong, Howard? You jealous?"

Amelia scoffed. "Right. You wish, Creed. I just..." she toyed with the pen in her hands, words she could never say racing through her mind.

You deserve better. Dating girls like that is going to catch up with you. Be careful.

And the most hidden whisper of her heart: *Why not me?*

"You just what, Amelia?"

Something about his soft tone rippled through her. She bounced her gaze off of his then to the hall outside the open door.

"You can't really be mad that I don't want to study," he said. "So what is it, Amelia? What were you going to say? You just..." he prompted.

"Warning! Warning! Get out fast," her coward heart screamed.

Amelia slammed her book shut. With jerky movements, she rose to her knees and jammed books and pens into the satchel beside her on the floor. "Just nothing, Creed. I have to study. If you don't want to take this seriously, then please stop wasting my time."

She stood and strode from the room, taking the stairs in rapid succession, ignoring his calls for her to come back.

A few hours later, she sat on her bed, clutching a pillow to her chest, blasting her stereo, staring at nothing. When she got home she had asked her mom to tell Creed she wasn't home if he called. Which he had. A few times. Amelia heard the doorbell ring downstairs. She paused the country album, listening to the muffled conversation in the living room below her. A creak on the stairs prompted her to swipe fingers under her eyes. She dove across the room to her desk chair and flipped open a textbook and fixed her face into a mask of concentration. A few seconds later a light knock rapped on her bedroom door.

"It's open," she mumbled.

Creed walked in, a large, flat box from their favorite hole in the wall pizza café in his hands.

Amelia leaned back in her desk chair and crossed her arms. "I thought you had a date."

Creed shrugged. "I cancelled it. You're right; you came over to help me study and I wasted your time. So," he lifted the box, "what do you say we study for a few hours, then walk to get ice cream as our reward?"

Amelia bit the insides of her cheeks, trying to hide a smile. She stood, arms still crossed. "Well, I guess that depends on what kind of pizza you have in there."

Creed grinned and moved to lift the lid. "Barbeque chicken, of course. With chopped tomatoes." He hated tomatoes, she loved them. It was a constant game between them: whomever ordered the pizza won out.

She stepped forward and grabbed the box. "Aww, you must really love me."

Creed grinned and lightly punched her shoulder. "Of course I do, buddy. Now let's get the torture over with..."

Izzie giggled and called out to them from the bouncy house, sucking Amelia back to the present. She blinked and stood suddenly, smoothing her jeans.

"Well, I'm going to rustle up some grub," she said and walked away.

Rustle up some...? Seriously, Amelia?

Creed caught up with her at the food table and grasped her elbow. "Sorry I got quiet back there. I'm a little embarrassed about that video and, truthfully, I cannot decide if I'm all that pleased to have Izzie's face all over the internet."

Amelia pulled in a breath, thankful he had no idea where her mind had just been. She handed him a paper plate before plopping a spoonful of potato salad onto her own.

"I understand that, Creed. The nice thing about trending videos is that, from what I understand, they are a dime a dozen. Your sweet song will soon be replaced by a laughing baby or dancing dog or a laughing baby riding on a dancing dog and America will forget all about you."

"Gee, thanks."

Amelia laughed at his wry tone. "I, however, will have to see a therapist once that happens, I will be so lonely for the sweet Daddy/Daughter song of yore."

Creed laughed.

"You always could make me laugh, Amelia," he said, locking eyes with her. Amelia's breath caught at the years of memories dancing within those gold-flecked orbs.

Chapter Nine

Whoa, Williams. How long have you been staring?

He took a step back before he could fill up his plate and muttered something about getting Izzie ready for dinner. He strode to the bouncy house, his mind racing.

Since Izzie entered his life, Creed had not dated or so much as lingered on thoughts of women. Well, at least not serious thoughts. He worked hard, served on the worship team at church, and took care of Izzie. Romance wasn't on his radar.

Every so often he thought with a pang of guilt that Izzie was missing out on the influence of a mother, but then he would think of Hailey: her flat eyes and emotionless voice as she walked out on her own flesh and blood. He could not—would not—risk another woman walking out on his daughter.

The thought that Amelia would never walk out on anyone snaked through his mind. She was loyal, honest, and exceedingly trustworthy.

No, in their story, *Creed* had been the one to walk out on *her.*

"Will you be on my team, Creed?"

Amelia's sweet voice from their senior prom night rang out across the years and pierced his heart.

He watched with unseeing eyes as Izzie jumped and laughed with her friends, cheeks flushed, eyes bright.

"Daddy," she called out, snapping him back to the present. The wisp of memory dissipated before it could fully develop. His daughter clung to the netting in front of where Creed stood, struggling to keep her balance as the kids behind her continued to jump.

"I'm hungry, Daddy," she said, face flushed.

"Yeah, I thought you might be."

Creed helped Izzie crawl through the low opening and locate her shoes on the side of the bouncy house.

"I saw you talking to Miss Howard, Daddy," Izzie commented. "Isn't she nice?"

"Hmm? Oh, yep. Very nice. In fact," he squatted down on his heels, elbows resting on his knees, "Miss Howard and I were good friends a long time ago."

Izzie's eyes lit up with excitement. "Really, Daddy?"

"Really. Scout's honor," Creed held up three fingers, lips twitching at her delight.

"Whoa. That's even better than being famous," Izzie slapped a hand on her forehead, eyes wide. Creed stood with a laugh and reached out a hand to lead his daughter to the food table. As Izzie loaded up her plate, Creed's eyes nonchalantly scanned the group, wondering where Amelia had landed with her *grub*. He snickered inwardly as he recalled her wide eyes and pink cheeks.

He located her in the center of the crowd eating dinner with Lucy and Chad. Before Creed could choose where to sit, Izzie's adoration for her new teacher made the decision for him. She insisted on sitting with Miss. Howard and Uncle Chad. Creed took a deep breath and braced himself for a distracted dinner.

He needn't have worried. Chad led the conversation and Amelia was invited to play volleyball before Creed had a chance to talk with her. He watched as nonchalantly as he could until it was time to take the stage and play a few songs for Worship in the Park.

Their church had gathered there the last Friday of every month since the beginning of summer. With the air turning colder, the sun setting earlier, and autumn officially on the calendar, this would be their last Friday.

Creed made sure Kate had her eye on Izzie before he gathered the rest of the worship team and led them in a quick prayer. Creed noticed that Amelia faltered a serve when he took the stage. They locked eyes and Creed winked at his old friend before he turned to the gathered crowd.

"It's been a great season of Worship in the Park. I don't know about you all, but I'm not ready for it to end. Thank you to everyone that has faithfully come every month and served our community with free dinner and fellowship. Let's worship our Lord together, shall we?"

*   *   *

There was that pesky quiver in her belly again. Amelia nonchalantly pressed a hand to her stomach, desperate to squash the butterflies taking flight there.

Does he have to wink at me like that? And since when does Creed lead worship? Amelia's mind clogged from so many questions. Annoyed that she had faltered the serve, she tossed the ball to the other team.

She remembered clearly that Creed had not exactly been a religious guy in high school. He went to church because his parents made him, but in their friendship, she had been the one begging him to attend youth group events with her. And their discussions afterward were often heated and less than amenable.

Her volleyball game suffered with Creed's voice pulsating from the speaker placed right next to the sand pit. Her teammates had to repeatedly remind her to rotate positions, and teased when they caught her watching Creed. She couldn't help it; he sang with a humble passion he hadn't possessed in their teens. Amelia blushed when one woman on her team smiled knowingly.

"I have a hard time concentrating when Creed leads worship, too," she whispered. "Have you seen that adorable video of him and his daughter, yet?"

Amelia swallowed hard and moved to her place without answering. Minutes later the ball was flying right for her when the music shifted and Creed began to sing her favorite worship song from their high school days. His deep voice distracted her once again and the so-called poised, organized teacher got beaned right in the face with the ball, losing the game for her team.

They all laughed good-naturedly and shook hands, but Amelia's head was spinning, and not from the hit.

The sun sank low enough for the park lamps to switch on, signifying the end of the evening. Once again Amelia found Lucy and sat with her while Chad, Creed and others from the worship team packed up the sound equipment.

"So, you ready to go?" Amelia asked, all too ready to slink away and never see these people again.

"No, silly, we haven't had dessert yet," Lucy answered, not at all concerned with her older sister's humiliation.

"But the sun is going down. Parks close at sunset," Amelia pointed out, inexplicably panicked when she saw Creed, Chad, and Izzie walking toward them.

Those blasted butterflies in her stomach just would not let up!

"Thirty minutes after sunset. Anyway, we made arrangements with the city. Some people put away the sound equipment while others clean up everything but dessert, so we have plenty of time to enjoy brownies or cookies or whatever and then we'll leave. Rebecca over there—" Lucy pointed, indicating the woman from the volleyball game that had confided that Creed affected her as well "—is having a card night at her house afterward if you are interested."

Before Amelia could vehemently reject that idea, Creed was at their table.

The butterflies took flight and Amelia stood suddenly.

"Brownie!"

The group turned toward her, varying degrees of confusion twisting their features. Amelia blushed. "Um, I'm going to get a brownie, would anyone else like one?"

"Can I come with you Miss H?" Izzie jumped up and grabbed her hand. Amelia smiled tenderly at the ketchup smudge on the young girl's cheek.

"Of course, kiddo," Amelia answered before nodding her head toward Creed. "But you should probably ask your Dad."

Creed cleared his throat, a strange look on his face. "Only if you bring me back a stack of cookies," he obliged.

Amelia and Izzie walked to the dessert table, swinging hands. Izzie was intent on giving her teacher the inside scoop on all the recess happening from the day. Amelia listened with rapt attention, amused by the conversation. This she could do: play the teacher role, focus on the animated girl next to her and pretend she was a regular student…not Creed Williams' daughter.

"Then Gracie chased Max down because he's 'posed to sit next to her at lunch, not with the other boys." Izzie shook her head.

"And did she catch him?" Amelia handed Izzie a plate.

"Yup. And she kissed him right on his face. Blech!" Izzie scrunched her nose in disgust.

Amelia laughed and dished a large corner brownie onto Izzie's plate. She also collected a variety of cookies for Izzie to take back to her father. "So, I'm guessing you are not ready to chase boys around the school yard?"

"No way," Izzie said. After a moment, she narrowed her eyes and twisted her mouth to the side thoughtfully.

"Well, if they took my lunch or bag or something, I would chase them down and punch 'em right in the stomach," she made a fist with her free hand and almost dropped her full plate when Creed's voice, sharp with disapproval, cut into the moment.

"Izzie Marie Williams!"

"Ah nuts," Izzie murmured.

"Oh dear. Middle name and everything," Amelia whispered to Izzie.

She suppressed a smile when she saw her student's dejected face. They both turned toward Creed, hands hung on his hips, eyes narrowed. Amelia gave a mock shiver.

"Oooh, that cold Daddy stare," she teased.

Creed's mouth twitched at the corners, yet his features remained hard. "Izzie, why don't you take our dessert and go sit down? Try to remember what I have said about you punching people."

Izzie whispered an apology and turned large doe eyes on Amelia as she walked away.

Amelia pulled at her top lip with her teeth to keep from laughing.

When Izzie was out of earshot, Amelia leaned close to Creed. "For the record, she didn't actually punch anyone. She only told me what would cause her to chase boys around the playground. And, honestly, you might prefer her tactic once she catches them over Gracie's."

Creed hung his head. "I don't even want to know."

"Hey, be happy you don't have a Mariah Watkins on your hands," Amelia said, referring to a very flirtatious girl they had gone to school with.

"Yeah, no kidding," Creed murmured, distracted, his eyes on the ground.

"Well, I better go sit." Amelia ducked her head and inched by him, suddenly shy again.

"Amelia, why do you keep running from me?" Creed asked abruptly.

She stopped and slowly pivoted to face him. "Well, I..." she fumbled, unsure of what to say. Finally, she shrugged and answered honestly, "I guess you make me nervous."

"But you were fine just now, before Izzie walked away." Creed tilted his head.

Amelia shrugged. "I'm a teacher, Creed. Kids are my safe zone."

He nodded and looked past her to the receding sun. When he didn't say anything more, words that Amelia had longed to say to him since the reunion welled up inside of her. Before she thought better of it, Amelia whispered them, hoping her heart didn't crack in the process.

"I wrote to you."

Creed winced. He faced her, his eyes clouded with an emotion she didn't recognize but could almost feel emanating from him. Regret?

"Will you come to coffee with me?" he asked, reaching out to grasp her free hand. "Izzie is spending the night with my sister."

Amelia's mouth went dry and she was unable to answer. She thought of the first letter she wrote to him: the one full of drippy confessions and pathetic declarations. The last one was even worse—how his kisses had affected her so deeply that she couldn't seem to conjure up romantic feelings for her own fiancé. Why-oh-why had she brought it up?

"I would really like to tell you about, well, everything," Creed murmured. His thumb traced a small circle over the skin on her wrist. Could he feel the wild tap-tap-tap of her pulse?

Amelia swallowed, and try as she might to remember her resolve to forget about men, the desperation in Creed's eyes broke down her resolve.

"Okay."

Chapter Ten

Creed waved good-bye to Izzie as she rode away in Kate's van, smiling when she blew him a kiss. He turned toward his own SUV to find Amelia waiting near the passenger door, an odd smile on her face.

"What's that look for, Howard?" Creed asked, the tension from earlier hanging in the air, but set aside for the time being.

She shrugged. "Just kind of amazing. You and Izzie. You as a father. You're good at it, Creed."

Unsure of what to say, he retrieved the keys from his pocket and reached around her to unlock the door. Amelia misread the movement and hugged him around his middle. Creed allowed his arms to settle around her shoulders. He closed his eyes and rested his cheek against the top of her head. It was so familiar he couldn't help himself. How long since he'd held a woman in his arms? Especially one that smelled amazing and fit just right?

"Um, thank you. I was just going to open your door for you," Creed chuckled softly against her hair.

When Amelia jerked away, her face cloaked in horror, he could have kicked himself.

"Oh my goodness," she breathed and placed her hands on her cheeks. She stepped back to let him unlock her door and quickly slid onto the passenger seat, the streetlight illuminating the blush that crept up her neck. Creed hesitated for a moment before he shut the door gently and jogged around the back to slip behind the wheel.

"I'm so embarrassed, Creed. I thought you were giving me a hug!" she punched him playfully on the arm.

There was the old Amelia.

He grinned. "Yeah, I figured that one out *when you hugged me.*"

He turned toward her and spread his arms wide. "I won't turn down another one, though."

Amelia rolled her eyes. "You already got one, Pal. So where are we going for coffee?"

"Actually, do we have to pretend to be adults and do the coffee thing, or can we just suck it up and get pie like we both know we want?"

Amelia chuckled. "You read my mind."

Creed started the car and backed out of the space. The car's headlights spanned across the few remaining cars in the lot. The beacon caught on Chad and Lucy where they stood side by side next to Lucy's car, deep in conversation.

"Looks like we're not the only pair that's catching up tonight," he commented lamely.

Amelia settled back in her seat. Silence settled around them until Creed finally cleared his throat.

"I owe you an apology, Amelia."

She turned toward him. "I'm okay with that. Shoot."

"When I got your letters—"

"Oh, so you *did* get them. I thought maybe they were lost in the mail. So, what—you needed time to respond? Ten years?" she joked, but the earlier twinkle in her eyes melted into a pool reflecting the hurt she carried inside.

Creed sighed and tugged nervously at the bill of his hat. "Hey, I'm trying to apologize here."

Amelia cringed. "You're right. I'm sorry." She folded her hands in her lap and watched his profile.

"When I got them, I just couldn't write back. At first it was just that new college thing, you know? Busy with classes and new friends and getting settled." Okay, so it wasn't entirely the truth, but it was the best he could do for now.

"I was dealing with all of that too, Creed, and I still wrote to you," Amelia pointed out.

"I know. But you were always so sure of yourself. Where you were going, what you believed, who you were."

"You didn't know those things about yourself?"

"Not really. Once I was on my own I realized my barely-there faith was my parents' and my drive had been you pushing me all of those years. When I was on my own I just didn't know who I was. And, unfortunately, the only thing that stood out was my ability to flirt. I became more and more distracted by parties and having fun. And, although I mostly stayed on track with school, I spent far too much time, uh, socializing."

Amelia nodded. "I get that, Creed, but I still don't understand why you couldn't write me back."

"I was just too ashamed. You wrote me letters reminding me of who I had been, or at least who you thought I was. I knew I wasn't really that guy and I definitely did not want you to know the kind of guy I truly was. So I just ducked my head in the sand, so to speak."

There was more to it, of course—much more. But it was too soon. Their barely recovered friendship too new.

Amelia stretched her arms out, fingers interlacing over one knee. "So, then…what changed? Because the single-dad I saw tonight—the one that buckles his daughter safely in her booster seat and sings worship music for a church picnic—doesn't look all that much like a partying frat boy."

Creed pulled in a breath and glanced her direction. A passing car illuminated Amelia's profile momentarily before shadows swallowed it up again. "Near the end of my junior year of college, a woman I had dated casually showed up at my apartment with a baby she claimed was mine."

"Izzie?"

"Of course, Izzie! What, you think I have a dozen kids running around?"

She had the good sense to cringe.

"Sorry. Stupid question. Where is Izzie's mom now?"

"That's a great question."

Amelia listened without comment as Creed explained the way that Hailey showed up with a baby and made a hasty exit. He shared how Izzie changed his life. He finished just as he parked the car at a local diner and cut the engine. A neon sign that advertised warm apple pie flashed on and off, casting Amelia's silhouette in red, then green, and back to red. She stared straight ahead, gaze fixed on the dashboard, her bottom lip pulled in thoughtfully. Finally, she nodded and grabbed the door handle. The dome light cast a harsh glow.

"I'm so sorry, Creed. I can't believe I was so snarky about a couple unanswered letters when you were dealing with all of that."

"No, it was wrong of me not to write back, Amelia. Especially after you told me—"

"It's all forgiven, Creed. Really. So are you ready to buy me a piece of that apple pie?" she exited the car abruptly and Creed stared after her in stunned silence.

Okay…apparently talking about the content of the letters is off limits.

* * *

Well now what do I do? All she could think of was getting out of the car. Once the cool night air hit her, Amelia's mind cleared slightly. After everything Creed had gone through, her emotional letters were hardly worth mentioning.

Please don't let him mention it.

She looked up as Creed slowly unfolded himself from the seat and locked the car. His legs swallowed the distance to the sidewalk in three long strides. Amelia waited at the door offering him a small smile.

Creed eyed her for a heartbeat, then opened the door, gesturing for her to go first. They entered the diner in awkward silence; the dull jangle of a bell alerted the staff to their entrance. A waitress in her mid-forties with long brown hair pulled into a high ponytail greeted them. Amelia couldn't help but smile at the waitress' cliché uniform: a blue dress covered by a crisp white apron and white sneakers.

"Looks like you have the run of the place tonight. Everyone else in town seems to be at the football game," the waitress said. A piece of neon green gum peeked out from where she'd tried to tuck it in her cheek. She reached an arm out toward the row of empty booths lining the windows, her gesture indicating that they could seat themselves.

Amelia led them to the last booth in the back corner. The waitress walked away after she plunked down two ice waters on the table and handed them plastic menus.

Amelia finally spoke up. "Creed, I—well, I'm sorry you went through that. I'm really proud of the man you have become."

"Surprised, you mean."

She playfully swatted at his folded hands resting on the table. "No, proud."

70

They locked eyes, warmth radiating across the table. His baseball cap cast a charming shadow across his eyes, cloaking him in mystery. Ten years' worth.

Creed opened his mouth to speak, but the waitress chose that moment to step up to the table, pen poised above an order pad.

"So are you two ready to order?"

Both Amelia and Creed glanced down at their untouched menus.

"Or do you need another minute?" the waitress asked, tapping her pen against the pad.

Creed pointed at Amelia. "You want pie, right?" he asked.

She nodded and glanced up at the waitress. "A slice of Dutch Apple please and a cup of decaf."

"I'll have the same, but make mine á la mode, please," Creed said.

He handed the menus to the waitress with a charming smile before he turned back to Amelia.

"If you have more questions, I'm happy to answer them, but I would also like to hear about you."

Amelia's heart tripped. Despite Creed's omission of the details in the letters she sent him, she still wondered if it would come up. Did he even remember? Oh, how she hoped all of his years of single parenting stress had blotted out the details. She sipped her ice water before setting it down with a loud, awkward *thunk*.

She folded her arms on the table and leaned in. "Me? Well, you know everything there is to know: I'm a teacher. That's all that has changed."

"That, and you have become even more beautiful, which I did not think possible," Creed said, taking a sip of ice water.

"Oh come now, who do you think I am? One of those silly girls in high school that turned to mush as soon as Creed Williams tossed them a compliment?" Amelia scoffed, hoping the blush she felt inching up her neck would not give her away.

"Seriously, though," Creed leaned back. "Tell me about you."

"What do you want to know?"

"Hmm, for starters where do you live?"

"Right now I live in a little basement apartment near the school. A sweet widow lives on the main level upstairs and has graciously kept my rent the same for the last five years. I just bought a house, though, and will be moving in just a few weeks. My new place has a much bigger yard for my dog, which is wonderful."

Creed tilted his head, surprise lighting his eyes. "I always figured you for a cat person. What kind of dog?"

"Olé is a golden retriever; he's basically the best dog ever. And I do love cats, I just never…" her throat closed and she stared at the table, blinking rapidly. *How do I explain to Creed that a creepy commitment I've had for some mythical future husband all of these years has kept me from getting a cat?*

The silence stretched for moment before Creed rescued her.

"Olé as in Café Olé?"

She let out a chuckle. "Yup. I do love my chips and salsa."

"I remember," he said. His lips melted into a fond smile.

Amelia looked away, then back. She dropped her eyes to the table, suddenly at a loss for words.

"I've always wanted to get Izzie a golden retriever," he said, rescuing her.

"You should; they're amazing with kids. I can set you up with the family I bought Olé from—they breed often. In the meantime, Izzie can play with Olé anytime she wants."

A shadow passed over his features. "Yup. That would be great."

"All right, folks. Two Dutch apple pies. One á la mode."

Amelia leaned back when the waitress set down their pie.

"So if you like them so much why don't you get her a retriever?"

"Why don't you get a cat?" Creed countered.

Amelia rounded her eyes at him, surprised.

"You think I didn't notice the weird way you clammed up back there?" Creed took another bite of pie.

Amelia hesitated, stabbing a chunk of apple with the fork before she finally set it down with a sigh. "It's just embarrassing, Creed."

"More embarrassing than being an almost thirty-year-old father that can't afford a home where his kid has room for a dog?"

"Hey, you're doing an excellent job caring for Izzie. You have nothing to be embarrassed about," Amelia protested.

He stared at her pointedly. "You're stalling, Howard."

She bit the inside of her cheek.

Really, what would it hurt? Better than the oversensitive nerves she was carrying around wondering how long they could tip-toe around the subject.

"Okay, fine. Do you remember in high school when I asked you to be on my team? To help me be loyal to my future husband?"

Chapter **Eleven**

Will you be on my team, Creed? The whisper of memory from earlier now hit with full force…

Creed was eager to get to Amelia's. He turned onto her street, the heel of his hand casually straightening the steering wheel of his dad's burnt orange '64 Impala. After swapping horror stories from their years of dance experiences, Amelia and Creed had chosen to attend their senior prom together.

"What better way to spend the dance to end all dances than with a friend?" Amelia had said. Creed couldn't have agreed more as he strolled up her front walk, feeling light and carefree.

Mrs. Howard ushered him into the wide foyer and he made small talk with Mr. Howard until Amelia appeared at the top of the stairs. Her hair was woven in a braid that crowned her head. She wore a navy blue dress overlaid with shimmery fabric that changed hues when she moved. It hugged her slender frame in all the right places. Her beauty sucked the moisture from his mouth.

Amelia struck a playful pose before descending the stairs on a half-run as she always did, the bottom of the dress balled in her fist. A pair of heels was waiting when she reached the bottom. She slipped them on with a wink and looped her arm through his, oblivious to his pounding heart. They posed for pictures in front of the stairs, then the fireplace in the living room before heading to Chuck E. Cheese.

The dinner location had been agreed upon weeks before, but suddenly, with Amelia sitting next to him, so bright and beautiful, Creed found himself wishing he had made reservations somewhere special. She chattered on about some book she'd read that week, but Creed found it hard to concentrate.

Pull it together, dude. This is **Amelia.**

Instead of a candlelit dinner in a romantic steak house, they loaded up on pizza and laughed their way through arcade games. Creed won enough tickets to buy Amelia a set of plastic jewelry. Her fragrance—vanilla and lilacs—was familiar, but as Creed leaned close to place the pink beads around her neck, he found it alarmingly intoxicating. He unceremoniously dropped the necklace into place and Amelia wore it proudly to the school dance.

They had as much fun together as they knew they would, dancing, joking, and seizing one last opportunity to just be a couple of kids before life hurled them into adulthood. Although Creed was much more distracted by her graceful moves than he expected to be, this was still the Amelia that had been his best friend for years. He began to wonder why they hadn't gone to every dance together before that one. Or how he had ever looked at another girl with her around.

Now Creed couldn't take his eyes off of Amelia. The soft shine of her auburn hair, the streaks of blue and green that mingled together in her hazel eyes, the way her face lit up when she smiled; no pretense, just joy—all of it—mesmerized him.

This was Amelia. His best friend. The one that could make him laugh and knew every one of his secrets and still stood by him, believed in him.

They were on the dance floor attempting to do the robot when a slow song came on. Creed seized the opportunity and, before she could protest, he pulled her into his arms. Every nerve was aware of the way she fit against him. There was a rightness to it.

The realization struck him. His heart pulsed in the palm settled against her waist. He pulled her closer.

Amelia leaned her head against his shoulder and sighed contentedly. "Can you believe it's almost over?"

A response stuck in his dry throat and he swallowed several times before he could answer.

"What do you mean?" his voice was like tires on a dirt road. He forced a light cough.

He felt her shoulders lift and drop. "You know: high school. Childhood. The end of carefree living, the start of college. The beginning of plans..." her breath teased his neck, the scent of cinnamon gum clouding his thoughts. Thousands of shared moments—seemingly insignificant chords and choruses—blended into one beautiful song. Like a tune he knew by heart, but had never stopped to listen to. He ached to tell her all that was in his heart. But how? He tightened his hold on her waist.

"Amelia..."

She lifted her head and pulled back to connect her eyes with his. Creed sucked in a breath, but forgot how to release it. Amelia crinkled her eyes at him.

"Creed, I have something I need to tell you," she said softly.

He tilted his head to one side, questioning, thankful for another moment to remind himself how to breathe.

"That book I was telling you about earlier? It changed my perspective on everything..."

Creed listened, his oxygen leaving him and threatening to never return, as she shared her decision not to date. To wait for God to show her the man He wanted her to marry. How she wanted to honor the Lord with her relationships and choose them carefully.

"This book just makes so much sense, Creed," she chattered on, obviously not experiencing any of the feelings he was fighting to stuff down in the wake of her revelation.

"The author said that when you let God take charge, you should tell your friends and ask them to be on your team, to help you stay true to your future spouse. I really want to honor him now. I've already begun to pray for him," Amelia said, dropping her eyes shyly to his collar, her dark lashes fanning across her cheekbones. She looked back up again to search into his gaze.

Creed glanced away hoping she couldn't read the feelings that surely must be written all over his face.

"You know me better than anyone. Will you be on my team, Creed? Will you help guide me through my future relationships until I find the man that God has set aside for me?"

Creed, overwhelmingly aware that he was not that man, could only nod.

Chapter Twelve

A decade later, Amelia was back in his life, asking if he remembered that moment.

How could I forget? That was the night that I realized our friendship was never going to last.

Creed squeezed the back of his neck. "Yeah, uh, I remember something like that. Why?"

"Well, at the reunion I realized that I have lived my life that way ever since," Amelia said.

He narrowed his eyes. "What do you mean?"

Amelia leaned back and shoved her hands under the table nervously. He could tell her knee was bouncing by the way her shoulders shook a little.

"The short version? I have lived like a married woman all of these years."

Creed titled his chin away, gave her a long side eye. "I think you better give me the long version."

Amelia took a sip of water and averted her eyes. "Well, after I asked you to be on my team, we graduated and I went to college."

He squinted. "I vaguely remember that."

She swatted lightly at the hand he rested on the table. "Anyway, I went with that resolve and by the end of freshman year I met the man I thought God had prepared me to pray for. C.B. was—"

"C.B.?" Creed interjected.

"C.B. Charles Brian Benton. The fourth."

Creed fought to keep his lip from curling in disgust, but if the look on Amelia's face was any indication, he was decidedly unsuccessful. He cleared his throat. "Go on."

"Anyway, C.B. was a junior. A hard worker. He was charismatic and passionate about the Lord. He came from a long line of pastors and authors. Influential family is an understatement. We were for all intents and purposes engaged when I finally met his mom. She considered herself the epitome of the Proverbs 31 Woman...and was quick to point out to me and to C.B. that I was no such thing. I was too ambitious, not wife material. C.B. agreed and broke things off," she shrugged as if telling him she had received an average grade in a theology class. But her eyes dimmed with the rest of the truth. Creed wondered where this C.B. and his mother got off being such idiots.

A mask had slipped over Amelia's earlier openness and he saw the years stretch between them. This was not Amelia his best friend. This was the Amelia he had abandoned to men like C.B. This was a woman that had been hurt in ways he hadn't been there to understand or fix. And he was no longer the eighteen-year-old fool that had disappeared. He, too, had shadows of memory filling the ten years that separated them. They were practically strangers. Creed shook his head and tried to find his way back to the conversation.

"How could you possibly—what kind of an idiot—what does that have to do with you not having a cat?"

"I don't know of many men that like cats. C.B. broke things off with me because he said I lived my life with no thought to my future. He hated cats, my future husband probably wouldn't like a cat, ergo I never got a cat."

"Okay. Well, that's...different. But not totally abnormal."

Amelia arched a brow at him. "I'm a teacher because I thought this career would best benefit a family life. I live in

81

a tiny basement apartment that I hate because it's cheap and enabled me to build a nest egg for when I do get married. I kept thinking, 'I'll be married soon and that's when I will move.' Years later, I'm still there."

"But you just bought a house, right?"

"True. But it took me five years. Anyway, I hardly ever date and when I do, I almost immediately feel guilty and retreat in panic that I might have somehow dishonored my future husband. I have stayed at my parents' church all of these years so that I wouldn't be settled somewhere that I love and have to leave when I meet my husband and he goes somewhere else."

"Okay, well, that's dedicated, Amelia, but not—"

She interrupted him, "I have three journals at home full of letters to him. I put myself through cooking classes at the kitchen supply store so that I could please him with good, home cooked meals. I have not traveled anywhere because I wanted to experience all of my firsts with him. I have Pinterest boards full of wedding themes and ideas and homemaking tips for when I am a wife." Tears pooled in her eyes and her voice turned wobbly. "I'm beyond pathetic, Creed."

Creed whistled low. Okay, yeah. That was extreme. Unsure of what to say he asked, "What's a Pinterest?"

Amelia smiled. Then giggled. Then laughed. She cracked up, shoulders shaking, tears streaming down her face, mouth open in hysterical laughter, her hand splayed out across her chest. She ran her fingers under her eyes, laughing until all of her tears were squeezed out. Finally, she took a deep breath, but with one look at his face she cracked up all over again. Creed froze, baffled at her behavior and wondering if he should call Kate. Or Lucy.

Amelia took a final deep breath and smiled at him. "Thanks, Creed. I needed that," she said and took a hearty bite of pie.

"Uh, anytime?"

They ate their dessert in contented silence before Creed finally commented on all that Amelia had told him.

"I think it is amazing that you have stayed so committed to your future husband—"

"I believe pathetic is the word you are looking for, actually."

"No, I said amazing and I meant it. But can I be honest with you? You don't seem happy this way. Not that all of life is about being sublimely happy, but it sure seems that you're sacrificing an awful lot for a maybe and missing out on life in the process. And for what? For some distorted picture a jerk in college gave you of what men want?"

Amelia nodded. "Yes. That finally hit me at the reunion, actually."

"And?"

"And what?"

Creed leaned forward, locking eyes with her. "And what are you going to do about it Amelia?"

Her eyes shifted, a subtle flare in her pupils before she looked away. "I don't know what you mean."

He flipped the hat backward on his head and lowered his chin to look up at her through thick lashes. "Come on. You can tell me. I bet you have new journals full of new dreams. Spill, Howard."

Amelia rested her chin in her hand and rolled her eyes toward the ceiling, a small smile curling the corners on her mouth. "I don't know Creed. I want to say the cliché thing: I'm going to write a novel. But I don't have a book in me, as they say. I thought I would have all of these plans, too, but the Lord isn't leading me to uproot my whole life. I really do enjoy teaching. And I did buy my house. I guess that's the next adventure."

She hesitated. Creed reached out to lightly pinch her chin.

"What kind of house did you buy?"

She became animated for the first time in the last hour. She told him of an old farmhouse she knew about next to an apple orchard a few miles outside of town.

"I've admired it for years. Every time I drive by I could just see it in a restored state. It might be too much land, but I don't care." She described the two-story building, the upgrades on the inside of the house, and the surrounding acreage in finite detail.

Creed watched her eyes glow with new promise and hope. As he listened to Amelia dream aloud, he experienced the same sinking feeling he had years ago during their dance.

How ironic. Years ago I held her as she told me of her plans to honor her husband—a title I knew then that I didn't deserve. Now she is telling me that she is leaving thoughts of marriage behind…

Chapter Thirteen

The thought nagged him through the rest of the evening as they laughed over pie and old memories. Creed paid the bill and they walked to his car. He opened the car door for her and closed it gently once she was settled in her seat. He walked slowly around the back of the car. The autumn air was heavy with memories of high school hayrides and bonfires with Amelia at his side. When Creed slid behind the wheel, he opened his mouth to ask if Amelia would like to join him and Izzie for a pumpkin patch outing in a few weeks, but before he could he noticed his phone lying on the driver's seat.

Must have fallen out of my pocket when I got out of the car, he thought, picking it up before he sat down. The small device rattled in his hand, a silent indication that he had missed a call.

"Sorry, I have to see if this is Kate. Sometimes when she spends the night, Izzie likes to call me before she goes to bed," Creed explained as he swiped his thumb across the screen. He had missed five calls and one text from Kate. His heart sank when he read the text:

Call me ASAP—EMERGENCY!

She'd sent the text an hour ago.

He showed it to Amelia, then dialed his sister, his heart settling into his stomach like a heavy rock in a lake when there was no answer.

"Amelia, I have to check on Izzie. My sister never sends me texts like this. Something has to be wrong."

"Of course," Amelia said, her face white.

Creed backed out of the spot and left the parking lot in a rush. As he raced toward his sister's home, filled with dread, he barely registered Amelia whispering a desperate prayer in the seat beside him.

* * *

Amelia had a student fall to the ground with a seizure the year before and needed to call for an ambulance while keeping her class calm.

Two years before that, she lost a student for ten earth shattering minutes on a field trip to the discovery center.

She performed the Heimlich on a student during snack time her first semester of student teaching.

But never had she experienced the stinging fear that swept through her now, starting with a tingle that spread from the back of her legs and up her neck to her cheeks. The look on Creed's face had caused the fear: the absolute desperation of a parent that couldn't get to his child fast enough.

She whispered an incoherent prayer and braced her hands against the dashboard as Creed steered his car through sharp corners, barely, it seemed to her, keeping all four wheels on the ground.

They finally roared to a stop in front of a brightly lit craftsman style home in a cozy neighborhood. Creed leapt from his seat, slamming the door shut behind him. Amelia was close on his heels as he dashed up the front walk. He tried the knob, slamming the heel of his hand on the door in frustration when he discovered it was locked. He pounded twice more before turning toward Amelia, eyes wild with panic, raking his hands back through his hair.

At a loss for words, Amelia glanced around the porch, wondering if one of the little statuettes or smooth river stones was really one of those hide-a-key devices. She kicked over a suspiciously large, flat rock that was painted like a turtle.

Pay dirt. She leaned over to pull out the key wedged inside, smacking her head against Creed's as he bent to do the same. They leapt apart, Amelia grasping her forehead. Creed pressed on as if nothing had happened, his fatherly concern overshadowing everything. He was so rattled he missed the lock on the first try. When he finally opened the door, they charged into what appeared to be an empty house.

"Their car is out front. If they are not here, that means they went in the ambulance," Creed's voice was strained with emotion.

Amelia tried to keep her cool when all she wanted to do was cry. "No, the whole family couldn't have gone in one ambulance, Creed. There has to be some—"

A flicker of unnatural light beyond the glass French doors off the kitchen caught their attention. Creed marched through the open living room and kitchen, swung the door open and charged into the backyard.

"Daddy!"

Amelia wilted with relief when she heard Izzie's happy greeting. She stepped outside as well, quickly taking in the scene: a movie screen had been set up in the corner of the yard. On the ground before it was a pile of blankets and pillows with a tangle of Izzie's cousins piled on top. A cartoon plane flew across the screen.

Kate and her husband, sat up abruptly in lounge chairs placed behind the kids. A pile of red embers glowed from the fire pit between them, a row of roasting sticks leaned against the edge of the stone ring.

"Creed, what are you doing here?" Kate asked, her brow knit in confusion.

Creed's face was nuzzled in Izzie's neck, his shoulders rising and falling around deep, calming breaths. He shifted Izzie to the ground, but kept her close. He turned to his sister, voice dripping with annoyance.

"What am I doing here, Kate? You called me a dozen times and texted that it was urgent. In fact, I'm pretty sure you used the word EMERGENCY. When I tried to call back there was no answer. What was I supposed to think?"

Kate shrank back, her shoulders coming up to her ears. "Whoops," she said.

"Whoops? That's all you have to say?" Creed forced the words through clenched teeth.

Kate held up her hands in defense, "I'm sorry Creed. When you didn't answer I just figured you were…busy." Her eyes flicked to Amelia with sisterly interest.

"Daddy, can I go back to the movie?" Izzie asked, her excitement over seeing her Dad losing out over the pile of giggling cousins.

"Of course." Creed softened his stance and leaned to plant a kiss on top of her head.

"What was so urgent, Kate?" he crossed his arms, calmer, but still annoyed.

"Come inside," Kate unfolded her long form and stood. She waved at him to follow her. "You, too, Amelia. Good to see you by the way."

"Thanks, you, too." Amelia chuckled, but clenched her jaw and swallowed hard when Creed pinned her with an accusing glare.

"Traitor," he whispered, gesturing for her to pass in front of him. She held up her hands in playful surrender.

Kate led them into a warm kitchen decorated in red and black—and roosters. Lots of roosters. A framed photo of a rooster with crooked feathers poking out everywhere with bags under his eyes and an empty coffee cup in his hand hung above the coffee pot. "Hand over the coffee before I show you my bad side," was the bold caption printed on the bottom.

Kate grabbed her phone from where it was charging on the counter and pressed the speaker button before a voicemail clicked on.

"Yes, I'm looking for Kate McDonald. This is Natalie Gossard from *Trending Topics of the Day*. I understand that you can get me in touch with the father in that adorable video that has gone viral. We would like to speak with him about both he and his daughter being guests on our show in New York next week. You can reach me at…"

Creed twisted his features in confusion. "What is *Trending Topics of the Day?*"

The voicemail beeped and Kate shushed her brother as another voice clicked on.

"Yes, this is Robert Callahan in New York with *But First the News*. I am hoping to get in touch with the father in that video…"

Creed and Amelia stood near one another in shock listening as one voicemail rolled into another with producers anxious to have Creed and Izzie on their shows.

"They all called you today?" Creed asked in disbelief.

"Yes. My battery died while I was running errands today. I'm trying to be better about not being on my phone, so I left it here for the picnic. I heard all of these when we got home and called you right away."

Her eyes roamed over Amelia again. "I didn't want to interrupt your date, but I—"

Amelia felt her face flame. "Oh no, it wasn't a date. Just old friends catching up."

*   *   *

Creed vacillated between annoyance at Kate, disbelief at the voicemails, and disappointment that Amelia had rushed to assure Kate that they were just friends. The panic he had felt for the minutes leading up to that moment crashed in on him and he sank down on a stool at Kate's breakfast bar.

"Okay, Sis. Repeat after me: 'Next time there is not an emergency, I will call or text Creed once and *then leave it alone* so as not to give him a heart attack'."

Kate rolled her eyes. "You're such a baby." She slanted a look at Amelia and lifted one brow as if to say, "Am I right?"

Amelia coughed and scratched her upper lip.

"So which show do you think you'll go on first?" Kate asked.

"Uh, let's see. None of them," Creed pinched his forehead between his thumb and two fingers then smoothed it out again. The action did little to ease his growing headache.

"Are you kidding?" Amelia and Kate protested in unison.

Creed looked between them in surprise. Both women planted their hands on their hips, taking on a fighting stance. He was used to Kate, but Amelia was almost too adorable to argue with.

Almost.

He turned to his sister first. "I can't take my daughter to another state right now, Kate. You know I can't afford that."

90

He then looked to Amelia. "And, Miss Howard, I'm surprised at you. I can't take my daughter out of school this early in the year."

"The shows pay for it."

"Of course you can!" Again, the women spoke in unison.

Amelia placed a hand on his arm. "Creed, what a wonderful opportunity for you and Izzie. I think it would be incredible for her to be able to tell her children one day that she was on television."

Kate nodded, eyes rounded. "She's right Creed. And she's a teacher. You can trust her."

Creed couldn't believe what they were suggesting. Why would he be on T.V. just to talk about some silly video he and Izzie made? A video he never intended for anyone other than his family to see. His headache sharpened by the minute and he decided he needed to sleep on it.

"I need to get to bed," he muttered and slipped outside to kiss Izzie good-bye. She had fallen asleep on the blankets, a mess of strawberry blond hair curled against her cheek. Creed smiled down at her and tenderly brushed his hand across her cheek.

"Night baby girl," he whispered.

He turned to head back in the house, and caught sight of Amelia through the glass doors nodding along and laughing at something Kate said. He paused, just drinking in the sight of her before walking back inside and bidding Kate goodnight. They walked silently to the car parked at, or rather *on*, the curb. Creed opened the passenger door. Once Amelia was settled in the seat, Creed rested his hand on the frame and leaned in.

"Thank you," he said.

"For what?" Her upturned nose practically begged him to plant a kiss on it. He cleared his throat and leaned back.

"For being there tonight. For pie and catching up and…well, just thanks."

A small dimple appeared in her cheek. "Anytime, Creed."

He shut the door and jogged around the back.

Creed followed Amelia's directions, surprised at how close she lived to his parents. He pulled into the long circular driveway and shifted his car into park. Amelia opened the door and the dome light illuminated her auburn hair, casting irregular shadows across her face. She paused, but whatever it was she wanted so say, she chose to keep to herself.

"Goodnight, Creed," she whispered.

"Night," he answered, his hand gripping the steering wheel. He watched the graceful way that she followed a stone path around the side of the house before she turned to wave at him.

His chest tightened as he backed away, which irritated him. He could not fall for Amelia; she deserved more than a man who had lived fast and loose in college. She had lived her life for another, in hopes of honoring him and it was her turn to live her own life, not step into a ready-made family.

And yet…

His mind slipped into a dream on the drive home. One of finding Amelia and Izzie laughing together over breakfast in the morning. Of cuddling as a family on the couch to watch a movie. One of he and Amelia kissing Izzie goodnight and leaving instructions for the baby-sitter before heading out for a date night.

The dream carried him home, but settled like a rock in the pit of his stomach when he pulled into his carport. Creed entered the empty townhouse forlorn. He loved that Izzie was able to spend special nights with her cousins, but the house echoed with emptiness on nights that she was away.

The scent of Amelia's perfume on his sweatshirt teased him, magnifying his loneliness. Everything within him wanted to pursue a relationship with Amelia, but he wanted to honor her and do what was best for her. He snapped off his hat and tossed it across the room before he fell face down onto the couch with a groan.

Another topic to sleep on.

Chapter Fourteen

Amelia had not been to another church since she came home from college. In a long line of what she now saw as meaningless, ridiculous decisions she had made as part of her "honor him all of your days" lifestyle, was the choice to stick with a church that would not have been her first choice. Not that it was a bad place, but she had grown up there and constantly felt out of touch with the mix of young families and older members. She knew she needed to step out of her comfort zone and truly serve in a church, not just take up space volunteering in the nursery.

She joined Lucy when she invited her to Grace Bible and told herself that it had nothing to do with the fact that Creed was one of the worship leaders there.

And when her heart flip-flopped as Creed greeted everyone from behind his guitar on stage, she reminded herself again: *It has nothing to do with him. It's just new church nerves.*

The pastor was engaging; he spoke with conviction and truth. It was obvious that he wanted to lead them into a closer relationship with the Lord. She scribbled notes on her bulletin long after the closing prayer and song, anxious to remember all that he had said. It had been a long time since she had learned so much from one sermon.

"Wow, someone is making the rest of us look bad," a deep voice spoke above her.

Amelia sucked in a breath and looked up into Creed's smiling face. He stood in the row in front of hers, leaning over a chair, reading her notes.

"You don't take notes?" Amelia asked, stuffing the paper—and hopefully those blasted twitters that fluttered in when Creed was around—into her purse.

He laughed. "Not that many. I'm glad you came. Are you here with Lucy?"

"Of course, she's standing right—"

Amelia gestured to the chair next to her but stopped short when she realized Lucy wasn't standing nearby as she'd believed. She stood herself and spun in a circle before she found her younger sister talking with a group of women on the other side of the building.

"That stinker. She abandoned me," Amelia protested.

"In her defense, I stood here clearing my throat for a full minute before you noticed me," Creed said.

"No, that can't be true," Amelia responded. Her jaw dropped open when Creed nodded solemnly.

"Sorry. I just haven't heard that passage explained so well before."

"Miss H!" Izzie squealed and ran down the aisle to hug Amelia around the middle, knocking a small "Oof!" out of her with the intensity of her embrace.

"Ease up, Kiddo," Creed said, tapping Izzie on the arm.

"She's fine," Amelia said, squeezing the little girl back. She took in the black and green flower print dress Izzie wore, with little black tights, shiny shoes, and a deep green headband arched over neat pigtails.

"Well don't you look beautiful? You must have stayed another night at your Aunt Kate's."

"No, I was home last night. Daddy made pancakes this morning," Izzie announced, not noticing the look of shock on her teacher's face.

But Creed noticed.

His eyes twinkled when he asked, "And why would you assume that she spent the night at Aunt Kate's Miss Howard?"

Amelia's cheeks grew warm. The snake. "I just, uh—oh, there's my sister. I better go track her down before she forgets me."

Amelia made a move to leave the row, but Izzie grabbed her hand.

"Will you sit with me at family dinner?" The little girl scratched the side of her face, eyes trained on Amelia.

"What's family dinner?"

"It's where they have all the food that you don't have to eat, but have to be polite," Izzie answered.

Amelia looked to Creed for help.

"We have a potluck after church today. We always have snacks and coffee after the service, but today we have the full blown deal," he explained.

It was then that Amelia noticed the savory aroma of chili and bread. She also took in the emptiness of the chapel and the line forming at the back of the church. It wound through the hall and around the corner.

"Yup. And if something looks yucky, we don't haffta eat it, but we can't say yuck or scrunch our face or stick out our tongue. We just walk on by," Izzie moved her hands like a ground tech helping to land a plane.

"Oh, I see. Well, I came with my sister, so I will have to check with her first."

"Yeah, you're not going anywhere for a while," Creed commented, his face turned toward the line.

Amelia followed his gaze, rolling her eyes at the sight of Lucy standing next to Chad in line, hand in hand, eyes locked together as if no one else existed.

"Looks like I'm sitting with Izzie for lunch," Amelia said as she turned to her young student, enjoying her squeal of delight.

It turned out that eating with Izzie really meant that she would help her dish out her food. Izzie ate a total of three bites before she hopped down to run around the large gym with the other children.

After Creed refilled his plate with seconds, he took Izzie's place next to Amelia. She tried not to look too admiringly at his dark jeans and gray button down collared shirt with sleeves rolled to his elbows.

"So, Teach, are you still on board with Izzie going to New York next week?" he asked.

"Of course. Did you finally decide to go?" Amelia asked excitedly.

Creed sighed. "Yeah, I did. I think you're right—definitely a once in a lifetime experience. Would you mind sending her work with me for Tuesday through Friday?" Creed hedged.

"Absolutely. I already made permission slips for the students to be allowed to watch one of your shows in class. We're going to have a popcorn party and cheer on our Izzie," Amelia smiled wolfishly and popped a bite of roll in her mouth.

"You need a permission slip for that? And wait—you already made one up?"

She ignored his second question. "It's just easier to get permission now than to apologize later. Some parents really don't want their kids to see T.V. at all and some don't care enough about what their kids see, unfortunately," she answered, buttering another bite of roll.

"These are so yummy," she commented, closing her eyes.

Creed's gaze dropped to her mouth. A small dab of butter glistened on her bottom lip before she licked it off. He looked away.

"I'm glad you like them. Izzie and I couldn't decide which ones to make," Creed took a bite of chili, not-so-secretly watching from his peripheral as Amelia rounded her eyes at him.

The roll stuck in her throat and she coughed. Amelia took a drink of lemonade to help it down.

"*You* made these rolls?" she demanded in disbelief. "These buttery, flaky, wonderful, airy, heavenly rolls?"

"Wow. Are you sure you don't have a novel in you, Teach?" Creed laughed.

She arched a brow at him, impatient for a response.

"Yes. I can dress my daughter in proper church attire. I can style her hair. I can bake rolls. I can take care of us," he leaned over to nudge her with his shoulder. "I am capable."

Amelia popped the rest of the roll in her mouth. "I never doubted," she said, her voice muffled. Creed winced; he had spent most of the lunch telling Izzie not to talk with her mouth full. Amelia caught the look and grinned, pushing the remnants of her roll through her teeth teasingly and leaning close.

"What? Does this bother you?"

Lucy found them this way, laughing together. She grinned down at them, a wicked triumph in her eyes.

"I was coming over here to apologize for ditching you, but I see that I needn't have worried."

Amelia swallowed and wiped her mouth with a napkin. "You should be ashamed of yourself, Lucy. Thankfully Izzie rescued me or I would have been some lonely, pathetic woman hiding in the corner."

"And mocking your old buddy with your 'A.B.C. food' isn't lonely and pathetic?" Lucy asked.

"A.B.C. food?" Creed asked, brows knitted.

"Already Been Chewed," Amelia answered before turning back to Lucy. "He deserved it for teasing me," she sniffed.

"I'm sure he did," Lucy remarked with a wink.

Amelia sobered, embarrassed by Lucy's look. Before she could respond, an older woman stepped close and asked to be introduced to Amelia.

By the time the potluck was over, Amelia had met more members and been invited to a Bunco night the following week, a monthly book club, and a weekly Bible study.

"Wow, that church has a lot going on," Amelia commented as she and Lucy drove home.

"They really like to spend time with one another," Lucy replied. "I love that."

"Me too," Amelia said, staring thoughtfully out the window.

Lucy opened her mouth to tease her sister about love, but took in her pensive profile and closed it again.

Chapter Fifteen

Amelia stood with a handful of mothers near her desk on Monday morning, handing out printed maps with directions to the apple orchard.

"Now, it's about a twenty-minute drive from here. You will feel like you passed it after all of the signs advertising different farms. We are headed to Sweet Picks. It's the fourth farm on the left once we pull into town," Amelia explained.

"Do you have a list of the students and how many seats we have available?" Daria asked. Every year Amelia had one mother that became her right hand and Daria was this year's model.

"Yes, I do." She opened the top drawer of her file cabinet and pulled out a folder. She handed it to Daria.

"Could you line those up for me while I jet down to the office and make copies of your licenses and proofs of insurance?"

Amelia waited while the ladies found the information she needed and turned toward the door. Just then Creed stepped in with his hand on Izzie's shoulder, and Amelia stopped short.

She had woken that morning, deliciously swoony after having a dream about Creed. She remembered it was snowing and he brought her bbq chicken pizza. And started a fire in her new fireplace before wrapping his arms around her middle and pulling her close. He had been so sweet and tender, telling her he loved her. That he had thought of her as much as she had thought of him over the years.

And now here he was, standing in her classroom.

He's probably just dropping his kid off, Amelia, she assured herself. But she could hardly hear the thought over the sudden pounding in her ears. Despite their interactions over the weekend, something about Creed stepping into her teaching world rattled her.

Um, possibly the romance of her dream?

"Hiya, Miss H," Izzie offered her typical greeting and Amelia gave a high five in response.

"You ready for some fun apple picking?" Amelia asked, working to steady her trembling knees. If this was how her nerves were going to react every time Creed was around, it was going to be a long year. She had never been this nervous in his presence in high school. Of course, Creed didn't go around singing classic songs with his daughter or walk with such masculine assurance back then, either.

"Yeah! And guess what, Miss H? Daddy-O is going to be a 'perone," Izzie rubbed one foot against the other leg.

"He is?" Amelia rounded her eyes in excitement for the young girl's sake, avoiding Creed's watchful gaze.

"Chaperone, Izzie," Creed corrected before he dipped his chin to catch Amelia's gaze. "Is that going to be okay, Teach?"

His look reminded her of the smug-yet-charming way that he would become around girls with obvious crushes on him.

Amelia squared her shoulders and met his gaze head on. If blushing schoolgirl was what he thought he was getting, then Miss Howard was going to be a big surprise.

"Of course, Mr. Williams. I was just headed to the office to take copies of the drivers' licenses and proofs of insurance of all of our carpoolers. Are you planning to drive or just tag along?"

He blinked at her cool, professional tone. "Uh, I was hoping to drive."

Amelia tilted her head back toward the group of moms. "Great. I need a copy of your license and insurance card. I'll need you to go chat with Daria over there and she will assign kids to your car."

She watched his face pale slightly at the hungry looks of the moms who all huddled together to watch their interaction.

Ha, take that Mr. Big Shot. Serves you right for being a devastatingly handsome internet sensation.

Amelia left and took his smug smile with her.

She returned from the office moments later and gave the drivers their things before she called out above the dim of noise. No one heard her, so Amelia called out louder, clapping her hands together, "One, two, three—"

"Eyes on me," the students finished, turning toward her and quieting down instantly.

"Great job class. Okay, Tommy's mom will tell you what car to ride in. No arguing with her. I expect you all to be well behaved on the ride. At the apple orchard, we will first hear all about the varieties of apples, how they grow, and what they are used for. Then the farmer is going to show us the different ways to make cider and apple juice. Put on your best listening ears and take it all in. We will have an assignment later about our trip. I expect you to be able to answer questions. Let's be their favorite guests this season, shall we?"

The students cheered enthusiastically and broke into groups. Amelia helped organize and find coats, buckle kids into seats and be sure all of the drivers had directions. She usually found a parent to ride with once she was sure everyone was ready, but by the time she got to Daria's suburban, she saw that it was full. Another mom was in the front seat and rolled down the window.

"Izzie's father had a third row, so we combined my crew with Daria's. I think he had room for you, though," the mother added with a teasing wink.

Amelia would rather strap herself to the roof of Daria's rig than spend twenty fumbling minutes with Creed. But it looked as if she had no choice. She slowly walked down the line of cars, beginning with the last one, double checking students against the list on her clipboard to be sure everyone was accounted for. Creed's small SUV was first in the line. She opened the passenger door and leaned in, her feet planted firmly on the pavement.

Good grief, did he have to put on that baseball cap again?

She took a shuddering breath and focused on her students, "Okay, you should have four kiddos in here: Izzie? Gotcha. Gabe? Ok. Louisa? Got you, Sweetie. And, Hannah. Great. All kids accounted for."

She tucked the clipboard under her arm and tilted her head at Creed and the kids, "You all mind if I ride with you?"

Creed led the kids in a loud cheer and clapped as Amelia climbed in.

"The best car always has the teacher," he winked, catching Izzie's eye in the rearview mirror.

"Yup!" she called out, giggling with Hannah.

Creed looked to Amelia as he shifted into drive. "You ready, Teach?"

"As I'll ever be."

* * *

Creed was greatly amused by Amelia's red face and flustered responses, though he was baffled by them. He thought they had settled her nerves over the weekend. No matter how hard he tried, he couldn't understand women.

He drove silently, following Amelia's directions and drinking in her camaraderie with the students. As much as she would probably attribute her choice to be a teacher to that whole "Honor thy husband" bit, it was obvious to Creed that the Lord had greatly gifted her to teach. She was calm and steady, fun but firm. The students adored her.

The trip to the apple orchard flew by with Creed and Amelia leading the car in silly songs and telling knock-knock jokes. They were seamless in their interaction with the kids, even as they avoided conversation with one another.

At the orchard, Amelia was quick to hop out of the car and walk quickly up the long dirt driveway to where a man and woman were waiting in front of a sprawling ranch house. Creed helped the kids out of the car, smiling when Izzie ran ahead with her friends in excitement. He trailed behind the moms that kept sneaking glances at him.

He hated the popularity of that video more and more.

Amelia gathered everyone around and introduced the farmer, Marty, and his wife, Bev, before stepping back for the demonstration. Creed enjoyed watching the man use an old machine to make cider. He helped Amelia and the moms hand out the samples that the wife brought out and then it was time to pick apples. Izzie and her friends were back at Creed's side, recognizing the advantage his height offered them. Izzie handed him the pole with a basket welded to the top and marched toward the orchard.

Creed followed his daughter and her friends for the next hour, laughing with them and asking questions. If these were her playmates, he wanted to know them better. By the end of the day, he knew which kids he appreciated and which he would try to steer her away from. That Gabe had a crush on his daughter was obvious: he would blush when she looked his way and then run off mid-conversation.

While he immensely enjoyed his time with Izzie, Creed couldn't keep his eyes from drifting to Amelia. He instinctively knew where she was at all times. From beneath the rim of his hat, Creed admired her way with the kids. Her black leggings, tall black boots and long, fitted red and black gingham dress with a wide black belt around her thin waist certainly didn't hurt, either.

Amelia crouched down to tie a student's shoes. She lightly patted the little girl's leg and smiled into her eyes. Creed's chest squeezed. The student skipped away and Amelia rose and looked around. Creed kept his gaze on her until she noticed him. She froze. Her fingers rubbed the side of her neck, then fidgeted with her silver necklace.

Marty and Bev approached her just then and Amelia turned to give them her full attention.

"Daddy-O, our sack is full," Izzie tapped his leg, breaking Creed from his stare. When he glanced up Amelia was still deep in conversation with the proprietors and Daria was waving her arms and calling out to the students. The group gathered near a long row of picnic tables and again Creed helped to pass out snacks from the coolers a few mothers had set out. He kept busy the next twenty minutes opening fruit snack wrappers, spearing organic milk boxes with big round straws, and reigning in the wayward students that had a hard time keeping still.

Through it all, he continued to sneak glances toward Amelia and her intense discussion. Her brow was furrowed but a smile played across her lips, exposing tiny dimples near the corner of her mouth. He didn't think he'd seen that look on her face before; deep concentration fighting against unbridled excitement. Finally, she hugged them both and turned her attention back to the class.

"Alright, kiddos! Are we all ready?" she called.

Once the kids were circled up, she encouraged everyone to tell the farmer and his wife a big thank you.

At the cars, Amelia went through the same routine, checking students in each car, helping where she could. Creed didn't know how she managed to be so organized. Of course this was the girl that could keep him focused on his Economics homework. Creed started the van and waited for Amelia to join them. He could see her in the rearview mirror, talking with Bev once again, accepting a brown pastry box with a hug. She jogged back to the van and set the box on the floor before scooting in and turning her legs to avoid crushing it. The sweet smell of cinnamon and baked apples drifted toward Creed.

"Mmmm, what's that?"

Wordlessly, she glanced toward the back. Izzie and her friends were turned toward one another, playing rock-paper-scissors and giggling uproariously.

Amelia twisted back to look him in the eye. "Homemade, award-winning apple turnovers. Tell no one," her low voice sent a delicious shiver through him.

She slowly reached a hand back for her seatbelt, hazel eyes trapping him in their gaze.

"You're going to share with me, right?" he raised a brow. "I expect payment for my silence."

Amelia pinned him with a look. "Are you threatening me, Williams?"

In the back of the van the children continued to play and chattered excitedly about their trip. In the front the only noise was the click of Amelia's seatbelt. Creed had never heard her voice drop to that octave before. He swallowed.

"I guess not."

A wide grin lit up her face and broke the mean teacher glare.

"That's what I thought. I would love to share," she said.

Creed whistled low. "Yikes. Did a cold breeze just blow through here?" he teased.

"I never pictured you as a chaperone guy, Creed," Amelia said, changing the subject.

"It won't be often that I get to go on Izzie's field trips so I wanted to make it count and be helpful. I also needed to check out these friends she talks about all day," he whispered.

"Wise move, Daddy-O," Amelia commented, eyes on the road.

The car rolled to a stop at the main road, where traffic had picked up since they arrived that morning. Amelia stared out her window, pensive. Creed followed her gaze, while waiting for a line of semi-trucks to pass by. A dirt packed driveway met with the gravel road they were on and trailed back through an empty field to a small two story house. Something about the front porch and stone chimney spurred something in his memory. He remembered her excitement from the other night.

Her words and the strange meeting she held with the proprietors of the orchard dawned on him.

"That's your new dream out there, isn't it, Amelia?"

She turned back to him, her eyes rounded and vulnerable. They caught glances for a heartbeat before her lips curled ever so slowly upward, flashing those subtle dimples his way.

"I believe it is, Mr. Williams. I believe it is."

Chapter Sixteen

Creed didn't have time to analyze the weekend or field trip or Amelia's new dream; he had too much to do before he and Izzie left for New York. At least that is what he continued to tell himself. But as he packed their bags, arranged his schedule with various producers, and rescheduled photo shoots, Amelia's lovely face continued to play in the corners of his mind.

And that house. She had said it needed work the other night, but her excitement had painted a lovely, sturdy farmhouse in his mind. The sagging porch, overgrown weeds, peeling paint and crumbling chimney was not as charming as she had earlier presented. The image of Amelia huddled up in the corner as snow fell through a giant hole in the roof haunted him.

Did she seriously buy that place? And how was it any of his business? A courtroom drama of sorts ran through his thoughts the rest of the day, with him arguing both for and against Amelia's dream, then switching to defendant and prosecutor with his own misplaced feelings for Amelia.

By the time he arrived to pick up Izzie from school and retrieve her packet of homework, he was exhausted. He had hoped to speak with Amelia for a few moments, but she was deep in conversation with a student and her mother. The mother's face was pinched and her hands moved wildly in agitation. Amelia glanced up as Creed approached and held one finger up.

"Just one second, Mrs. Layne," she said, turning to Creed. She handed him a red folder and white paper sack with an apologetic shrug.

"Have a wonderful time, you two. We'll see you next week!" Amelia hugged Izzie, offered a small smile to Creed, and turned her full attention back to the disgruntled Mrs. Layne.

In his car, Creed opened the sack to find two apple turnovers. He grinned and turned to hand one to Izzie, thinking how much he liked that Miss Howard.

Kate drove them to the airport, Izzie chattering about the trip to the apple orchard the entire way. Creed and Izzie bid his excited sister goodbye at the "Kiss and Fly" zone. Izzie kept up her excitement as they checked in and endured the security line before finally boarding the plane. Creed encouraged Izzie to finish all of her work on the plane instead of trying to do it during the week of shows and sightseeing.

Amelia had left notes on the pages of homework for Izzie and for him; explaining certain assignments, encouraging them both to have a good week and not be nervous. She had finished each one with a circled smiley face and bold "Miss H."

The whirlwind week passed quickly. They barely had time for sightseeing in between tapings and interviews. With every show, Creed couldn't help but wonder if Amelia found a way to watch. Was she on the other side of the camera? Did she have a Facebook account—why had he never asked her?— and if so, did she see the little arrow at the side that pointed to the headline, *Trending Now— father/daughter take the morning talk show scene by storm with adorable routine?*

As the week drew to a close, with Creed and Izzie packing up the memories of a lifetime, Creed had decided that he would find a way to renew his friendship with Amelia. Even if she never wanted romance, he knew that, in whatever capacity she would allow, he wanted to have Amelia Howard in his life.

Chapter Seventeen

Amelia set her DVR to record every show.

She told herself it was just to screen which clips would be appropriate for her students and their popcorn day on Friday. But the way her stomach curdled when a very attractive hostess flirted with Creed and lightly touched his arm told her the truth.

I have a thing for Creed, she admitted. She rolled her eyes at herself. Duh. Hadn't she always?

"Good gracious, Amelia. What happened to your single woman power plan? Just me and Jesus. These feelings of jealousy have no place. Be gone," she karate chopped the air for emphasis, thinking as she did that she'd spent too much time around first graders.

Olé came trotting into the room, tail high in the air.

"No, I didn't call you, Pup. But I will take you on a walk," Amelia said, gathering the leash she kept on a hook by the door and her tennis shoes. Olé jumped up and down on his front feet, his tail bashing against the wall.

Outside in the dusky night, Amelia pulled her jacket close to ward off the cold evening. Last week at the picnic it was warm enough for a long sleeved t-shirt and jeans. But the day after the apple orchard trip, rains had come and with them autumn and its early evening chill.

This was Amelia's favorite time of year. She thought back to the cold morning at the orchard. If she was honest with herself, she had loved watching Creed interact with his daughter and her friends on that trip. He shared in their joy with each apple that was plucked and added to their stash. She thought too long about the way the cool air painted his cheeks a charming red beneath his baseball cap.

Catching herself, she quickly moved her thoughts to the other excitement of her week: the move. Bev and Marty gave her permission to work on the house before closing day. She had been working on her farmhouse little by little, painting the kitchen and sanding and staining the floors. She was glad she had chosen to do the repairs and stay in her apartment so the paint fumes had time to air out. That week the carpet would be installed upstairs over the existing wood floors. She couldn't bear to remove the original floors, but liked carpet in her living spaces. For the living room, she settled on a large rug that accentuated the newly stained floors. She and Lucy planned to go furniture shopping the next day for her living and dining rooms.

Aside from Creed, Amelia had thought and prayed about little else the rest of the week. Her savings was hefty, thanks to her frugal, wifely living, and she was having an exceptionally wonderful time spending a big chunk of it.

But could she really take the plunge?

She drifted back to her favorite daydream of coffee and her morning devotions on the wrap around porch. Of course her vision included plenty of sunshine, white, distressed wood furniture, a steaming cup of coffee and a plate of Bev Forrester's famous apple turnovers.

Amelia's scattered mind wondered if Creed had liked the pastries or if the gift had been cheesy. She was tempted to go back and buy another dozen for when Creed and Izzie returned from New York, but immediately disregarded the idea. Would he find her kind of pathetic? Or think she was being a nice friend?

Olé tugged her further down the walk and Amelia noticed one tree beginning to change its colors. Just one among a dozen, but it was a start. She couldn't wait for the valley she lived in to be ablaze with the fire of orange and red and golden brown leaves.

Somewhere in her neighborhood someone must have started up their fireplace; the smell of wood smoke reminded her of her childhood and calmed her spirit. But the calm didn't quite reach the recesses of her heart where thoughts of Creed dwelt. They had been dormant for so long that Amelia had truly thought they had left altogether. But since the reunion, and even more so since they had spent time together, the memories and dreams of her sweet teen years came rushing back.

Only this time, she was facing a mature, godly Creed. One that dressed his daughter for church so that her headband matched her dress, made scrumptious yeast rolls, and sang sweet songs with his child that became internet sensations overnight.

This Creed was going to be much harder to forget.

Chapter Eighteen

The morning arrived for Creed and Izzie's debut in her classroom, via their last morning show appearance. Amelia and the principal had spoken with the parents of her students and sent out permission slips; all involved felt that this particular show would be the most family friendly version of their small tour.

Amelia made popcorn for the students and rolled a television in from the teacher's lounge. She shook her head with a giggle at how many of her female coworkers checked in to see how it was going. She knew they all hoped to catch a glimpse of Creed and Izzie, even though they, like her, had been watching their DVRs all week. The children in the class were thrilled to have a special day and to see their classmate on T.V.

"Miss Howard?" Gracie, dressed up for the occasion, tapped her on the arm.

"Yes, Gracie, what do you need?" Amelia asked absentmindedly, frowning at the remote in her hand. The T.V. did not want to cooperate with her. *T.V. Input. Channel. Annnnd...nothing. Drat.*

"Hmm? I'm sorry, Gracie, what did you say?" Amelia set the remote down and turned to give her full attention to her student.

The little girl took a deep, long suffering breath, before she repeated herself, "Now that Izzie is on T.V., does that mean we're all famous?"

"Well, not quite, Gracie. But it sure will be fun to see someone we know on this thing, won't it?" Amelia rapped her knuckles on the old screen. Gracie let out another sigh, her shoulders dropping in disappointment. The dejected girl joined her classmates on the story time rug and Amelia went back to the old television with an amused grin.

Maybe I should forget about the furniture and use my savings to upgrade the technology around here, she thought to herself. Working at a Christian school had been a dream come true, but because it was a school supported by tuition, their supplies were seriously lacking.

The T.V. finally clicked on and the object of her thoughts filled the screen. An anchor's voice was dubbed over a playback of the video that made Creed and Izzie famous. Amelia laughed as her students joined in the song, all of them imitating Izzie.

"Quiet everyone! It's starting," Amelia announced as she sat back in her chair.

She couldn't tear her eyes away from a sharply dressed Creed seated in the studio. He wore dark blue jeans and a moss colored button down shirt with a skinny black tie. His short red hair was spiked slightly and, although he appeared a little tired, Amelia felt her knees go weak at how handsome he looked sitting next to the show host.

Izzie fidgeted in the chair next to Creed in a near matching green and black polka dot dress and black leggings complete with knee high boots. Where Creed looked worn, Izzie looked downright bored slumped down in her chair with her chin tucked close to her chest, legs swinging in small circles. Amelia snickered. *And baby girl is* done *with all of this nonsense.*

The children in her class squealed and squirmed, excited to see their friend, calling "hello" and pretending to be offended that she wasn't answering them.

"Oh, I see. Izzie gets famous and forgets all about the little people," one student, Kris, called out. Amelia laughed out loud. *Where did he come up with that one?*

She clapped three times. When the students clapped back their "we're listening," response, she nodded her approval and turned up the volume. The host was asking the typical questions:

"Izzie, how does it feel to have your video trending all across the world?"

Izzie shrugged and rolled her eyes up toward Creed. He laughed, his smile charming.

Amelia's heart misbehaved again.

* * *

Just twenty more minutes, dude, keep it together. Even when they ask your daughter stupid question after stupid question…you can do this.

Creed turned to the anchor, wondering if she had followed their progress through different programs all week and just decided to repeat all of the same questions.

"Izzie thinks New York is fun, don't you, Sweetie?" Creed made a silly face at his tired daughter. Izzie answered with a bored, teeth only, smile before he continued, "But she doesn't know what trending means. All she cares about is being famous for her classmates."

"Oh, are they watching at home, Izzie?" the anchor struck a pose and smiled into the camera.

"I dunno," Izzie sighed, but seemed to perk up at the idea. She sat up in her chair and smoothed her dress, something the wardrobe fanatic in the back had picked out.

Creed saw the chance to brighten her mood and get the interview over with faster. "Why don't we wave for them and sing a song?" The producer had mentioned that she wanted Creed and Izzie to sing live; he hoped she didn't mind that he grabbed the opportunity to get Izzie to cooperate while it was there.

"That would be fun," Izzie grinned. She picked a camera to look into and waved, "Hi Gracie!"

Creed grabbed the ukulele that someone had placed next to his chair and they sang a few lines from Izzie's favorite Etta James song. When they finished, the interviewer asked how such a young girl had come to know so many classic songs.

"I listen to them while editing photos and Izzie plays in the room with me. Eventually we began to sing different parts together and found that we really enjoy doing that," Creed answered.

Now as he sat with his daughter on live television and thought back on their whirlwind trip the last few days, he couldn't believe that this was the result. So many days he had spent working at home, encouraging Izzie to be in the room with him so that he could have some time with her to make up for the hours that he had to be away on shoots.

The anchor bobbed her head as he answered more questions, but Creed thought she appeared distracted. She placed a finger against the earpiece hidden behind her expertly styled blond hair, and nodded.

"Well, Creed and Izzie. It has been amazing to have you on our show today. I know you are probably ready to head home here in a little bit, but we have one final surprise for you…"

Creed, not knowing what to expect, followed the host's eyes to the next set, where a woman stood and walked into the lights.

The years had been hard on her; that was obvious no matter how much make-up the studio had painted her with. She was rail thin and wore a ridiculous flowy top over leggings and black boots similar to Izzie's. She also wore the same bored expression that Izzie had been flashing his way all morning only with a cynical twist of a smile.

Creed felt waves of shock and anger course through him, blocking out the excited chatter of the anchor as she explained to the audience at home that her producers had found Izzie's mother.

"Hailey Anderson."

Chapter Nineteen

"Listen, Mr. Williams, you need to understand th-that we are a business. Ratings are our br-bread and butter, surely you can understand that."

Creed paced back and forth across the green room, praying fervently for the Lord to intercede before he took the producer's head in his hands and squished it like a blueberry. He was disgusted by the small man's backpedaling. It was bad enough that he had brought Creed and Izzie to his show under false pretenses, but to stammer and falter around, eyes darting to and fro? The whimpering man made Creed sick.

"Daddy?" Izzie tapped on his leg.

He looked down at her, annoyance flooding through him at her tired gaze. Not only had they shocked him; they had emotionally jolted his young daughter; and after a week of interviews and appointments, a week in a hotel room away from all that was familiar to her. She rubbed her eyes and began to cry. Creed sat down next to Izzie on a worn couch and pulled her close.

"Yes, honey?"

"I want to go home," she sobbed into his chest. Creed laid a hand against her head, and glared up at the man in the suit.

"Me too," he said, eyes locked on the producer's beady eyes.

The man sighed. "So you don't want to do the second segment?"

Creed laughed without humor. "You have got to be kidding."

The man sat across from Creed, and leaned in. "You know if she goes out there without you, she can say just about anything she wants and you won't be there to refute it."

"So?"

"So, America is hard to rewire later. Once they hear one side of the story, that's what they believe. And the vibe I'm getting from this chick is that she is all about the drama and attention."

Creed worked a muscle in his jaw. "Maybe you should have thought about that before you brought her into my daughter's life without permission or warning," Creed hissed through clenched teeth. "Now would be the time to call me a cab. I don't give one lick about what America thinks."

The little man—face red, lips pinched—stared Creed down for another moment before he finally turned and left the room. Thirty minutes later he came back in and informed Creed that a taxi was waiting downstairs, with the bags they had brought with them to the studio already loaded into the trunk.

It wasn't until after Creed had numbly led Izzie through security and found their gate that he realized that they hadn't spoken since they left the studio. He sank into a chair near the wall of windows and pulled his daughter into his lap.

"What are you thinking, Kiddo?"

She shrugged, eyes on the drawstrings of his worn sweatshirt. It felt amazing to be back in his own clothes after a week of dressing like some hipster.

Creed waited a moment, but when Izzie still didn't speak or look up, he asked, "Would some lunch help?"

Izzie nodded. Creed checked their boarding time. Still three hours to go; the only glitch in his insistence that they be driven straight to the airport. He had spotted a burger place just down the wing from them. After a milkshake, fries, and four bites of burger, Izzie pushed her food away and finally asked what he knew she would.

"Was that my Mommy?"

"Sort of," Creed answered softly.

Izzie crinkled her forehead at him.

Creed sighed and leaned forward. "Izzie, a Mommy is someone who stays with you when you are sick, who takes you to school and volunteers in your classroom, who loves you and dresses you and brushes your hair. A Mommy reads to you and snuggles you and puts you first. That woman has not done any of those things. She could have, but she didn't."

"So…you and Aunt Kate and Grandma are my Mommies?"

Creed chuckled. "Ah, no. But family does step in sometimes," Creed said. He took in her wrinkled nose and sighed. "I hope someday I can explain it better, but for now I'll just say you never have to see that woman again."

"But she's right there," Izzie pointed to something over his shoulder and Creed's heart sank. *Hailey wouldn't have followed us to the airport, would she?*

Thankfully when he followed Izzie's line of sight, it was to a television that was airing the show they had just left. Creed couldn't imagine why the show would still be airing the segment with Hailey this long after they walked out— did people truly care that much about their personal business?

He let his gaze linger just a moment on the woman that walked out on his daughter. Hailey sat on the edge of the couch, one ankle crossed in front the other, hands folded regally in her lap. Gone was the smug gaze that she had reserved for him, in its place she wore a demure expression, full of self-pity. *What could she possibly gain from this?* Creed turned away but the woman stayed in his mind. She was blonde, tall and willowy. Opposite of Amelia's petite frame and dark coloring. *Now why am I comparing her to Amelia?*

Long after Creed and Izzie boarded the plane and coasted toward home, Creed thought over the day and his conversation with Izzie. He knew the reason Amelia's sweet, lovely face wouldn't leave his mind: when he described what a true mother was to his daughter, visions of her and Amelia doing all of those things together taunted him.

* * *

Amelia watched in confusion as a woman about her age with smug and calculating eyes joined Creed and Izzie on the set. Once the host explained who the woman was, Amelia jumped up in front of the screen. It took every ounce of willpower she had to turn off the T.V. and shield her students from the drama the producers had obviously worked hard to create.

Hours after she had pressed the off button and forced herself to put on a brave face to get through the rest of the day, Amelia walked through the front door of her apartment and flopped back onto her couch, feet hanging over the arm rest. Olé excitedly licked her face, but she barely noticed. Creed's ashen expression and rigid back stayed vivid in her mind for the remainder of the day.

When Amelia woke up Saturday morning, she watched the full segment with a mixture of insecurity and confusion. Izzie's mother was beautiful in all of the predicable ways that Creed's high school girlfriends had been: blond, tall, thin. Creamy skin, dramatic makeup, and a smart wardrobe. Amelia would have referred to her as "Fancy Pants" were it not for the flat eyes, and deep shaded pockets of sleep deprivation that hung below them.

Just as Amelia wondered if that haunted look could be a sign of great regret for leaving Izzie, the news anchor asked a similar question. She turned up the volume and leaned forward on the couch.

Hailey drew in a shaky breath, "Oh, every day. Every day I miss my baby girl."

The anchor nodded solemnly, her eyes large with sympathy. With calculated tact, she crossed her long legs and rested her chin in her hand. "Why then, Hailey? Why did you leave her?"

Hailey looked toward the ceiling, blinking her eyes rapidly before she answered, "I still hear her crying as I walked out that door, reaching for me. It haunts me." Hailey took an offered Kleenex box from someone off camera and wiped under her eyes.

"Way to not answer the question," Amelia muttered under her breath.

A knock on the door startled her and she paused the show. She pulled back the curtain on the French doors to find Lucy standing outside. Her little sister caught her eye and held up a brown bag and a drink carrier that held two coffee cups. Amelia smiled and dropped the curtain before she opened the door.

"Well, this is a treat! I thought you weren't coming until close to lunch." She took the drink carrier from Lucy and stepped back.

"Please tell me you watched it." Lucy breezed past Amelia into the living room and spotted the paused television with Hailey's upturned face frozen on the screen.

"Oh good," Lucy said as she unwound her knit scarf and plopped down on the couch. She held the bag in the air. "I brought donuts. We need some serious sustenance to watch this chick."

"How did you know I would be watching this?" Amelia asked.

"Are you kidding? Who *isn't* watching this? Chad's family is so freaked. I wanted to come see how you are doing."

Amelia gave a dry laugh. "Why would I be upset?"

Lucy shot her an unamused glance as she set the donut bag on the coffee table. She pulled out a maple bar, the bag crinkling.

Amelia walked to the kitchen for a stack of napkins and two plates. "Why is Chad's family so distraught?" Once she asked the question, she realized how ridiculous it was.

Lucy answered her thoughts back to her, "Well what could she possibly want? Does she plan to file for custody? Does she want to be in Izzie's life? What has she been doing, and how can they be sure that she will be safe for Izzie to be around?"

Amelia handed Lucy a napkin and sat beside her on the couch. She pulled out a buttermilk donut and asked, "Chad's worried about all of that?"

Lucy swallowed her bite of donut, shaking her head. "No, we were invited to dinner at their house last night and that broad got the whole family worked into a tizzy. Chad's mom and sister are pretty worried. Creed doesn't seem to be too concerned, but that could just be that he's tired and surprised. I mean, they really land blasted that guy."

Amelia's hand froze midway to her mouth, the donut between her finger and thumb. "You saw Creed?"

Lucy nodded, eyes on the T.V., oblivious to the strange ache her sister was experiencing.

"He came home and went right to their house. Izzie missed her family and I think Creed just needed to check out for a little bit. He and his Dad went on a pretty long walk after dinner. Hey, where is the remote? I didn't really see this, just the end."

Amelia numbly handed it to Lucy and ate the donut in silence. It tasted like cardboard.

Well what did you expect, Amelia? You and Creed have only had a few encounters; it's not like you two are best friends anymore. Why would he call you?

No matter how much truth she spoke to herself, the lump in her throat proved she wasn't listening. She had spent the week watching him on television, day dreaming about the possibility of a new house, new life, new…romance? Friendship? Whatever it was, having a close up of his handsome face on the screen night after night certainly hadn't helped her tangled emotions.

"Are you listening to me?" Lucy interrupted her pity party.

Amelia blinked. "Sorry, still waking up. What did you say?"

"This bit about Izzie crying and reaching for her. It didn't happen," Lucy rewound and played that section again. Amelia watched closely and noticed that, while Hailey blinked rapidly and wiped at her eyes, there were no actual tears.

"How do you know that it's not true?" Amelia asked, although she had been teaching first grade long enough to spot a liar when she saw one. Hailey certainly came across as dishonest.

124

"When Creed got Izzie she was just an infant sleeping in her carrier. She couldn't have been reaching for her. There is no way Hailey saw her do that."

Amelia turned back to the show, troubled. *What game was this woman playing?*

They finished their coffee and spent the rest of the day shopping together. The sisters shared a great comradery in spite of their age difference. Lucy had grown up too fast, marrying some scum bag after high school only to have her husband walk out and disappear a few months later. Amelia had spent a lot of time that very difficult year praying for her sister, letting her sleep over, and just sharing tears with her.

Lucy would say that the whole painful experience had served to drive her to the Lord, to make her faith real in a way that it hadn't been before. It had also forged a deeper relationship between Lucy and the rest of her family; one of transparency.

Over lunch at a small café, Amelia grew quiet. Lucy leaned over her citrus chicken salad and stared into Amelia's eyes. "Spill, Amelia. What are you thinking about? Creed?"

Amelia hesitated. "Oh, Lucy. My heart is involved here, and I am afraid it has rendered me stupefied. You know? I mean, the guy has enough going on. And all I can think about is scratching that woman's eyes out. But why? He's not mine. Why am I so consumed with jealousy?"

Lucy chewed her bottom lip thoughtfully. "Well, Sis, maybe it's that all of this time that you thought you were waiting for your future husband…Creed is who you were thinking about."

Amelia didn't answer. She wasn't ready to let herself think about how true that was.

Chapter Twenty

Creed had known that the trip would be tiring; he had never expected the emotional toll it would take on both him and Izzie. When they arrived at church Sunday morning, he held his young daughter's hand through the parking lot and into the church. He swore he felt the tension leave her as soon as they crossed the threshold. His shoulders loosened as well; this place was home and full of people that loved them. It was safe.

Creed greeted a few friends on his way to their usual spot in the sanctuary. His eyes found Amelia right away, sitting with Melba—an older woman in the congregation that was a grandmother to everyone she met. He admired Amelia's long gray dress and hip-length purple cardigan from where he stood. She kept her eyes on Melba, listening with rapt attention as if no one else in the room mattered.

Izzie gasped in delight when she saw her teacher. She wriggled her hand free and ran straight for her. Creed took one step in her direction when Gary, the man who ran the soundboard, called out to him. He surreptitiously watched Amelia's face split into a wide smile of joy. She dropped to her knees to receive Izzie's hug. They held one another for a moment and Amelia pulled back to look into Izzie's eyes and speak with her. She tucked a stray curl of red hair behind Izzie's ear and nodded, eyes wide while Izzie waved her arms animatedly. Melba said something to them both and Izzie's attention was diverted.

Gary asked Creed a question and he forced himself to turn away from Amelia and concentrate. After he agreed to run the sound board that morning—Gary's wife was home sick and needed help with their young children—Creed's eyes found Amelia again.

She was still crouching in front of Izzie, but chose that moment to rise to her feet. She rubbed her arms, and glanced around the room. He could tell the moment that she found his eyes on her. Her cheeks turned pink and she dropped her eyes. Eventually she brought them back to his unyielding gaze.

Not for the first time since the awful experience in New York, Creed wondered if Amelia had watched the shows. Somehow he was certain that she had and he wanted her opinion. Before the service started, he pulled his mother aside and asked if Izzie could sit with her while he ran the sound and if she would like to take Izzie home with her after church while he ran errands.

"She's not in the mood to drive around with me, I'm sure," Creed explained. "We're in dire need of groceries. I'm also hoping that I can talk Amelia into going with me to lunch. As Izzie's teacher, I'd really like to get her opinion on this whole mess," he added. He hadn't thought of it until now and was pleased with the idea.

His mother smiled up at him, a glow in her eyes. She patted his cheek. "I always did want you to end up with Amelia," she whispered knowingly.

Creed grinned and shook his head. "Just wanting to get her take on things," he said as he kissed her cheek.

She gave him a sly look that assured him he wasn't fooling anyone.

One woman down, one to go, Creed thought as the music started.

The sermon was on love. What love was and what love was not. Two points made by their pastor hit Creed square in the chest and deflated his plans: love is forgiveness and love is not getting your own way. For all of his frustration with Izzie's mother, Creed knew he owed her forgiveness. After all, he had been forgiven so much.

And for all of his rekindled adoration for Amelia, he needed to remember that she had other plans. Plans that she had put off for years. Plans that most definitely did not involve romance. Who was he to charge in and interrupt them?

Once the sermon was over and Creed had buckled Izzie into his parents' car with the promise to pick her up later, he fought down the desire to ask Amelia to lunch and left the parking lot alone.

*   *   *

Amelia felt like a fool. Creed made no effort to come and talk to her. She was certain after the intensity of his gaze that morning that he would seek her out. That at the very least he would say, "Hello." Instead, he and Izzie had left in a hurry.

Lucy invited Amelia to join her and Chad for lunch out, but she declined. She drove home and made a turkey and avocado sandwich instead. She used the last of her turkey and realized that she was low on almost everything else.

Looks like a grocery trip is in order today. I certainly can't afford to eat out very much once I start paying my mortgage.

Her stomach twisted. Reality of the leap she had made was finally settling in and her emotions were at war. On the one hand, her hopes were tied up in the excitement of actually living in her dream house. Of working hard to make it her own.

On the other hand, it was a terrifying step. Was she ready to commit to a mortgage? Was this really what the Lord had in store for her, or was she rushing ahead, making plans of her own without stopping to consult Him?

She knew that wasn't true this time. She'd prayed more about that house—that the doors would be closed if it wasn't right for her, that He would have His hand over the entire process—than she had in a long time.

Standing in her kitchen in thoughtful silence while she ate, Amelia barely noticed if the sandwich had any flavor. She gave Olé her crust and stepped into her bedroom to change into jeans, a sweatshirt, and sneakers.

"Sorry, Olé. They won't let you in the grocery store," she said when she exited the room and Olé began to dance around her feet in excitement.

"I'll take you on a long walk when I get back," she promised.

Amelia ruffed up his ears and told him to kennel up. She slipped him a treat after she closed the door, then left and locked her apartment behind her.

She was half way through her shopping, still lost in thought, when a deep voice called out from behind her.

"Amelia?"

She turned slowly, a tingle creeping up the back of her neck. Creed took a few steps toward her, pushing a half-full cart. She almost dropped the salad dressing bottle she was reading.

"Creed," she breathed dumbly. Oh, how he affected her.

"You shop here?" he asked.

"I guess so." she answered. *I guess so? As if I don't know where I shop?*

A woman steered her cart around Creed and stepped between them. She snatched a bottle of Italian dressing off the shelf, glaring at them both and then marching away in a huff.

"Oh my, we're totally breaking grocery store etiquette here, aren't we?" Amelia asked.

"How much shopping do you have left?" Creed asked, glancing at her cart. She breathed a quick prayer of thanks that she hadn't needed any embarrassing items for his eyes to feast upon.

"I'm just about done."

"And do you have plans later?"

"Yes, I have a date," she answered, thinking of her promise to Olé. She was surprised when Creed's face fell.

"With my dog. I promised Olé I would take him on a walk, but I could do that after," she rushed to add, in awe again at the change in his expression. His dark eyes brightened, the flecks of gold flashing as he stood taller.

"Well, I only have a few things left to get here. Could we go for coffee? I was hoping to talk something over with you. What do you say we have a little contest and the winner buys the other a treat at check out?" The twinkle in his eye was irresistible.

"Deal."

*　*　*

Creed rushed through the rest of his shopping, grabbing all the wrong brands and not caring one bit. So Izzie would get crunchy instead of creamy peanut butter, the kid needed some variety in her life. His happiness at running into Amelia both warmed and alarmed him. Hadn't he just resolved that she deserved better? *But that doesn't mean we can't be friends,* he assured himself, knowing that disaster awaited him if he truly thought he could just be friends with Amelia. But he didn't care. Time spent with her was worth the pain of possibly losing her one day.

Amelia suddenly appeared beside him and practically knocked him over to grab a jar of chocolate hazelnut spread. She grabbed the front of his cart and yanked hard, turning him sideways, before she took off toward the registers.

"Hey!" he called out, straightening his cart and chasing after her as fast as he could while being careful not to hit anyone. Amelia speed walked in an adorable stride, nodding and smiling angelically at other customers. Creed couldn't help but admire the sway of her hips. He shook his head.

Focus, Williams.

They arrived at check out at the same time and Creed laughed in triumph when the checker in the line Amelia chose put out the "Next Checkout" sign before she could reach the conveyor belt. She chose another—longer—line and Creed could taste the victory.

"Hey Amelia!" he called out. She rolled her eyes in his direction, looking as unamused as Izzie did during his niece's piano recital. "I'll take those jalapeño chips right there," he pointed with a smirk.

She opened her mouth to answer when another man called out her name. They both turned to see an employee wave her over to his lane as he turned on the light above his register.

"I can help you here, Darlin'," he said.

Amelia flashed Creed a saucy grin.

"Sorry, Creed. I guess you'll have to get your own chips. Oh, and uh, I'll take one of those dark chocolate almond bars. Thankyouverymuch," she winked and turned a one-hundred-watt smile to the cashier.

Creed chuckled and grabbed a couple of the bars. *Touché, Howard,* he thought. *Touché.*

"One problem with this plan, Creed," Amelia said when they rejoined in front of the store minutes later.

"What? That I ended up being suckered out of my win because some guy has a crush on you?" he asked dryly.

"Guys over seven years old don't get crushes on me, Creed. No," she continued swiftly, embarrassed at how true that statement was, "I bought cold stuff, and I'm assuming you did, too. Where were you planning to go? Because I can't risk my chocolate melting," she wiggled her eyebrows at him.

"You mean in this cold, sixty-degree air?" he asked, holding out a hand as if he could capture it.

"Well, what were you thinking for coffee?"

"Didn't you say you had to walk your dog? I could take these home, pick up the coffee, and meet you at your apartment for that walk. How does that sound?"

Salad Dressing Lady walked out of the store and glared at them for being in her way. Again. Creed pushed his cart closer to Amelia and offered the woman an apologetic smile. She rolled her eyes and marched past them both, her heels clicking sharp disapproval on the pavement.

Amelia arched a brow at him. "Well, well, well. Looks like your charms don't work on everyone," she teased. Then, picking up on something he said, she added, "Wait, Creed, do you live around here?" she asked in amazement.

"Nope. I live about twenty minutes that way—just a few minutes from your farmhouse, actually," he said, pointing north.

"Then why are you shopping here?"

"It's close to my mom's house," he answered, smiling into her eyes.

132

"Oh, duh. So will you have to drive home to drop off groceries, or…?"

"Well, I figured I would store my cold stuff in my parents' outside freezer and come back to get you. I do it all the time since I have to squeeze grocery trips in when I can and can't always get home immediately after," he explained.

"Okay. You take your stuff home and pick me up. Olé and I will be out front waiting for you. Feel free to bring Izzie, too."

"I love my daughter, but we've been together in a hotel for a week. I'm going to let her play at my mom's."

"Oh. Yeah, that makes sense." Shoot. Izzie was a great prop to hide behind when she got nervous. "Then I will gladly give you an adult only outing. Oh, and please make my coffee decaf. I'm an old lady now, you know. I can't handle caffeine after one in the afternoon."

After dropping off his groceries in his parents' garage, he chose The Hut for coffee, hoping Amelia still liked the same thing she had in high school, although he doubted it. His tastes had certainly changed over the years. He thought maybe the nostalgia of it would be enough to win him points as he ordered the decaf caramel mocha for her and black coffee for himself.

When he arrived at her apartment, she was sitting on the home's front steps, a large golden retriever at her side. When Creed parked and walked toward them, the dog's tail swayed back and forth, shaking his rump violently, but he stayed right by Amelia's side. Creed handed over the coffee, delighted when she took a sip and sighed with pleasure.

"I haven't had one of these in forever," she said, taking another drink.

"I'm just glad I remembered what you used to like," he said, pleased to have made her happy.

133

Olé stared up at him, tongue hanging out of his mouth, tail shaking his whole body.

"Are you still a dog fan?" Amelia asked Creed.

When he answered in the affirmative she softly said, "Ok, Olé," and the dog rose and walked next to Creed to nudge his free hand with a large, wet nose.

Creed crouched down to scratch behind his ears and talk to him for a moment before he rose to his feet.

"Wow, he's friendly," he commented.

"Yep, he's a love," Amelia smiled down at her pet, eyes warm. She glanced back up at Creed as she stood. "Ready?"

They walked along one of the oldest streets in town. Century old homes lined the street on either side. Large elms and willow trees hugged the sidewalk, roots breaking up the cement in some places. Leaves had begun to fall, cloaking the ground beneath them, creating a melodious soundtrack to their conversation as they crunched through the colorful carpet. Creed was impressed with how obedient and calm Olé was and said as much to Amelia.

"We were in a wonderful obedience class when he was a puppy," she said. "I wanted to be sure—" she cut herself off and turned a red face away from him.

"Wanted to be sure he would be a good dog for your future husband?" Creed ventured.

She only nodded, obviously embarrassed.

"You know, I think part of the fun of marriage will be learning stuff together with my wife," Creed commented, taking a sip of his coffee.

When she didn't answer, he continued, "My parents always tell about this season of their early years where all they could really afford were potatoes. My mom said they had a

134

great time figuring out all of the different ways they could eat potatoes. I'm sure at the time it was a real trial, but when they talk about it now, they get this tender look between them. You just know that the meat of their marriage is in those moments."

"I guess I never thought of it that way," Amelia said softly. Her eyes flooded with an emotion he couldn't define. Her thoughts had found their way to a memory—one that didn't include him, he was certain. How many years of memories were stacked between them when they were apart?

They walked in silence for a few minutes before she changed the subject. "Was Izzie upset that she couldn't come?" she asked, pulling Olé away from a tree he'd been diligently sniffing for the better part of a minute.

"Not one bit. She needed a break from me," he said with a wink.

"I've seen that girl with her Daddy. She does not want breaks from you."

"Well, she needed a break from errands anyway. She, uh, she had a rough trip," Creed stepped carefully into the subject that he had longed to talk over with Amelia and hoped that she would have insight for him.

Chapter Twenty-one

Amelia sucked in a breath, thankful that her hair covered her red ears. Could he tell that she had watched the show? Would he care if she did? Amelia had noticed the news still listed the encounter on the show as a trending topic. She wondered how long Creed would have to put up with being in the spotlight.

"You saw it, didn't you?" his deep voice interrupted her thoughts and Amelia felt her shoulders drop.

"I saw it. In fact, we were watching you at school. The principal and I had decided that particular show would most likely be the safest, cleanest one for my class to watch. I had to send a letter home to the parents letting them know that I had jumped up and turned off the T.V. before any of the kids picked up on the drama." She flattened her mouth. "I still had a few heated phone calls."

She suddenly stopped and rounded her eyes at Creed. "I'm so sorry, Creed. I am not blaming you and I certainly don't think talking to a few upset parents in any way compares to what you are going through, I just—"

Creed stopped as well and turned to her, his free hand on her upper arm.

"Amelia, slow down. I didn't take it that way. As a parent, I'm really thankful that you turned it off. As your friend, I'm really sorry that you had to."

He stared into her eyes, searching.

They stood that way, a slight breeze ruffling her hair. Creed moved his hand to cup Amelia's face and rubbed a finger over her cheekbone. Olé sat down as Amelia had taught him to do when she stopped walking, but she barely noticed. The gold flecks in Creed's chocolate brown eyes flickered like a campfire. The smell of wood smoke rising from a nearby chimney added to the affect. A warm glow began to rise from Amelia's toes and up to her cheeks.

"You, Amelia Howard, are a kind, fun, and loving teacher. Those kids—and their parents—are blessed to have you. You have every right to tell me how it affected you," he murmured.

His warm coffee-scented breath filled her senses; the look in his eyes rendered her speechless.

Olé whimpered up at them, breaking Amelia from her daze. She stepped back and tripped over a crack in the sidewalk. Her mocha flew in the air as she fell back. It smashed to the ground next to her, splattering the pavement—and her pant leg—with the sticky sweet liquid. Creed reached out to catch Amelia but tripped over Olé. He turned just in time to cushion her fall on the sidewalk. They lay that way— Creed cradling her in his arms, Amelia half sprawled on his chest—laughing until they were breathless.

"Now there's my clumsy old friend," Creed tossed out.

Amelia playfully smacked him on the shoulder. "Hey, I wasn't that bad," she protested.

Creed speared her with a knowing look and she relented. "Well, okay. I have always been a bit on the clumsy side, I suppose."

She laughed again, but sobered at the clouded look in Creed's gaze. His hand reached out to gently wind a section of hair that fell forward around his fist. Her scalp tingled; she labored to keep her eyes from closing in pleasure.

He's held you like this before, Amelia. Remember? And then he stomped all over your heart. Don't be a fool.

The chiding didn't calm the squeeze in her stomach or the warmth spreading through her chest.

"I missed you, Amelia. I've really, truly missed you."

She played with the string of his sweatshirt, feeling like the high school girl that had been so smitten with the man in front of her. The breeze shifted the branches of the trees above them and the sun shone brightly in her eyes, reminding her that they were sprawled on the sidewalk and part of a stranger's lawn in broad daylight. She rolled away from Creed and rose to her knees, wiping off her pants and sweatshirt. Creed groaned and did the same before he stood and offered a hand to help her up the rest of the way.

"Well, looks like we're out of coffee," she said, gathering the now empty cups and lids that had popped off.

"I'll take those for you," Creed said, stacking them together and shoving the lids inside. He plucked a leaf from her hair.

They walked on in awkward, stiff silence before Amelia asked what she had wondered since she saw Hailey on T.V.

"Creed?"

"Hmm?" he answered, eyes on the sprawling old house they passed.

"Were you and Hailey together very long?"

"No, not really. We went out for a few weeks, but never really clicked," he answered.

Amelia stopped and stared at him; her jaw unhinged in disbelief.

"What?"

"You have a child together, Creed. You must have clicked a little bit."

He stopped as well and shoved one hand in his pocket. He waved the coffee cups in a wide, helpless gesture.

"Amelia, I am not proud of that period of my life. I made decisions, that I'm not...I just...I screwed up, okay?"

138

Amelia wished she hadn't said anything. Her mind raced to come up with a way to back out of the conversation and go back to their easy banter.

Creed turned back to her before she could, his voice even and sure, "I wasn't like you, Amelia. I didn't think my future through. In fact, gave no thought to my future at all, let alone the spouse I hoped to have one day. I didn't live the deliberate way that you chose to, and I am deeply ashamed." The flecks in his eyes had cooled to a muted, muddy brown. She wanted to breathe life into him again, see the embers of light and life return after her careless words had snuffed them out.

"But you have Izzie."

A slow smile crept onto his face. She watched in amazement as the embers did, indeed, begin to glow again.

"Yes, I have Izzie, and I am so thankful. It amazed me how generous God is, in spite of my desperate wandering."

"I've never thought of that, Creed," Amelia admitted, thinking again that all of her preparing to be the perfect wife in the name of God had kept her from a meaningful relationship with the Lord. The realization troubled her and she told Creed as much.

"I think that's normal, Amelia. It is painfully easy to be distracted, even when what we are doing is the right thing. I can get very caught up in being a godly father without remembering to go to Him for that direction first."

Amelia appreciated his honesty. Without thinking, she looped her arm through his, the way that she used to, and they continued down the street at a lazy pace.

"Tell me about Izzie as a toddler, Creed," she demanded.

"Ah, you are on dangerous ground. This Papa is pretty enamored with that girl. I'll bore you," his eyes twinkled at her, obviously pleased that she wanted to talk about Izzie.

"Try me," Amelia said.

For the next hour Creed shared stories of the little habits Izzie used to have and how he had balanced spending time with her while building his business. Creed's family rallied around the single father and cheered him on, giving him time to breathe when he needed it, but mostly supporting him and Izzie as a complete family unit. No matter what anyone said about the way that Izzie had been conceived, the girl was loved well by Creed and his family.

Amelia's heart flickered with disappointment when at last they found their way back to her street. Creed walked her to her French doors around the back of the house, but before she could insert her key in the lock, he reached out to lightly cup her arm.

"Hey, Amelia?"

His touch was burning through the jacket. "Hmm?"

"What do you think of Hailey suddenly appearing on that show? I mean, do you think there's a chance she'll try to be in Izzie's life?"

Okay, if I am going to be grown-up Amelia I'm going to have to concentrate on his mouth—er, words, and not the way my inside are all squeezy right now. For goodness' sake, pull yourself together.

She scratched at a pretend itch on her opposite shoulder and his hand fell away.

"I definitely think it's odd that she showed up. And lied"—her face grew warm, and she rushed to cover her blunder—"or, er, Lucy told me that she lied. About Izzie reaching out for her?"

Creed worked a muscle in his jaw. "Yeah."

140

"Anyway, that's strange Creed. But has she tried to contact you at all since then?"

He shook his head, eyes fixed on a spot over Amelia's left shoulder.

She shrugged. "Then maybe that was just her seeking her ten minutes of fame? I honestly don't know. But I know you can't worry about something that hasn't happened yet."

Right, Amelia. It's only his daughter we're talking about here. Like you would understand.

"What I mean is, you know the Lord is with you and Izzie, and even Hailey. And only He and Hailey know her intentions. I think you should seek Him. He knows better than I, that's for sure."

Creed shifted his glance to hers, the corners of his eyes wrinkled softly.

He slowly nodded his agreement. Then he took a step back, his eyes still on hers.

"Thank you for the walk, Amelia. I really needed this."

"So did I, Creed. I—" she cut off. She had been about to say, "I really needed a good ending for us after the way you left. A restart." But she couldn't say that. Couldn't ruin their friendship now with remnants of her teenage emotions.

Hormones, she corrected herself. *That's all it was. You're a mature woman now. A teacher, for goodness' sake. Again— pull.yourself.together.*

"I needed a walk," she said lamely.

Creed eyed her wordlessly for a long heartbeat before he bid her and Olé good-bye.

Amelia had a lot to do in the following weeks with painting the new house and packing. She saw Creed at church each Sunday but she was either deep in conversation when he was free, or he and Izzie were slipping out immediately after the service. Izzie was back to riding the bus to school most days and the one time that Creed had picked her up, Amelia was busy with parents and students.

Although they hadn't seen one another much, Creed had begun to text her almost every day. Sometimes about something funny Izzie said, or some snarky remark about stories in the news. Most often he would text her some insight about his devotional in the morning.

She couldn't believe how different he was. The more they texted, the more she saw his heart. How humble he had become, and how much he truly loved the Lord and lived to be a man after God's own heart.

The crush she had on Creed in high school was nothing compared to the one she was developing as an adult.

Chapter Twenty-Two

The first morning of parent teacher conferences, the buzz of Amelia's phone brought a smile to her face. Not many people would text her so early. She finished drying her hair and put the hair dryer away before she read his text.

Pharaoh is a real delight, isn't he?

She laughed and texted back: **I always thought so**

She added a silly face emoji and applied her mascara.

I mean, what kind of leader lets his people suffer like that?

A terrible one, obviously. But God said he would be hard-hearted. Because of it the people of Israel and Egypt saw the amazing wonders that God performed. But I agree with you—he was a real loser ;)

I hope your conferences go well today. Watch out for your 4:00—I hear he's a real charmer.

Nah, he's just a guy that's too big for his britches. I can handle him.

Hey!

See ya at 4, Creed ;)

With Creed's reminder, her heart fluttered in anticipation of the afternoon appointment. Amelia chose her clothes carefully. She wore gray pinstriped dress pants and a cream colored blouse with gray ribbon woven in the modest scooped neckline. She carefully worked her bangs into a delicate braid pinned just above her left ear.

Most of her meetings for the day went smoothly. She really enjoyed meeting with parents and learning more about her students and how she could best teach them. There were certainly meetings that didn't go well, but for the most part each parent she met appreciated what she had to say.

In the short break before her time with Creed, Amelia stopped short of spritzing herself with the perfume she kept in her desk while she waited for him to arrive. *Too much, Amelia.* She rubbed a small drop of scented lotion into her hands instead.

Creed walked into her room five minutes late, face ashen, his smile—if one could call it that—not reaching his eyes. He slunk into the chair in front of her desk.

"Whoa, what is the matter with you?" Amelia asked, leaning forward in her desk chair.

"My lawyer just called me," Creed murmured, dazed. "Hailey wants to be in contact with Izzie."

*   *   *

Creed didn't know what to make of the situation. Didn't know what to do.

Hailey had her lawyer contact the lawyer he had used when Hailey dropped Izzie with him in the first place. Back then his attorney, James Q. Peabody, had counseled that unless he wanted child support from Hailey, he could go about his life with Izzie without contact. After all, Hailey had abandoned the child and Creed could file for custody. Creed hadn't known then what he wanted to do. He had barely been keeping his head above water in the new role of father, but he had filed—and won due to no contest—full custody.

Now Hailey had a change of heart and wanted Izzie in her life?

What if he allowed Hailey in and she did more damage? Izzie might have a wonderful family, but Creed knew once

144

Izzie had contact with her mother, her heart would be involved. It was only natural. And what if he said no? Creed had heard horror stories about the court system and their almost automatic favor for the mother in these situations. What if he said no and Hailey filed for custody—and won?

When he arrived at the school for his conference, and told Amelia about the phone call, she sent him home.

"Creed, we can do this another day. You just focus on this."

Creed nodded numbly and rose, barely acknowledging Amelia's tender squeeze on his shoulder as he walked out.

The next morning, a Friday, after a fitful night of sleep agonizing over what he should do, Creed finally rose and made a pot of coffee. He had a meeting with his lawyer later that day to seek his advice.

Before he could do anything, make any decisions, he needed time in the Word, seeking counsel from the only One who knew and loved them all.

He had finished reading two chapters in John, and was getting ready to head to the kitchen for a second cup of coffee when Kate called him in a tizzy.

"They're following you Creed! It's, like, the paparazzi. You need to warn Amelia or get a bodyguard at the school or some—"

"Whoa, whoa, whoa, Kate. Slow down. I haven't even had my second cup of coffee yet. What are you talking about?"

"Creed, turn on your computer and go to the *But First the News* website. They have pictures of you and Amelia, um, cuddling? Outside on a sidewalk or something?" her tone changed to sisterly curiosity.

Creed sat at his desk in the living room and ran a finger over the square pad to wake up the laptop. It only took a few seconds to find the site. His blood ran cold at the picture of him and Amelia at the top of the page. It was the day of their Sunday walk and the picture was obviously taken after they fell. He clicked on the article and another image came on the screen of him holding Amelia's face in his hand and staring into her eyes. A little "play" icon showed that the article was a video news report.

"I'll call you back, Kate."

He tapped "end" on his phone and tossed it on the desk. Creed clicked the icon and sat back with his arms crossed, clenching and unclenching his jaw as a young male anchor with skinny jeans and a snug t-shirt enthusiastically delivered the "Trendy Snippet."

"Creed Williams of the popular Father/Daughter video was seen canoodling with his daughter's teacher last Sunday. Williams and his daughter took social media by storm when their video went viral after it was entered into a contest for grand prize money totaling fifty thousand dollars. Last week they made the morning show circuit in New York, but ended the last interview abruptly when the child's mother, Hailey Anderson, appeared on set. Williams claimed to not know Anderson was coming and left New York immediately. Maybe to get back home to the teacher? Yesterday Ms. Anderson posted on Twitter that she is seeking more time with her daughter. Certainly Williams will have a response, just as soon as he disentangles himself from the pretty brunette. We'll keep you posted on this and all of the Trendy Snippets we come across on But First the News."

Creed groaned and closed the website. Questions raced through his mind, chasing one another with no resolution.

Why on earth was this news?

Why did anyone care one bit about his personal life?

He rubbed his hands down his face, pulling at the skin on his cheeks, and stared at the pictures again. Most disturbing was that he had not noticed someone with a camera following them on the walk. How would Amelia ever feel safe with him after this?

He groaned. *Amelia. Dangit.* He texted her.

Hey, you up? I need you to call me when you get this.

When she hadn't answered five minutes later, Creed tried calling. It went straight to voicemail. He remembered that she'd told him on their walk that she turned her phone off every night.

"I started getting really weird calls from telemarketers at night. One even called at three in the morning! I finally got in the habit of turning my phone off when I go to bed. I hope no one ever needs me in the middle of the night because I'm not changing it any time soon," she had said with a laugh.

He checked the time. 5:23 am. There was no telling when she would turn it back on. He had his sister back on the phone in no time.

"Kate? Can you do me a favor and come over here? I won't be long, but I need to go warn Amelia; her phone is turned off. She has parent meetings all day and I don't want her to be caught off guard."

"Already in my car and on my way, Creed. I'll see you in a few," Kate said, breathless. The line went dead.

Creed laughed. How often had Kate badgered him to date Amelia in high school? No doubt she thought that embrace was something steamy and found great delight in the thought. He couldn't wait to tell her that Amelia had knocked him over by accident and that she had no interest in him whatsoever.

Chapter Twenty-Three

The knock sounded again and Olé growled low in his throat. Who would be at her door so early? Watching a true crime show the night before had definitely been a bad idea. Amelia looked around for a weapon. Her eyes landed on the heavy iron skillet she kept on the wall above the stove.

Worked for Rapunzel in that movie.

She grabbed the skillet and crept toward the door, hoping she wouldn't have to use it.

A deep, muffled voice called out through the door, "Amelia, it's Creed. I need to talk to you."

Still unsure, Amelia glanced down at Olé. "If you really are Creed, then what is my dog's name?"

"Right now your dog is Olé. Your first dog ever was Blue, and the dog you had when we were in high school was Stormy," came the steady reply.

Amelia pulled back the curtain to see Creed standing on her stoop with his hands shoved in his front pockets. She breathed a sigh of relief when his lips twitched up in their familiar way. She dropped the curtain and smoothed a hand over her hair. She looked down at her snug t-shirt and flannel pajama pants. Great. She opened the door and Creed shook his head.

"Really? I could have been a serial killer that's been stalking you for years! I can't believe you opened the door."

"What on earth are you doing here, Creed?" she asked, stepping back to let him in.

"What are you doing with *that?*" he countered, eyeing the skillet in horror.

"You could have been a serial killer, remember?" she volleyed, her back to him as she hung the skillet on a hook above the stove. He didn't comment.

She turned back to the living room where Creed was scratching behind Olé's ear, eyeing her apartment. She tried to see it through his eyes: small living room with a kitchenette along one wall, a short hallway that led to her room and bathroom. She had set up a small round dining table with three mismatched chairs near the wall between the kitchen and the bedroom. Other than her couch, an overstuffed chair and her coffee table, she didn't have much furniture. Just a bookshelf and T.V. cabinet that had been her parents'. In fact, most of the furniture in the room had been her parents'. She wondered if Creed might recognize it. Her coffee cup sat on the table next to her chair, an enticing curl of steam rising from it. Her Bible lay open next to her coffee.

The spicy scent that followed Creed into her apartment mingled with the rich brew hanging in the air from the coffeepot. For all of the years that Amelia had dreamt of a husband, she had never imagined how wonderful the fragrance of cologne or man soap or whatever it was and coffee would be when entwined together in the wee hours of the morning. Her face flushed. She might need to get Creed out of her apartment and never let him back in.

He looked up at her just then, causing her stomach to flip. As always.

Could he tell that she wanted to snuggle up with him and watch *When Harry Met Sally* every Friday for the rest of their lives?

"You might be upset with me in a minute," he said softly.

"Why?" Amelia struggled to tamp down her emotions.

Instead of answering, he gestured to her open laptop on the coffee table, and asked, "May I?"

Confused, she nodded and Creed sat down on the couch. He typed for a minute before turning it to her.

Amelia gasped out loud when she saw the pictures of them together on a major news website. Well, not news, necessarily. What was her face doing on a gossip rag? She sunk down on the cushion next to Creed.

"Is that from our walk?"

"Yes."

"And someone took pictures of us?"

"Looks like it."

"Why?" she turned to Creed, heart trembling at the stricken look on his face.

He turned to her. Seemingly on their own his hands reached out and settled on the tops of her knees. "Amelia, I don't know. I have no idea if Hailey has something to do with this or not. I don't know why anyone cares about my personal life. I don't understand any of this. I wanted to come here and warn you before you went to work today so that you wouldn't be blindsided."

Amelia laid her hands over his. He slowly rotated to meet her palm to palm. "Thank you. I appreciate that, Creed."

They remained frozen for a moment, hand in hand, the quiet of the morning giving both a hope that neither was willing to let go of. The faint rhythm of their heartbeats thumped messages to each other through their warm fingers and palms; whispering what had been left unsaid for more than a decade. Their gazes avoided and met, then fell away before skirting back to one another and holding. Amelia felt that she could sit that way forever. She found herself gently sweeping her thumb up the edge of his pinky finger and back again. His fingers tightened around hers and his eyes went almost black. She cleared her throat and pulled her hands back.

"You need to go," she whispered.

Shadows played across his face. A muscle danced near his jaw.

"Not because I'm upset," Amelia felt the need to assure him. "Well, I am, but not at you. You couldn't have known that someone would do this. We both know how innocent that walk was. But Creed?"

"Yes?"

"You smell amazing. I'm confused and still waking up…and that picture of me looking up at you while you hold my face is just too much. It reminds me of…well. And you being here in my apartment this early with just the two of us doesn't feel appropriate. I hope you understand that I need you to leave."

His Adam's apple bobbed. His eyes skittered away and met hers once more. He rose and walked to the door, opening it wide before he turned back to her.

"Would you join Izzie and me for dinner tonight, Amelia? We would love to cook you our specialty."

"I would love to. On one condition," she answered, following him to the door.

"What's that?"

"You need to make those amazing rolls." She winked, trying to lighten the electricity that pulsed between them.

* * *

Her sleepy eyes and mussed hair were too hard to ignore. The slowly awakening dawn and the threshold between them emboldened him. He leaned forward and brushed a lingering kiss against her cheek. She jumped slightly, her breath fluttering across his lips. He pulled back quickly, before he could take advantage of his emotions, or the early morning, or the memory that she had surfaced.

"Deal." He grinned and took a step back.

Amelia shut the door and Creed waited for her to lock it before he walked away. He was thankful that he had been able to warn her about the sudden publicity, and even more thankful that she had kicked him out. Her warm apartment smelled like oranges and cinnamon and the feminine touches throughout had filled him with a strange and sad longing. He wanted Izzie to have a mother; a woman to braid her hair and shop for her and bake her cookies. Sure, he could do those things, but a woman—Amelia, if he was honest about where his heart was headed—could do it all with a flare that Izzie needed. With the love that he longed for.

Lord, why did I have to fall for a woman that spent the last ten years of her life preparing for her husband...only to change her mind about all of that just as I am ready to be the man that she has been preparing for?

He drove back home and opened the door to the townhouse quietly. Kate sat on the couch, his laptop balanced on her knees, scrolling through Facebook.

"Creed, it's not even six in the morning and I have a dozen messages about this news article. The little 'Trending now' section on the side of the screen has you and Izzie and Hailey at the top under 'Father/Daughter Duo Custody Battle'."

"Great," he muttered, tossing his keys on the desk.

"That was fast," Kate commented, fishing.

152

He sunk into his recliner, feet sprawled apart, elbows digging into his knees. He stared at the floor thoughtfully before he responded to his sister.

"She's amazing, Kate. And I think I'm too late. Or at the very least I am too complicated. She deserves so much more than this nonsense," he said, waving his hand toward the computer.

He laughed without humor. "Amelia doesn't even have a smartphone—or at least she didn't until last week, I guess. She must be the last person on earth to purchase one. She is simple. Down to earth. She deserves so much more than what I can offer her." He punched a fist into his open palm lightly, thinking.

"But…she's coming to dinner," he said.

From the corner of his eye, he saw Kate's face split into a wide smile.

Chapter Twenty-Four

"Creed, I really don't think she has much of a case if she chooses to make one. You are a good father that has provided a stable home for Izzie. As for Hailey, she is a giant question mark. She has moved around and dropped off the radar so frequently that she would make a fly dizzy," Creed's lawyer, an older gentleman with thinning white hair and a rail thin frame leaned back in his desk chair with a squeak.

Creed nodded, his eyes on the "James Q. Peabody" etched into the frosted glass on the top half of the office door.

"So what about this, photographer or reporter or whatever he is, that took these photos of me? Should I be worried about that?"

James scoffed. "No. You are certainly allowed to date, Creed. And I think you should," he added, winking. "But this is just a gossip rag. If it becomes troublesome, come see me and we can do something about it. If anyone is in the wrong, it's them; not you. In the meantime, trust your gut on whether Hailey should see Izzie or not. Legally, I don't think you need to be concerned. You are a great father, Creed," he said again and rose, his hand outstretched.

Creed shook the offered hand and thanked James before he let himself out. The law office was located in the heart of downtown in an old building. Creed loved to bring clients to the alley behind it for photo sessions. The red brick and a vintage, faded advertisement for laundry soap made for a charming backdrop.

The autumn air had turned even colder and Creed zipped up his black fleece jacket before he shoved his hands in the front pockets. The meeting with Peabody had taken less time than he anticipated. He was pleased that he had time to walk around downtown for a bit before he met his client for coffee around the corner.

The senior and her mother were waiting for him at the coffee shop when he arrived ten minutes early. Creed apologized for not beating them there.

The mother grinned, "Not a problem; we're early."

Her smile was uncharacteristically bright. Maybe she was just one of those perky yoga types. She certainly dressed the part.

"Were you with your girlfriend from the internet?" the daughter blurted out. She jumped slightly and whispered, "Ouch," rounding innocent eyes at her mother with a shrug.

Creed forced a tight smile. "I'm afraid that was a misunderstanding," he answered. He turned to the large menu mounted behind the cash registers.

"What do you ladies say we grab a drink to keep us warm and get started? Do you have a special place in mind where you want to take pictures today?" he rushed on, hoping he could avoid the subject of Amelia. His mind was far too cluttered where she was concerned.

Creed had never photographed such a distracted subject, including the family portraits he had taken for a family with triplet toddlers the month before. His senior seemed to be star-struck, her mother no better. He resisted the urge to roll his eyes when his client not-so-nonchalantly snuck in a selfie with him in the background and spent the next few minutes posting it somewhere online.

By the end of the session, Creed had a headache and stiff neck from waiting frozen in position while the girl texted or tweeted or whatever it was she was doing. He stored his equipment in his car and noticed a green light blinking on his phone. He had eight new messages from potential clients, all recommended by the distracted teen. Well, at least this was good for business. No doubt they all hoped that the website where he posted teasers of his sessions was just as popular as the trending video. *I can make them all famous!* he thought with sarcastic enthusiasm.

He tossed the phone onto the passenger seat and hoped Amelia was faring better with her parent-teacher meetings.

At least the parents are only worried about their children and not her weekend activities.

He drove to his mom's to pick up Izzie. Once they were back in the car, he waited patiently for her to buckle her seat belt before he caught her eye in the rearview mirror.

"Missed you today, Kiddo," he crinkled his eyes at her.

"Miss you, too, Daddy. Nana made me eat soup for lunch." Izzie stuck out her tongue in disgust.

"Well, we should make up for that at dinner."

Creed shifted the car into reverse and backed out of the driveway. They both waved at his mom who stood blowing kisses from the large picture window.

"With pizza?" Izzie sat up excitedly.

"I was thinking we could make something fancier than that for our guest tonight." Creed pulled forward and drove in the direction of the grocery store.

"Who's our company?" Izzie asked distractedly, digging through the backpack of toys she had taken with her.

Creed paused and once the car was stopped at a light he caught his daughter's gaze again.

"Miss Howard."

156

He scrunched one eye closed and twisted his mouth to one side under his wrinkled nose at the shriek of excitement that hit him full force from the back seat.

* * *

"I assure you, Mr. McClary, it's not what it looked like," Amelia leaned forward in the chair across from her boss' desk, hands clasped to her chest.

The entire day had been a train wreck. From the moms that were intrigued by her relationship with Creed to those that were clearly offended by it. None of them seemed too interested in discussing their child's progress. By the time noon rolled around, a headache began to pound behind Amelia's eyes, her shoulders taut with anxiety.

Now she sat across from the principal who said he had received numerous calls from parents concerned that the publicity of the first grade teacher would put their students in danger. While McClary assured them and Amelia that he in no way anticipated that being the case, he did care about the bad publicity.

"We're not here to discuss the truth behind the article, Amelia. I'm more concerned with the reputation of this school. I have a meeting today with members of the school board; I'll find you at the end of the day to discuss this further."

He looked over wire-rimmed glasses at her, making her feel like a student that had been sent to him for throwing spit wads across the cafeteria.

The stress of the morning caught up with her and welled in her throat, holding a response in its grip. She nodded and rose.

Chloe called out to her in the hallway just before Amelia stepped into her classroom.

"What did he say to you?" she whispered, her dangly skeleton earrings dancing with the shake of her head.

Amelia shook her head. She glanced behind her and back at Chloe. *Not here.*

Chloe understood the look. "Hey, I have a break between parents, how about you?"

Amelia finally had her breath back, "Uh, yeah. My parent for my next block of time cancelled and then I had scheduled a lunchbreak."

"Then, girl? Let's get out of here," Chloe said.

Over chicken salad sandwiches at a small deli around the corner, Amelia shared some of what the parents and the principal had said. Chloe, as Amelia expected her to be, was outraged.

Chloe was usually outraged over something.

"Good grief, Amelia, where is this law that says you need to remain unmarried or that dating is going to affect your job? What do they all think you are going to do, give your students a play-by-play of your relationship?" Chloe shoved a chip in her mouth, and munched angrily.

Amelia shrugged. Although she felt raw and uncertain, Chloe had a point. In what world was she not allowed to date? Just because she had behaved like an old maid doesn't mean she was one. But there was more to it, of course.

"It's because of the position we were in when the picture was taken and the colorful spin that reporter gave on it. Not exactly a great advertisement for New Hope Christian School, you know?"

Amelia picked up her sandwich and set it down again. She really wasn't hungry.

Chloe chewed thoughtfully for another moment. She bounced her eyes from Amelia to the window next to their table and back again, a barely contained question in her eyes.

"Oh, just ask, Chloe," Amelia said, a small smile curling her lips.

"Well, was it, you know—a steamy moment?"

"If you consider tripping and knocking a guy over by accident steamy, then yes. It was quite scandalous," Amelia answered dryly.

Chloe laughed. She rested an elbow on the table, chin in her hand.

"And how is your heart, Amelia?"

Amelia gave a small, self-deprecating laugh. "Gone, Chloe. It's gone."

Chloe wrinkled her forehead, "And why is that bad? The ex-wife thing?"

"Not an ex-wife. Ex-college-fling," Amelia corrected, hoping she didn't ask for more details. Amelia had no desire to share Creed's personal business. "And no, it's not that. It's me. This is when I was supposed to really go after all of the things that I've ignored for these years. I finally get to change my life. I'm moving into my new house tomorrow, and looking for ways to serve people in all of that space. I don't want some guy in my head making decisions for me like I've had all of these years. I want to get a cat…"

Amelia stared out the window, her voice drifting, leaving Chloe to wonder about the significance of cats. Time ran out and the women wrapped up the remainder of their lunches and drove back to the school. Chloe parked, but stopped Amelia before she could open the door.

"I just have to say: maybe Creed is your new dream. And who cares if it is too much like the old one? Maybe you have been living like an old married woman to protect yourself from falling in love. And here love has found you and I think your new dreams—the house, the independence, the, uh, cat?—could possibly be your new protection—your new reason to hide from love. Or maybe to hide from something bigger altogether—the scary unknown."

With that she exited the car, leaving Amelia stunned. *Could Chloe be right?*

Amelia made it through the rest of the afternoon, mind more muddled than before. Thankfully most of the afternoon parents wanted to actually discuss their students. Still, it seemed that there had been a shift in the air. A quiet disapproval in their eyes. Almost every couple she met was stilted and unnervingly quiet. They asked very few questions, making the fifteen minute sessions shorter, the breaks in between longer.

Amelia coasted through the remainder of the day on auto-pilot. When the last parent finally left she chose to stay another few minutes and write out instructions on the board for Monday. When she was done, she gathered her things and straightened up her desk.

A knock sounded on the open door.

Amelia jumped slightly and turned to see Mr. McClary standing tall, his hands in the pockets of his pants. His frown matched the downward pull of his eyes.

"Miss Howard, I need to see you in my office when you're finished," he said.

Chapter Twenty-Five

"Daddy! She's here, she's here, she's here!"

Amelia laughed, in spite of a piercing headache, at the banshee wail that rang out from the depths of the house. A male voice answered and pounding steps grew louder. The door handle twisted and snapped back in place a few times, followed by inaudible whispers. Amelia bit back a smile at the sound of Creed's voice near the door. The lock squeaked loudly and at last Izzie opened the door. Creed stood with his hands in the back pockets of his worn jeans behind her.

The little girl giggled, her face red. "I forgot to unlock the door," she rolled her eyes toward the ceiling and slapped her hand against her forehead.

Amelia flashed Creed a grin and looked back at Izzie. "That was silly, Miss Izzie."

She sobered at that. "Hey, you called me Miss, just like you're Miss. Miss Izzie and Miss H.," she babbled excitedly.

"Hey, Miss Izzie and Miss H., what do you say we move this indoors?" Creed suggested, pulling Izzie out of the way so that Amelia could enter. She stepped into their home and handed Creed a small brown sack, but held onto a large leather photo album that she had tucked under her arm.

"This is for you; thank you so much for inviting me to dinner."

Amelia hoped her voice didn't give her frazzled nerves away. She had almost called to beg off the invitation but changed her mind when she imagined a crestfallen Izzie. And truly, after her day, Amelia found herself craving Creed's steady presence. She had taken three aspirin tablets, but they didn't seem to have an effect on the ice pick pounding her between the eyes.

Or the tight fist of fear that was squeezing her insides.

She allowed her eyes a quick look around their home, admiring the warm and cozy feel of it. The front door opened into a small living room, with stairs running parallel to it along the far wall. If she walked straight, she would find herself in a corner kitchen. The living room was simply but smartly furnished with a burgundy leather couch and matching recliner. Two short bookshelves flanked a small desk with a closed laptop set in the middle. Creed had mounted framed pictures, mostly of Izzie, along the wall beneath the stairs.

"Your home is lovely," Amelia said, making sure her eyes crinkled in the corners. *Take that, headache.*

Izzie, suddenly a formal little lady, offered to take her coat and purse. She hung them on a set of hooks anchored to the wall next to the door. A few Izzie sized coats and a pink backpack dangled from the hooks haphazardly. Amelia resisted the urge to straighten them.

"What is this?" Creed asked, hooking a finger on the rim of the sack to peek inside. He stood close enough for her to see a small freckle on the edge of his full lower lip. Funny how she had never noticed that before.

"Nothing big. Vanilla ice cream and something for Izzie," she answered, feeling a blush threatening to bloom. She placed a palm against her abdomen, desperate to squash her nerves. Creed pulled out the small container of gourmet vanilla bean.

"For me? What did she bring for me, Daddy?" the poised little hostess disappeared and Izzie was back, dancing from foot to foot excitedly.

"Hmmm," Creed set the ice cream down on his desk. He closed one eye tight and peeked in the bag again, holding the top with both hands before he looked back at Izzie, one eye still shut. He looked in the bag again and hid it behind his back.

"That depends. What are you going to give me for it?" Creed asked Izzie.

She responded by planting both of her fists on her narrow hips.

"Daddy." Izzie's chin dipped and she looked up at him through long lashes, her mouth flat.

"It's okay Izzie," Amelia interjected, holding out the photo album, "I brought something that's even better than the playdough in that bag."

Izzie laughed as Creed dramatically let his jaw hang open.

"I can't believe you ruined my game," he protested indignantly, handing Izzie the sack. "Here," he sniffed, his nose turned toward the ceiling, "you can have it."

Izzie giggled again and pulled out the container of purple glitter playdough, three plastic cookie cutters tied together with ribbon and a small rolling pin. Remembering what Amelia had said, she looked up and eyed the album skeptically.

"Why's that better?"

Amelia crouched down to Izzie's level. She opened the book to the first page so that only they could see it. Izzie's eyebrows rose and her mouth opened in delight. She looked to Creed.

"That looks like you, Daddy," she whispered. "Only you look little."

Creed leaned over to see the picture; he and Amelia stood back to back in their prom attire, arms crossed, trying to look tough.

"Wow, there's a blast from the past," he winked at the girls. "Izzie, why don't you take Miss H. to the couch and you can look at what she has there. I'll finish dinner."

Amelia rose. "Can I help you with anything?"

Creed shook his head no and picked up the ice cream container. "You just enjoy embarrassing me in front of my daughter with pictures of my awkward years. I'll try really hard not to burn the rolls in retaliation." Creed tugged lightly on Izzie's hair and walked down the hall toward the kitchen.

Amelia allowed Izzie to lead her to the couch where they sat together for the next ten minutes, looking through pictures of Amelia and Creed's teen years. Izzie asked a dozen questions about every photo and her teacher answered each with as much enthusiasm as she could muster.

"I am not comfortable with my child being in the class of someone who is so obviously immoral."

The accusing tone of her first appointment that day rang out over the pleasant evening, threatening to bring Amelia to tears. McClary's regretful tone fought for a place in her thoughts as well.

Creed stepped into the room and paused, his eyes on her face. A shadow passed over his expression. He tilted his head slightly, questioning. The compassionate fix of his gaze was almost Amelia's undoing. She closed the book.

"Izzie, looks like it's time to eat," she said softly.

"Why don't you set the table, Kiddo," Creed said to his daughter, eyes never leaving Amelia's face.

Izzie hopped down from the couch and ran past Creed into the kitchen. Amelia rose slowly to her feet, the lump in her throat and stinging in her eyes threatened to take over.

164

"Amelia?" Her name on his lips was a soft embrace.

She stopped next to him, her eyes fixed on his t-shirt collar.

"Rough day?" Creed ventured.

A nod. It was all she could manage.

Plates clattered; Izzie setting the table.

"Because of the pictures." It wasn't a question.

She couldn't respond. He had no idea. Did he even know about the rest?

Water kicked on; Izzie filling glasses.

Amelia sucked in a sharp breath as his arms came around her back. She closed her eyes at the feel of his cheek against hers. He moved his face slightly and her toes tingled at the scratch of his stubble against her skin. He held her tight for a moment, lips near her ear when he spoke at last, his breath warm against her hair.

"I am so sorry."

Amelia couldn't form a rational thought. All she could think about was the feel of Creed's arms around her back. Her hands slipped up his arms, over his shoulders, lacing behind his neck. The hug lingered, their bodies melding together. Amelia blushed. She should pull back; surely he hadn't meant for the embrace to stretch out this long. She was making a spectacle of herself. Before she could convince herself to release her grip, Creed tucked his nose into the hollow near her collarbone and she stopped thinking altogether. She could feel the steady staccato of his pulse through the pads of her fingers, noting that it's sudden increase matched hers.

"What are you doing?" Izzie's voice jolted them apart; the electric current that hummed beneath the surface lashing out with white hot force. Amelia's knees shook. She opened her mouth but nothing came out.

"Miss Amelia looked sad, so I thought I would give her a hug," Creed answered, the thick bass of his voice husky.

Izzie snorted. "Daddy. You called her Miss Amelia. And your face is all…droopy."

Amelia's cheeks tingled.

Creed blinked stupidly. "Is it?"

Izzie looked between them, arms akimbo.

Creed finally cleared his throat and clapped his hands together. "Well, did we promise *Miss Howard* dinner or what?" he asked. He walked to the kitchen without waiting for an answer.

Izzie's animated chatter at dinner eased the tension.

They laughed at her antics over grilled pork chops, garlic mashed potatoes, rolls, and a green salad. Creed had placed a small round table, just big enough for four people to fit comfortably around it, near the back door of his townhome. Amelia imagined Creed and Izzie enjoying many meals in that kitchen.

"This pork chop is incredible," she commented, taking a bite. The tender meat practically melted in her mouth.

"It's our specialty, isn't it Izzie?" he winked at his daughter while cutting a chop into smaller bites for her.

"Mmmm, 'Poor Man's Steak' is my favorite," she added, loudly smacking her lips together.

Amelia laughed at that. Creed raised a brow at Izzie.

"This is definitely better than any steak I've ever had," Amelia said. She stabbed another bite with her fork.

166

"Forgive me, but I was expecting boxed macaroni and cheese topped with canned chili," she admitted.

"That's Daddy's favorite!" Izzie gasped.

"What's so funny?" she asked her teacher who sat with a napkin over her mouth, her shoulders shaking.

Amelia swallowed her giggles and shook her head. She returned wordlessly to her meal, relishing the creamy potatoes and airy rolls.

"Honestly, Creed, where did you learn to cook like this? I took a cooking class years ago and I can barely pull off edible meals."

"Well, when Izzie and I first moved here, we were either at my mom's or eating out. I realized quickly that starting a new business was not going to allow our budget to eat out that much. My mom watched Izzie a lot more back then and I got the impression that she would rather we eat more meals at home."

Creed buttered a roll and put it on Amelia's empty plate. A smile played at the corner of her lips when he continued, completely unaware of what he had done.

"So I asked my mom to teach me some things. Turns out I have a knack for cooking which was a good thing for us, wasn't it, Izzie?"

She turned somber eyes to him. "Not really, Daddy."

His jaw dropped. "Why not?"

"Because when I ask if we can go out you tell me you can just make the same stuff at home. You took all the fun out of life," she rested her cheek in her hand, elbow on the table, and pushed the salad around her plate.

Creed rolled his eyes toward the ceiling.

Amelia really laughed at that. They finished the meal in companionable silence. Once father and daughter leaned back contentedly in their chairs, Amelia stood to stack their plates.

"Hey, what are you doing?" Creed jumped to his feet and took the plates from her.

"You cooked, it's only right that I clean," Amelia protested, taking the plates back.

"Does anyone ever take care of you, Amelia?" his voice was soft, his brown eyes piercing.

* * *

Creed watched her shoulders slump slightly.

"Daddy, can I play with the playdough Miss Howard brought?" Izzie asked, holding the tube in her hands, trying to open the lid with her teeth. Creed took the container from her and popped the lid off.

"You can play with it at the coffee table since the kitchen table isn't clean. We'll do the dishes and join you in just a bit, okay?" He handed back the playdough.

The patter of her feet running excitedly to the living room faded.

Amelia stacked the dishes next to the sink before she turned on the hot water and squirted dish soap into the stream. Each plate was rinsed off before being placed in the soapy water. Creed opened a drawer next to the sink and pulled out a towel. He stepped next to Amelia and held out a hand for a plate. She handed one to him wordlessly and he rinsed and dried it. They washed the rest of the dishes in silence.

"Remember in high school when you were dating Sophie Senada?" Amelia rinsed the soap from the sides of the sink as the water drained out. She turned off the water and dried her hands on the towel. She leaned back against the counter, her palms resting on the counter top, delicate fingers curled over the side. Creed finished putting the stack of plates away and turned to face her, mirroring her stance on the other side of the narrow kitchen.

He narrowed his eyes. "Vaguely."

"I remember because that was right in the middle of our obsession with horror films. There was a special midnight showing of *Chucky* at that old theater downtown, remember?"

Creed remembered the showing and how much fun he had with Amelia that night, but he couldn't understand what it had to do with some girl he barely remembered...or why they were talking about it now.

"I remember because apparently Sophia or one of her friends saw us downtown that night. The next Monday at school I was cornered in the ladies' room and Sophie told me to stay away from you. Apparently her friends had greatly embellished what they saw and she was convinced that I was some tramp trying to take her man. I didn't want to cause drama for you so I did my best to avoid you— which was the hardest thing I had ever had to do up to that point in my life, by the way."

"Amelia, I didn't—"

She interrupted him, "When you two broke up a week or so later, she approached me in Biology."

Amelia gave a small laugh, her eyes on the cupboard above his head. "She pushed my backpack off of my desk—"

"What? Why didn't you tell me?"

"—and told me I could have you. Today was a little bit like that. Only much, much worse."

"Why?"

Amelia poked her tongue into her cheek thoughtfully. Her voice dropped an octave, "Uh, I got fired today, Creed."

"You what?!" Creed pushed up on his hands, straightening immediately. "What are you talking about?"

Amelia glanced toward the living room, her look reminding him to keep his voice down. Amelia came to stand beside him where they could both watch the doorway. Her arm brushed against his as she crossed it over her stomach.

"My principal talked to me early in the day about not bringing drama to work. I guess quite a few parents called about that article," Amelia spoke quietly, her eyes averted. "I definitely got the cold shoulder from the parents I saw today, but tried to just ignore it. But after the second article was published—"

"Second article? What are you—"

Amelia held up a finger and walked into the other room. She said something to Izzie, her cheerful voice—almost believable—sharpened something in his chest.

Amelia came back into the kitchen, phone in her hand. She swiped a thumb across the screen, then tapped a few times before handing it over to him.

"The second article showed that I am not living up to the high moral standards they expect from teachers at New Hope Christian School. Parents of students from all grades called and complained. The board members had an emergency meeting; they fired me, Creed." Amelia's chest rose and fell.

The picture on the screen was blurry, as if taken from a distance and blown up; the headline was short and to the point. Beneath Amelia's porch light that morning when Creed leaned forward to brush an innocent kiss against her cheek, someone had been there, waiting to catch an innocuous moment and knit it into a stimulating story. Creed skimmed the article, lip curling at the insinuation that because of the early hour and Amelia's pajamas that something more sordid had been going on.

He felt a flush creep up his neck. Of all the…

He handed the phone back to Amelia. "And your principal believed this? And the other parents? Seriously?"

Amelia raised one shoulder, dropped it again. "I guess so." She finally let her gaze meet his, a wall of water rising on her lower lids. He brought his hand up to cup her face, the pad of his thumb catching the first tear that fell.

"I'll talk to him—to all of them. I'll set this right, Amelia. I swear it." After all, if it weren't for him she wouldn't be in this mess, would she? No, if not for the stupid media. Or was it Kate he should be angry at?

He let out a breath long and loud through his nose. When did everything get so complicated?

Amelia sniffed and turned to lean against the counter, his arm brushing against hers as it fell from her face.

"You know the crazy thing? I've been so careful and planned everything for so many years. I've been the epitome of chaste. And now that I finally stepped out of my comfort zone and bought a house, I lost my job because my so-called sordid lifestyle is giving the school a bad name. How's that for irony?"

Creed stared at their feet, side by side on the linoleum, hers small in their black boots next to his sneakers.

Lord, I don't understand this. I don't. And now Amelia's been hurt. She deserves so much more than this.

Amelia took a deep shuddering sigh. "I'm so confused, Creed. About everything."

"Hey guys! Are you done yet?" Izzie bellowed from the living room. Amelia straightened and ran her fingers under her eyes with a sniff.

"Here we come," she called.

Creed followed her out of the kitchen, wondering how he was going to focus until Izzie went to bed.

Izzie had placed the couch pillows around the small coffee table and set out the game Memory. A few smudges of playdough remained on the table and under her fingernails, but for the most part she had cleaned up everything. The proud grin on her face warmed Creed. By the look in Amelia's eyes, it was just what she needed as well.

"What have we here?" Creed asked, kneeling next to Izzie.

"I thought we could play a game," Izzie shrugged, looking up at Amelia shyly.

"Izzie that sounds like a lot of fun" Amelia smiled. She sat on one of the pillows with her legs crossed, and asked Izzie to explain the game. Creed settled on the other side of the table and watched Izzie and Amelia closely.

The tension in Amelia's hunched shoulders faded after a few rounds of Memory with Izzie. Creed had to check himself not to dwell too much on how much it felt like the "family game nights" his parents had insisted on in his childhood. He and Izzie had played plenty of games alone and with family, but that evening with Amelia, the mood shifted. Creed could see the longing in Izzie's eyes and ached over it. He would need to have a serious talk with her in the morning about her heart; he never wanted to neglect her feelings or disregard them. It was natural for her to long for a mother. The thought pulled at him. Maybe it was time to let Hailey in.

But he just didn't feel a peace about that.

At last Izzie's lids began to blink slowly and Creed nudged her to go upstairs and change into pajamas. She stood slowly, not happy with the idea, but obviously too embarrassed to throw a fit in front of her teacher. Suddenly she brightened.

"Miss H., will you read to me?" she asked.

"I would love to," Amelia answered sincerely.

Creed interjected, "But only if you go straight upstairs, brush your teeth and get on pajamas first. No complaining."

Izzie bolted for the stairs, slipping on the first step, then pounded up a few more before falling again and finally making it to the top. Her rushing around upstairs echoed loudly above their heads.

"Yeah…we're not a quiet family," Creed said dryly.

Amelia chuckled. She helped Creed sort the little cards into a red divider and placed it in the Memory box. They sat on the floor, the coffee table between them. Amelia fidgeted with her hands.

"Creed, I—"

"Okay, Miss H. I picked a good one. You are gonna love it!" Izzie ran into the room in a Snoopy nightgown with bright blue sweatpants underneath. She waved a book in the air and presented it to Amelia.

"Izzie! That's a chapter book," Creed stated the obvious, brows raised at his daughter.

"You didn't say what kind of book, Daddy-O," Izzie crossed her arms in defiance. Creed reached out to uncross her arms.

"No sass, young lady. And I think it's a given that when you ask our guest to read to you, *Junie B. Jones* is not what you come downstairs with. What about *Goodnight Moon*?"

"Daaa-aad. That's a baby book," Izzie whined. She shot an embarrassed look to Amelia.

Amelia nodded her head solemnly. "She's right."

"Not helping, *Miss Howard*," Creed hissed at her.

Izzie and Amelia stared at him, unblinking.

"Ladies, it's bedtime. There is no way I am going to let you read that entire book," he held up his hands and leaned back slightly, feeling cornered.

"Well, surely we could just read a few chapters, right?" Amelia asked taking the book from Izzie and lifting herself onto the couch that she had been leaning against. She patted the cushion and Izzie sat next to her. She cracked open the book, brow raised in triumph toward Creed. He gave a slow smile and shook his head, settling into the recliner to listen.

After a few moments he wished he had given them the go-ahead to read the entire book. Amelia's voice was animated, bringing the spunky Junie B. to life, imitating the bored, exasperated teacher from the story hilariously. He was sure he had never heard Izzie laugh so hard at a book. Amelia couldn't seem to keep from cracking up herself. But she respected his wishes and closed the book after three chapters.

"Well, should I do the teacher thing and tell you to write me a report about this book, Izzie?" Amelia asked. Creed heard the crack in her voice, even if Izzie didn't. Her eyes dulled briefly, as if just remembering that she wasn't Izzie's teacher anymore.

"Miss H., that's second grade stuff," Izzie protested.

"Then how about we find a way to finish this book together sometime, huh?" Amelia countered.

"Yeah!"

Creed cleared his throat. "Alright, Izzie, thank Miss H. and off to bed with you. Don't forget your drink; I don't want you coming down here again."

"Okay, Daddy."

Izzie hugged Amelia and then Creed, before she ran into the kitchen for a drink of water. She sprinted past them with her arms waving wildly in the air, showing off one final time for her beloved Miss Howard.

"Bed," Creed called after her, wondering how many times he would have to go upstairs to settle her down. Izzie giggled and darted up the stairs, only tripping once. Creed winced when her door slammed, echoing through the small house. Her feet thumped across the room, then nothing until—thwump—she landed on her bed with a squeaky thud.

The house pulsed with silence.

Amelia stared at her feet, Creed at the top of her head. Finally, she looked up.

"I guess I better go—"

"Want to watch a movie—"

Creed spoke again first. "Do you really need to go? I thought we could watch a movie."

Amelia seemed to consider it for a minute. But her face turned somber. "That sounds fun, Creed, but not tonight. Not with the possibility that someone is out there, right now, waiting to take our picture and imply the things they do."

"We can't do everything based on what some stupid gossip column online might say. We know we're not doing anything wrong, Amelia."

"I know, Creed. But I don't want to give even the appearance of evil. Isn't that a verse somewhere?" She unfolded her legs and stood. "Anyway, I'm beat. I'm officially moving tomorrow, so I better get some rest."

"Do you need help?" Creed stood with her.

"I think my parents and siblings have it covered. They owe me—I've moved Lucy and my brothers at least once."

She retrieved her jacket and purse from the rack by the door. She slipped her arms in the jacket and looped the purse strap over her shoulder.

Creed rose to join her. He gently took her hands in his.

"Amelia, I am so sorry for today. I wish I would have known or could have prevented it." Creed traced her knuckles with his thumbs, staring into her eyes, searching for her thoughts in the depths of green and gold.

Amelia shrugged. "It will all work out. Right?" She didn't allow for a response. "Creed, I had such a good time. Thank you for the meal and for game night and for letting me read to Izzie. I think that is the first time I have really relaxed in a while," she assured him, her voice soft. She withdrew her hands and opened the door.

"Goodnight, Creed," she said and stepped outside.

But before she walked away, Amelia rotated slowly. "Creed?"

"Hmmm?"

Amelia's chin trembled slightly, but she held his gaze. "It's really nice to be friends again."

Her words came in a rush, as if she needed to unleash them before she lost her nerve.

Creed stepped out on the stoop and flashed a genuine grin. "It really is."

She dropped her eyes, pulling her bottom lip between her teeth, the corners of her lips curling slightly.

"I was an idiot before, Amelia." he said, reaching out to grasp her shoulders, waiting for her to meet his gaze. He sucked in a breath at the pained shimmer in her eyes. Without thought, Creed leaned forward and pressed a gentle kiss to her forehead. Amelia tensed and Creed remembered her fear that someone was watching them. "Sorry," he whispered and quickly stepped back.

Amelia shrugged, her eyes shimmering with tears, before she turned away.

Creed stood on the stoop, watching to be sure that she made it safely to her car. He waited while she started the car and backed out of the parking space. Both hands were shoved in his front pockets, but he raised one in the air when Amelia waved. He watched her drive down the road, her taillights winking at him one final time before she turned the corner and sped off. Creed lowered his hand thoughtfully and put it back in his pocket. He stood that way for another few minutes, before turning to go inside and be sure Izzie was staying in bed.

Chapter Twenty-Six

That night Amelia slept fitfully. Dreams danced around her subconscious, of reporters with large cameras following her around. Of parents looking down on her, of McClary calling her names. After a while she drifted into a place between sleep and wakefulness. Memories of a summer day before her junior year in high school floated to mind, playing before her closed eyes like a movie on a screen...

> She couldn't remember why she was on the day trip, other than Creed had made some crack about her never joining in on the fun. When Christy Wilson called to invite her to join a big group at the reservoir for swimming and a late night bonfire, she jumped at the chance to prove Creed wrong.
>
> Especially when she heard that Carter Adams would be there, too.
>
> Carter sat next to Amelia in English and they'd carefully danced around an attraction for weeks before school let out. Carter was unquestionably out of her league. A lean basketball player with a reputation nearly identical to Creed's, Amelia dreamt as teenage girls often do, of being the one that turned him around. Of course she knew he was most likely leading her on, toying with her. But her stomach quaked whenever he looked her way, clogging all rational thought.
>
> When she and Christy arrived at the docks, her eyes sought him out, splashing in the water with Creed and a few others. Amelia waved back when Creed greeted her,

nodded to Carter, and spread her towel on the hot planks. She slipped the sundress she wore over her bathing suit down over her hips and stepped out of it before tucking it in her beach bag. Carter had eyed her appreciatively before diving in the water to race with a group of guys, including Creed.

She and Christy stretched out on their stomachs, making progress on their mid-summer tans. Amelia raised her head and rested her chin on her folded hands, watching the guys across the way easily lift themselves out of the water to the dock that floated in the middle of the reservoir. Creed sat next to Carter, joking around and eying their dock right back.

Amelia wasn't a fool, she knew they were all elbowing each other over Christy and Vanessa and the rest in their barely-there-bikinis. She found herself wishing she were brave enough to flaunt a two piece. She blushed just thinking about it. Maybe that's what would be the clincher for Carter.

The thought was unsettling. She'd been reading books lately about dating—or not, actually. About being mindful of the decisions she made and how they could affect her life later on.

Tired of sunbathing, tired of thinking, Amelia rose from her towel and walked to the coolers, in search of a soda. She wasn't surprised to see that someone had loaded one with wine coolers and cheap beer. Amelia rolled her eyes.

Carter's twin sister sat on the dock, separate from the rest of them. Amelia frowned at the droop in the girl's shoulders. Grabbing another soda, she walked over to Taylor and lowered herself onto the dock.

"Yowza, that's cold!" Amelia squeaked, as she slipped her feet into the water.

Taylor's eyes were puffy, her cheeks streaked with tears.

"Guys are such jerks," she muttered.

Amelia didn't comment, only popped the tab on a root beer and handed it over. It must have been all the prompting Taylor needed. Amelia listened as she unburdened herself of her sorrows. It was a story Amelia heard over and over from friends: Girl meets Boy. Boy charms Girl. Girl and Boy get intimate. Boy loses interest. Girl ends up brokenhearted and bitter. Boy moves on, either unaware or unconcerned for the damage left in their hormonal charged wake.

Those books were making more and more sense.

Amelia sipped her soda, watching the boys on the dock. She sucked in a breath when Creed suddenly leapt to his feet, towering over Carter, his stance threatening. Her brows furrowed as Carter stood as well, earning a shove from Creed.

"See?" Taylor commented, a small hiccup escaping her lips. "Guys are jerks. Even to each other."

Amelia gave a soft laugh and turned back, pensive. Vince jumped up and stood between the two friends and the fight was over as quickly as it had begun. It wasn't like Creed to fight. She'd have to ask him about it later.

When the guys swam back, Carter all but ignored her and headed straight for the beer in the cooler. Amelia's attraction had cooled, but wasn't entirely snuffed out. There was just something about him. Apparently Christy agreed. She sauntered over and made a show of pulling a wine cooler out and taking a long pull on the bottle in front of Carter. A sick feeling snaked through Amelia at the look that passed over Carter's face.

Bikinis and alcohol. If that's what it took to win Carter's approval, Amelia was out of luck. She felt ill just imagining the smell.

By the time the fire got going, Taylor and her boyfriend had made up, Carter and Christy were thick as thieves, and Amelia was wondering what she had been thinking when she found Carter good-looking.

She sighed. Okay, so maybe she was just a little jealous.

Her eyes met Creed's from where he stood across the fire and a pleasant squeeze worked from her chest down to her toes.

The light flickered over his face, shadow
and light chasing one another across his
square chin as he moved toward her.

Amelia sighed. As long as Creed was around,
she couldn't imagine ever truly having
feelings for anyone else. From the corner of
her eye she noticed Carter and Christy
slipping away from the group.

Carter's indirect rejection stung just the
same.

The idea of having Creed look at her
romantically was as remote as Carter
untangling himself from Christy and coming
over to declare himself a man of virtue.

Amelia shook the memory away and gave up on sleep.
Tiredly puttering to her kitchen, she noticed a distinct chill
in her small apartment. The thermostat read sixty degrees.
A far cry from the heat of her dream.

Her dream? Who was she kidding? The heat of that day
didn't compare to what she'd felt holding on to Creed the
night before.

She made a pot of coffee and opened her Bible, the words
blurring and running together. When they still didn't stick
in her mind after two cups of coffee, Amelia gave up and
set her Bible aside. *I'm sorry, Lord. I just can't concentrate.* She
had wanted to enjoy one last morning in her apartment, but
she realized her family would be there soon.

She hurried to shower and had just finished twisting her
wet hair into a messy bun and getting dressed when the
doorbell rang.

She and her family spent the next few hours packing her
small apartment into a few trucks and unloading at her new

house. Her oldest brother drove her to the furniture store to finally retrieve the items she and Lucy had picked out a few weeks before.

Her mom and Lucy stayed to help her wash and put away kitchen items and arrange her furniture. When at last everyone left, Amelia paced her house with restless energy. It was dinnertime, but she didn't feel like cooking. On impulse, she texted Creed.

Any way you and Izzie want to grab pizza with me?

A few minutes passed and Amelia began to regret her boldness when at last he responded.

We never say no to pizza. Want us to bring it to you?

She looked around her house. There hadn't been much to move, but it was still a cluttered mess. And there wasn't much for Izzie to do.

I thought pizza at Flying Pie would be more fun since they have arcade games. I have a jar of quarters burning a hole in my desk drawer.

Deal. See you there in an hour?

Amelia rushed to shower and dress. Not wanting to waste time on styling her hair, she twisted it into a long braid and looped it through her favorite baseball hat.

She beat Creed and Izzie to the restaurant and ordered their bbq chicken pizza—minus tomatoes—and a cheese for Izzie as well as a pitcher of root beer. Father and daughter walked in a few minutes later and slid into the booth across the table she chose.

"Hey guys. I already ordered the pizza." Creed opened his mouth to protest but Amelia held up her hands. "No, it's my thank you for dinner last night. My family wouldn't let me buy them pizza today, so I needed to blow it somewhere." She winked at Izzie.

"We have a few minutes before it's ready, you want to go play a game with me?" Izzie nodded eagerly. Creed offered to stay with their coats and Amelia's purse.

The night stretched into a full evening of games, good pizza, and laughter. Amelia relished it. She and Creed were falling into a comfortable rhythm. She thought she might like their new friendship even better than the old one.

Each time he glanced her way, Amelia worked hard to tamp down her growing attraction. That was one part of their old friendship that she refused to bring into the new.

A week after she moved, Amelia walked the perimeter of her new land with Olé. They had fallen into a comfortable routine at their new place and she couldn't imagine going to back to living in a neighborhood with sidewalks and fenced yards when she and Olé could roam freely around the orchard.

She wondered absentmindedly if they would receive trick-or-treaters that night. Though she wouldn't be home, she wanted to be ready. Maybe she would leave a bowl of candy on the porch just in case. The church she had been attending with Lucy had a Trunk or Treat ministry that night and Lucy had talked her into handing out candy together.

"We'll use Mom's van and decorate the back. It will be so fun!" Lucy gushed.

Amelia had to admit it sounded better than her usual Halloween tradition of renting Alfred Hitchcock movies and staying home alone eating apple slices and caramel dipping sauce with the lights off.

She walked Olé for over an hour, loving the crunch of leaves beneath their feet and the harvest tang in the air.

184

They finally made their way back and Amelia heated tomato soup in her new kitchen, staring out the window at the peaceful landscape while she ate.

Lucy arrived after lunch, the back seat of their mom's van full of bags from the party store.

"Good gracious," Amelia said when she saw it all. "Did you clear out the store?"

"Just about. I thought it would be fun to make our car look like an enchanted forest and we can dress up like princesses. The kids will love that don't you think?" Lucy's cheeks bloomed pink with excitement.

"Well that's better than sending all of the kids crying from us in terror tonight, I guess," Amelia muttered. "You didn't mention costumes, though, Sis."

"Didn't I?" Lucy asked innocently, retrieving two dresses from a hook in the back. She grabbed a large shopping bag as well and shut the trunk. "Let's go try these on to be sure they fit and then we'll decorate."

Amelia spied a wild, curly red wig through the plastic lining of the bag Lucy handed her.

"How do I let you talk me into these things?"

Chapter Twenty-Seven

Chad arrived at Creed's house in full Prince Charming attire. The tights. The small maroon, gold-stitched shorts. White billowy shirt. A short…dress jacket? Also maroon and stitched in gold designs. Poofy sleeves. A cape. A hat with a fluffy feather.

Creed opened the door a little wider, taking in Chad's garb with a smirk.

"Wow. I don't think I've ever wanted to punch you as bad as I do right this moment."

"Back off, peasant. There is an excellent reason I'm dressed like such a chump. And at least I'm in a costume unlike boring loser dad here." Chad strode in like some regal buffoon and flicked the bill of Creed's baseball hat.

"I'm in a costume," Creed protested.

Chad looked him up and down, taking in the sneakers, worn blue jeans, and faded sweatshirt. He cocked a brow at his older brother.

Creed rolled his eyes and pointed to the camera he wore on a strap around his neck.

"I'm the paparazzi. Obviously," he said.

"Oh, okay," Chad laughed. "Hey, what's going on with all of that? Seems that the whole 'trending' thing has moved on."

Creed flattened his mouth and gave Chad a long side eye.

"What?" Chad asked, blinking innocently.

"Have you not seen the pictures?"

"What pictures?"

Creed explained the ridiculous article about him and Amelia and the pictures posted first of their walk, then of him leaving her apartment.

Chad whistled low. "Okay, I stand corrected. So, the trending hasn't moved on, but do you think Hailey will?"

"I'm not sure. I told her I need some time to think it through. She asked if she could come by sometime or if we could go to dinner. The way she asked made it seem more like a date." Creed took off the camera and set it on his desk.

"No way, man. Why?"

Creed rubbed the back of his neck. "I don't know. It doesn't make any sense to me. She hasn't tried to contact me at all in almost six years. Now she's suddenly back and wanting to see Izzie, and me. What I don't understand is"—Creed leaned forward, his voice low— "what changed? And is she even genuine? Even at that show in New York she didn't so much as glance at Izzie. If she wants to see her as bad as she says, don't you think she would have been unable to look anywhere else? It's really strange. We've talked on the phone a few times, but she almost never asks about Izzie. Doesn't ask how she's doing or what she's like. I just can't get a peace about letting her into Izzie's life."

"That is strange."

They stood in silence for a moment before Creed snickered and punched Chad in the shoulder.

"Seriously, what is with this get up?"

"Uncle Chad!" Izzie, dressed in a puppy costume, ran into the room and leapt into Chad's arms.

"You look nice, Uncle Chad. So handsome!" Izzie fingered the clasp that held Chad's cape together.

"Why thank you, Izzie," Chad responded loudly, slanting a look to Creed. Creed shook his head.

Chad turned back to Izzie. "I need your help tonight. You see, Lucy is dressed like a princess and will be handing out candy." Chad leaned close to lean his forehead against hers. He whispered loudly, his eyes dancing. "I am going to ask Miss Lucy to be my wife tonight."

Izzie's mouth dropped open in a gasp, her eyes wide. "You're getting married tonight?!"

Chad laughed. "No, but soon. I hope."

Creed punched Chad in the arm again. "Wow! Really?"

Chad looked over Izzie's head to meet Creed's eyes. "I don't think I can wait another minute to ask that woman to be mine. I should have a long time ago. I was a real idiot."

Creed blinked, knowing just how Chad felt. He sobered. "Yeah, man. How can we help?"

Chad set Izzie down and put one hand on her shoulder, the other on Creed's circling them up in a huddle. "Okay, here is what I need. Creed, your pathetic excuse for a costume is actually perfect..."

*　*　*

Amelia couldn't believe how much fun she was having. Dressing up in a long flowy dress with wild, curly red hair, passing out candy and pretending to be someone else; it was magical somehow. She wasn't a teacher—or ex teacher in search of a job. She wasn't the woman from the internet. She wasn't some desperate fool that hadn't had a date in, well—never mind about that. According to Lucy, she was dressed up like Princess Merida—a woman that won her own hand in an archery competition to prove to her mother that she didn't need a prince.

Amelia liked that.

Lucy was ethereal in her pale blue ball gown. With her blond hair and pale skin, she made a perfect Cinderella. The sisters had parked near the end of the line and joyfully played their parts with each group of children that came by. The back of their van was decked out with paper trees, and rolling mountains made out of green and brown felt stuffed with pillows; bunny statues they had borrowed from their mother's garden were peeking out from the folds, and even a stuffed deer stood stoically behind a castle piñata. Twinkle lights were strung in the top of the van's trunk door, adding just the right amount of sparkle. Both sisters agreed it was cheesy, but the kids were eating it up.

Amelia was talking with a girl dressed in a hot dog costume when she noticed a man watching her. He stood a few cars away in the line and smiled softly when she met his gaze. Amelia blushed and looked away. After a few seconds she chanced another look. He was still watching. A small hand reached up to grasp the man's elbow and he turned his attention to the little wizard.

Amelia blinked. He really was watching her. How creepy was that? Some guy here with his kid ogling the princesses?

She felt more than saw when the man finally made it to their car. Still uneasy, Amelia focused all her attention on the little boy with him. She smiled and held out a bag of candy. He excitedly turned around and held his candy high in the air.

"Uncle Aaron, I got your favorite!"

Uncle? The man grinned over his nephew's head at Amelia. Oh, okay. Her nerves fluttered at the look in his eyes. And now that he was closer…

"Oh, hey I've seen you here at church, haven't I? You play the drums for worship?" Amelia asked, trying to keep her voice even. But those baby blue eyes he was flashing her way had tangled her nerves. Not that she was interested, just…well, it had been a while since a man had shown interest in *her*.

"Yeah, I thought I recognized you, too. I'm Aaron," he said, reaching for a handshake.

"Amelia."

"Hey, I know you're busy here, but, um…you should come to the singles group sometime." His face suddenly scrunched up. "I mean, that is if you're single."

Amelia laughed a little too loudly. He had no idea.

"Yes. I'm very single." *Very single? Really?* She fought to keep her eyes steady instead of rolling them toward the darkening sky. *Okay, so you can still talk to the opposite sex, right? You didn't completely forget how in your decade of seclusion?* "I've actually thought about it; I just haven't made it to an outing yet. But it sounds fun."

A wide grin broke over Aaron's face. "Then maybe I'll see you there." He held her gaze for a moment longer before looking around for his nephew. Seeing that the boy had moved on without him, Aaron winked at Amelia and took a few long strides to catch up.

Ok, what just happened? Did a guy honestly just show interest in me? And—oops—was agreeing to go to single's group like agreeing to go on a date? Amelia's thoughts raced around each other. And kept crashing on one memory: the feel of Creed's arms as they came around her at his home the week before.

But surely it was the same with Creed that it had always been. He wasn't interested in her that way. Just appreciated her friendship. There was—and never would be—anything between them. Right? The electric chemistry was all on her, in her own mind, wasn't it? He was just…being kind. If there was tenderness in his glances and warmth in his

190

touch, well, chock it up to comfortably familiarity. Plain and simple.

Amelia gathered the fragments of her thoughts and focused on handing out candy.

An hour into the parade, the line finally began to thin out as the activities in the church building started up. Amelia had been told that one of the men in church was a talented illusionist that liked to share the gospel with a carefully choreographed routine. She wondered briefly if the illusionist was Aaron and let her mind linger on the memory of his blue eyes and dark hair. Maybe she needed to work harder to get Creed out of her heart. Aaron wouldn't be a terrible distraction.

Just when her feet were beginning to pinch inside her ballet style flats, Amelia spotted Creed and Izzie coming their way.

And just like that she couldn't have picked Aaron out of a line up.

Creed's familiar gait stirred something deep in her belly. He wore his baseball cap backward—have mercy—and jeans beneath his hoodie. The frayed cuffs made her wonder if it was the same one she used to borrow in high school. His camera hung from a strap around his neck. Izzie jumped around excitedly next to him, stopping to lift the front paws of her puppy costume and pant. Her nose was painted with a black triangle and the costume had a hood with ears that flopped adorably over her little face. Chad trailed behind them, decked out in a Prince Charming costume. Amelia looked to see if Lucy had noticed them coming. Her sister was batting her fake lashes playfully at a little boy in line that told her she was beautiful, gazing up at her in wide-eyed wonder.

"Why thank you," Lucy blushed and shyly lowered her lashes, playing the part. "I was just saying to my sister here that the only thing I'm missing is my Prince Charming."

Amelia winked at Chad, who had stepped close enough to hear that comment. A hand wrapped around Amelia's upper arm and pulled her off to the side. She turned in surprise to Creed who flashed her an apologetic wince before he stepped in front of her with the camera raised to his eye. Amelia looked on in confusion, as the shutter on the camera began to click away.

Chad stepped forward and locked his eyes on Lucy as he knelt on one knee before her. Amelia brought her hands to her mouth, tears stinging the back of her eyes.

She couldn't hear what Chad said over the furious clicking of Creed's camera, but she watched with joy as Lucy smiled, tears streaming down her face, and nodded enthusiastically. Izzie stepped forward and held out her candy bucket, gripping the handle with both hands, her puppy-dog face lit up proudly. Chad retrieved a black box from it and turned toward Lucy. The lights Lucy and Amelia had strung on the underside of the raised van trunk shone down on the couple like stars blinking in approval.

Amelia stood on tip toe to see over Creed's shoulder as Chad eased a band onto her sister's finger. Lucy slipped her arms around Chad's neck, squeezing him tightly. Her diamond winked beneath the bright parking lot lights at the cheering crowd. Lucy pulled away to stare down at her hand, dazed. Well-wishers from those left in line and volunteers of the cars that were finished handing out candy rushed forward to congratulate the couple.

Amelia's eyes pooled with tears. Her sister had been through so much. The adoration in Chad's eyes was unmistakable: he loved her deeply.

A tap on her shoulder startled Amelia, and she turned to find Aaron standing to the side, his nephew no longer with him.

"Hey, sorry, didn't mean to scare you," Aaron said. His voice was softer than Creed's, more tenor than bass. And he was tall. Amelia's neck would cramp if she stared up at him too long.

"No, not a problem. I was, uh distracted," Amelia hooked a thumb over her shoulder, realizing belatedly that Aaron probably had no idea what she was pointing at.

Aaron's eyes twinkled, and he flashed her a bashful smile. He let out a puff of laughter before palming the back of his neck. "Listen, uh, I know you don't really know me, but I was wondering if you want to go out sometime? Maybe just grab some coffee?"

Amelia blinked. Go out? Coffee? She was still reeling from Lucy's proposal, from her own muddled feelings for Creed.

Creed! Why was his face filling her mind when this was her chance to move on, to shake off the ridiculous life choices she had made, to—

"Amelia!" Lucy called out for her and Amelia turned back to Aaron.

"I'm sorry, I have to go. My sister just got engaged, so…" as if that explained her hesitancy.

Aaron's eyes widened. "Oh, that's your sister? Wow, that's great. She and Chad are great. Yeah, I'll, uh…I'll just see you at church, okay?" He flashed her another smile and slipped into the crowd.

I could have handled that a lot better, Amelia thought. I'll just track him down at church next Sunday and…what?

She didn't stop to reflect on how relieved she had been to not have to answer his request.

Chapter Twenty-Eight

Focus, dude. Just focus.

But something clenched in Creed's chest as he watched Amelia smile up at Aaron out of the corner of his eye, at the way Aaron stooped over to talk to her. Creed didn't even know that they knew each other. Amelia was still new to their church and kept mostly to Lucy.

Aaron's voice floated above the crowd, "…coffee sometime…" and Creed strained to hear Amelia's response. Another swell of congratulatory shouts muted her answer.

Creed could have kissed Lucy himself when she called out for Amelia, interrupting her conversation and sending Aaron on his merry way. Chad must have informed his fiancé of the informal party they had planned at the Williamses house with all of the family to celebrate the engagement. Lucy waved Amelia over to inform her of their plans. Creed watched Amelia through the lens, snapping photos of the sisters hugging.

Click.

Amelia grabbed Lucy's hand, her mouth forming a perfect "O" as she looked at the ring, blinking back tears.

Click.

They hugged again, Amelia's red, curly wig pulling to the side, her cheek pressed against Lucy's, her eyes closed, lips curling upward.

Have mercy, she was beautiful.

Click.

Chad came forward to place his hand lightly on the small of Lucy's back, grinning like a big, dopey idiot in that Prince getup. Lucy turned to him and Amelia began to pack up.

Creed offered to help Amelia load up the van with the chairs and candy bags. Lucy and Chad were hopelessly worthless, gazing lovingly into one another's eyes. Creed asked Amelia if she would like to ride with him and Izzie to his parents' house.

"I see that your back seats are a little stuck under all of these woodland creatures, and I assume that Chad and Lucy will want to ride together," Creed said when Amelia looked at him in confusion.

"Oh, did Chad come with you?" she asked, realization dawning.

"Yes. The poor guy was so nervous he couldn't see straight. I figured he would calm down once she said yes," Creed winked.

Amelia looked distracted. "Yes, I would love to ride with you guys, I just don't know if there's more I am supposed to do to help with the festival."

Creed waved her question off. "Nah. Chad has been planning this for weeks, although he just told me about it a few hours ago. He let the staff in charge of this know that you two would be jetting out of here right after the Trunk or Treat."

Amelia dipped her chin. "Well, okay, then. Let's go to your parents'."

She took Izzie's offered hand and walked with them to their car. Creed lagged behind, admiring the look of the two of them together. And, if he was being honest, he admired the sway of Amelia's hips in her long dress.

He held her door open for her, handing her the bottom of her princess gown. She accepted it regally, her mood festive. After making sure Izzie was buckled properly, he jogged around the back of the car and slid into the driver's seat.

196

As soon as he had put the car in drive, Amelia squealed and lightly punched Creed in the shoulder. "Oh my goodness! Can you believe it?!"

She was positively giddy. Her wide smile brightened her face, the shimmer in her eyes infectious.

Izzie squealed from the back seat as well. Creed steered out of the parking lot, enjoying the excited chatter of the two ladies in his car. He was thankful that he didn't need to talk; Amelia's presence was heady that evening. The curly red wig—still slightly askew after all of the celebratory hugging—brought out the flush of her cheeks, the pretty pink of her mouth. She had glitter or something lightly brushed on her cheekbones and eyelids. Every time a car passed them, Creed found his gaze wandering to watch the way the headlights shimmered up her neck, to her eyes, and wig before falling away. She was radiant.

Though he hadn't seen her since they met for pizza a few days before, they continued to text every day. He had begun to look forward to her good morning emoticon wave—loved teasing her about how she was a smartphone junkie in the making. It had taken serious self-control to avoid texting her throughout the day as they fine-tuned the proposal.

Listening to Chad go on and on about Lucy all day had stirred a deep desire in Creed. It went beyond wanting a mother for Izzie, beyond his physical attraction to Amelia. While those were strong desires, it was the way they had fallen back into their old friendship so easily that appealed to Creed. The way that they could discuss things of the Lord in a way they hadn't before. He felt his soul being knit with hers, and his longing was becoming difficult to ignore.

Amelia turned to him with wide eyes. "Dude. It's kind of like we're brother and sister now."

He swallowed. What? That was not at all what—

"Isn't that so cool?" she laughed, loving the idea, apparently.

Um…no?

He felt her eyes on his profile and he forced a chuckle. "Um, yeah. Cool." A thought occurred to him. He glanced toward Izzie in the back seat. Her head was tilted to one side, her mouth hanging open, eyes closed. She was out. He wasn't surprised—she'd had a long day.

"Well, then as your big brother, I feel it's my right to say you were looking awfully cozy with Aaron earlier and I demand an explanation."

The smile died from her face and he could have kicked himself.

Oops.

Amelia sighed, offered a self-deprecating smile. "I know how ridiculous it is that I set myself up for a husband and lived like an old lady all these years. And you know that I'm trying to just accept the parts of that decision that shaped my life today. But now I wonder if it was just an excuse. A cover for my heart. Because honestly, Creed? It's not like I was fighting men off, you know? Up until thirty minutes ago, it's been years since I've been asked on a date. And I can't tell if it's a real date, or just a 'you and I can be good pals' thing. Kind of like when you asked me to senior prom. It was fun, but it wasn't real." Her mouth flattened.

Creed tightened his jaw. The conversation had taken a serious turn from lighthearted celebration to shadows of things unspoken and misunderstood. They'd dodged the subject fairly well over the last few weeks. Maybe it was time to clear the air?

"…up until thirty minutes ago…" So that was what Aaron had been up to.

He had asked her out? And, more importantly, what had been Amelia's response? Cold dread swept through him. He'd felt this frigid jealousy once before…

It took one comment from a guy the summer before their junior year to nearly ruin their friendship. Creed and his friends met a group of ladies at a nearby reservoir for swimming and a late night bonfire. Soon after they arrived, Creed and a few guys raced to a dock on the other side of the water. He came in third place, and hoisted himself up on the wood planks, a rush of water from his trunks splashing out beneath him.

"Oh man," his friend, Vince, held up both hands creating a mock frame pointed toward the other side where the rest of their group—mostly the girls—remained. "From here the ladies are on perfect display. Did you see Vanessa in that little black number?"

A few racy comments and whistles flew back and forth across the baseline of chuckles. Creed eyed their coed classmates appreciatively, enjoying the view as much as anyone else. He added his own quips here and there, loving his single, carefree status and the temptation of romance under the hot summer sun. Lately he had his eye on Christy Wilson, and based on the flirtatious content of their texts earlier that week, he was willing to bet he'd be snuggling up close when they had a bonfire later.

"Okay, okay, okay. Vanessa and Christy and Hannah and the rest are hot, sure. They always have been. But, seriously—can we talk about Amelia Howard? Where on earth did that hottie come from?"

Carter Adams' words cut through Creed's daydream of trailing kisses down Christy's neck. The fire that stirred in him sizzled and sputtered as surely as if Carter had doused him with a bucket of ice water.

The groans of appreciation around him snaked a different kind of heat through his veins. Ice and fire swept over him all at once and suddenly Creed was on his feet facing Carter, his stance challenging.

"Hey. Amelia's officially off limits." Was that *his* voice, growling with such menace?

The group, comments and laughter suddenly gone, smiles dropping off one by one from their faces, stared at him in baffled surprise. Creed's jaw clenched.

"Understood?"

A shadow passed over Carter's face. "No," he said. "Not understood."

He rose slowly, standing toe to toe with Creed. A muscle clenched in his jaw, his blue eyes now a steely gray. "Since when do you care who we date, Creed? Maybe we're all just a little tired of your leftovers."

Creed clenched and unclenched his fists, still grappling to understand the swift and unrelenting anger coursing through him at the thought of any one of these guys touching his Amelia.

Wait. *His* Amelia? Where had that come from?

Creed met Carter's stare. "You can have anyone—*anyone*. But Amelia Howard is off limits." He shoved Carter. Hard.

"Got that, Carter?"

"And what if I only want Amelia?" Carter challenged, shoving him back.

"Enough, guys," Vince jumped up and stood between them, holding his hands out to each. "Seriously. Do either of you think this is necessary? I mean, have you ever seen Amelia Howard so much as go to a dance? Or on a date for that matter?"

Creed knew there was more to that than any of them did. She'd been on dates with guys from their youth group and gone to plenty of dances—at other schools. Why that didn't bother him before now, Creed wasn't sure.

"Look, Carter. Amelia's a good girl. She's not your type." His eyes swept the rest of the guys who watched the interaction with open curiosity. "She's not any of our types. She's special, pure. Let's keep her that way. Understood?"

Carter considered Creed, that muscle still working in his jaw. He glanced across the water to the dock. Creed followed his gaze. Where most of the girls gathered in bunches, leaning back on the dock to show off their curves, Amelia sat on the edge in her modest one piece. She wore a baseball cap, the ends of her shoulder length hair dancing on the breeze. She sat next to Carter's twin sister, legs hanging off the dock, no doubt doing her best to cheer the girl up after an ugly break-up.

"She's like a sister to me, man," Creed muttered, knowing he could hit Carter right where it mattered. Sisters were off limits.

Carter met his eyes. He straightened. "Yeah, okay."

Trying to lighten the mood Creed reached out to shake Carter's hand. "I'll even back off Christy. She's all yours, man."

The earlier mood decidedly tarnished, the guys swam back to the rest of the group. By nightfall Creed was glad he'd given up Christy. She had easily turned her affections to Carter once they returned and he focused his attention on her.

Creed met Amelia's gaze on the other side of the fire and made his way to the log where she sat, staring into the flames, her gaze forlorn. She'd pulled a long sundress on over her bathing suit. Goosebumps pebbled her arms.

"Howard, where is your sweatshirt?" Creed asked, thinking he shouldn't be so aware of the way the soft material of her dress hugged her curves. Curves he had never noticed before Carter pointed them out.

The jerk.

She shrugged. "Amanda needed one. She forgot a bathing suit and swam around in her shorts and T-shirt all day. I think she was hoping one of the guys would offer to warm her up, but so far that hasn't worked out so well. I only hope she's smart enough to give up on her game and wear the sweatshirt I loaned her." She smirked.

"Meanwhile you're over here shivering," he pointed out.

Amelia pointed at the fire. "Not shivering, Creed. I am, however, getting eaten alive by these darn mosquitos." She slapped her arm just then, proving her point.

Creed sighed and tugged his sweatshirt over his head. "You're too nice for your own good, Howard," he said handing the hoodie to her.

She grinned at him, quickly tugging the hoodie over her torso. She left the hood in place, and flashed him a tough guy pose. The hat she wore shaded her eyes but Creed could see the playful pout of her lips. Funny how he'd never paid much attention to her lips before. Her bottom one was slightly bigger than the top. Full and—whoa. Why was he looking at her lips?

What's the matter with you, Williams? What happened to her being like a sister?

"Hey, Howard," he began, but her profile was turned to him, the firelight dancing on her sad eyes.

Creed followed her gaze across the fire to where Carter was leading Christy back to the cars, his hand hooked provocatively low on her waist. Christy turned to walk backward, reaching up to accept a kiss from Carter before they disappeared behind a crop of trees.

"Hmmmm?" Amelia answered.

Creed licked his lips, his throat suddenly tight, forgetting what he was about to say. He should feel slightly guilty, shouldn't he? After all, if he hadn't threatened Carter, maybe Amelia would be the one—

Creed's jaw tightened. No. That was *exactly* why he said what he did. Amelia was worth so much more than a steamy encounter that would end as fast as it had begun. She deserved much more than any of them—himself included—could give.

"Uh, nothing," he answered, hooking a friendly arm around her shoulders. "Didn't you come with Christy?"

Amelia snorted. "Yeah. Think you could give me a ride home?"

"Definitely."

When Creed dropped her off, Amelia gave back his sweatshirt. He watched while she jogged up the walk to her brightly lit house. She gave a quick wave at the door and slipped inside, carefree and happy. He drove home, trying to ignore the way Amelia's fragrance clung to his car. When he got home, he realized it was his sweatshirt that kept her fragrance so close. The wood smoke did little to cancel it out.

It took the rest of the summer to forget the pathetic way that he balled up his sweatshirt and slept with it that night, breathing deeply of Amelia and dreaming of her in a way that shook him to his core.

Chapter Twenty-Nine

The memories of that day—the jealousy that coursed through him, the sudden terrifying realization that his best friend was a beautiful woman—crashed around him. One glance at Amelia's face reminded Creed that now wasn't the time to be jealous that she'd been asked on a date. Though the very idea burned through him, he forced himself to swallow down his panic. After all, they were mature adults now. Not kids fumbling their way through high school crushes.

He squeezed the steering wheel, trying to remember what else she had said. About him asking her out?

"The prom was real, Amelia. Very real. In fact, that was the night I realized..." Did he dare say it? Silence pulled at them.

"Realized what, Creed?"

He slowed down and parked the car in front of his parents' house. Chad and Lucy hadn't arrived yet, but Creed knew they could drive up behind them any moment. He cut the ignition and turned to face her.

He reached to tug a lock of brunette hair that had fallen from beneath the red wig and caught in the corner of her mouth. Amelia scowled and took the wig off.

"I forgot I was wearing that, no wonder I suddenly feel like crying," she attempted a joke, and ran her free hand back through her hair. She kept her gaze aimed at her lap.

"Grandpa!" Izzie shouted from the backseat, startling them both. Creed looked past Amelia to see his father framed in the open front door.

Izzie unbuckled and reached for the door handle. "Let's go, guys!"

Creed chanced a look at Amelia. She fought to school her features, but was clearly losing the battle.

"Hey, Kiddo, why don't you run on in. Let Grandpa know we'll be there in just a minute, okay?"

He watched while Izzie ran up the lawn and jumped into his dad's arms. After they spoke for a moment, his father held up one hand to acknowledge that Izzie had delivered the message and shut the door.

Creed turned slowly back to Amelia. He captured her chin in his hand and lifted it gently to face him.

"Amelia," he whispered. She finally looked at him, the glow from the streetlight brightening her soft skin and tussled hair.

* * *

She felt so stupid. How had she gone from downright giddy about her sister's magical night to solemn and sad? It was like Creed agreeing that they were basically siblings and the punch that was to her gut had sucked all of the joy out of her.

Ridiculous. Hadn't she spent the majority of the last few months pressing thoughts of romance and marriage aside, pressing into the Lord more purposefully? And wasn't she the one that insinuated that they were no more than siblings now? So why the mopey dopey blues?

Get a grip, Amelia.

Creed's low voice pulled her out of her head.

"First of all, I remember plenty of guys that wanted to ask you out in high school. Plenty. But the ones that were wise enough to recognize that they weren't good enough for you stayed away. As for the rest? Well, let's say I gently persuaded them to leave you alone."

She felt her forehead wrinkle. "What? Why would you do that?"

"I could never stand the thought of one of those creeps dating you. I see now that it was none of my business, but back then, I guess I felt like your protector, your big brother. I didn't want them to spoil your innocence."

She scowled and lifted her chin. Something—fear?—flickered in his eyes.

"No, I knew you wouldn't make mistakes like I did, Amelia, but guys say stupid stuff, you know, to talk women into—"

She shook her head, staring out the windshield.

"You didn't want anyone to date me? You didn't want to—just kissed me and then left for college and never spoke to me again—but no one else could? That's ridiculous!"

And there it was. Plain as day and out in the open. Great.

She reached for the door handle.

"Wait. You don't understand." Creed balled his hand into a fist and gently pounded his chest. "*I* was one of those sleaze balls. You were stronger and wiser, more devoted to the Lord than anyone I had ever met. You still are that way. I wanted to protect you." He ran a hand through his short hair. "And then I messed everything up."

The regret in his voice stopped her. She let her hand slip from the door handle.

"What's your second of all?" she asked, folding her arms against her chest defensively, begrudgingly offering him a change in topic before she embarrassed herself more.

He blinked in surprise and narrowed his eyes, lips pinched. They sat in silence for a moment, Creed seemingly searching his memory for what he had intended to say. Finally, "Second of all, I wanted you with me at the prom.

Couldn't imagine anyone else that I wanted to be with, actually. Maybe we started out as just two friends having a good time, but prom is when I finally realized that I couldn't deny that I'd been harboring feelings for you for a long time. I wanted to tell you so badly."

The silence stretched between them, so still she could almost hear their heartbeats. Amelia's firmly crossed arms began to ache, her fingernails digging uncomfortably into her skin. She slowly released her grip, let her arms fall to her lap.

"So why didn't you, Creed?" Amelia asked, her voice soft, breathy.

Creed grabbed the steering wheel, twisting his hands around the leather. "Because that was the night you asked me to be on your team, Amelia. To help you stay true to your future husband. Your face was so open and honest. I knew you had no interest in me."

He paused. She sucked in a breath—he had no idea.

"Even more, Amelia, I knew then that I was not a man that deserved a woman as incredible as you."

He kept his face turned toward the windshield.

Amelia tentatively reached out to lightly stroke the back of his neck. He'd had feelings for her?

"Creed," her broken voice was barely audible, even to her own ears.

He turned back to her and she saw a depth of emotion crouching in the shadows of his dark eyes. The atmosphere in the small car shifted. It hummed. She'd experienced this same electric pause once before. Had thought maybe the memory had enhanced it beyond the reality. But no. No. It was as charged now—possibly more—as when they were kids.

His breath cut off, her heart sprinted ahead. He faced her and leaned closer, eyes melting like pools of chocolate when she met him in the middle. Their foreheads touched and she drank in his spicy scent. Her fingers tingled from the softness of the hair at his nape. She blinked slowly, drunk on his nearness. He moved his nose beside hers, his lips dangerously within reach. She savored the feel of cool peppermint from his gum competing with the heat of his breath and closed her eyes, not wanting to waste any sensation on sight when she could enhance *touch*. Amelia inched closer to brush her lips against his, an invitation. Creed responded greedily.

She'd dreamt of their first kiss for years. Remembered the cool feel of his lips against hers as they'd shivered at the reservoir. She'd been so confused then, her mind racing such that she couldn't enjoy it.

Now she just wanted to relish, to cast out all doubt, all thought, all negative arguments and just *feel*. She'd been given a second chance at his mouth, and even if it was foolish, even if it would end in heartbreak, even if it was the last time—she refused to waste it.

His lips were velvet. She cherished the feel of him. Drank him in. He moved his mouth over hers carefully, as if savoring this as much as she was. His hand cupped the side of her neck, fingers tucking into her hair, causing her to tingle all over. She rested her free hand against his chest, treasuring the rapid beat of his heart.

Lights flashed behind them and she jolted back from him, slamming her shoulder against the passenger window.

"Ow."

Could he hear the breathless timbre of her voice?

She rounded her eyes at him, chest rising and falling, trembling fingers pressed against her slightly swollen lips.

As endorphins waned, rational thought slammed in. Oh no. What had they done?

"We probably shouldn't have done that," she murmured.

She averted her eyes, fumbled for the door handle. They needed to get inside. It was Chad and Lucy's night. But she had no idea how she was going to concentrate when all she wanted to do was go on relishing his lips on hers. Or dig a hole and die of embarrassment. Her fingers finally brushed against cold metal and she tugged. The dome light came on, no doubt emphasizing her flushed cheeks. She slipped one rubbery leg out the door, wondering how on earth she was going to stand.

Creed's husky voice stopped her. "On the contrary, Amelia. I think we probably should have been doing that all along."

Her mouth parted in surprise and she turned back to him. Her stomach clenched pleasantly at the look in his eyes.

He exited the car quickly to shout out a greeting to Chad and Lucy as they came around the van hand in hand.

* * *

Did they all know? Could they see the after-effects of Creed's lips on hers?

Amelia kept drawing her lips together, rolling them inward. She wondered how long they would tingle from the pressure of his kiss. Continued to marvel at how much better the real thing was after years and years of living in memory.

She still didn't know what came over her. One minute she was spinning from all that Creed was telling her, the next she was staring at that freckle near his mouth, leaning closer and closer until she could feel the softness of his lips on hers. She blinked and cleared her throat, glancing around to see if anyone caught the dreamy look on her face.

Creed's mom had always been able to turn out a wonderful party. An eclectic mix of children in costume, as well as a few adults, the grandparents, and all of their siblings and their families gathered in the Williams' home. Izzie weaved in and out of everyone, amped up on sugar and cousins.

Amelia stepped into the kitchen to load a plate with appetizers that had been spread out on the island. She wasn't hungry, but desperately needed to collect her thoughts.

Creed's parents had remodeled since she had been there last. Amelia admired the white cabinets, gray quartz countertops and double stainless steel ovens, even as she relived that kiss over and over again. She leaned back against the counter, drinking in the moment.

Ohmygoodness. Creed and I kissed. She touched her fingers to her lips, half expecting them to feel as warm to the touch now as they had when they were pressed against his.

"Can you believe it finally happened?"

Amelia jumped as Mrs. Williams bustled into the kitchen with an empty tray. It clattered on the counter. She opened the fridge to retrieve a container of cheese cubes.

Amelia stuttered in disbelief. "Uh, believe what? There's nothing to uh—"

Oh. Duh. She took a deep breath, hoping to calm her swirling emotions. "I know. I am so happy those two finally found each other," Amelia commented lamely.

Mrs. Williams plunked a box of toothpicks on the counter and gestured to Amelia. "Sweetie would you help me with these?"

Amelia pushed away from the counter and came to stand next to Creed's mother. They stabbed cheese cubes with toothpicks in silence for a moment before the older woman sighed long and loud.

"Just one child left to go…" she commented, letting her statement hang.

Amelia blushed, drawing her lips inward again. "Um, yup. I guess so."

"You know, Amelia, Creed has changed so dramatically since you two kids ran around together," she shook her head. "He certainly went through a lot to get to where he is. I will never forget the day that he called, a screaming baby in the background. 'Mom, I need you,' was all he said. We were so disappointed for him—for the decisions he made. We worried, knowing how hard his life was about to be. And how hard it would be on Izzie to not be with both of her parents. But, oh, then we held that sweet baby," she grinned up at Amelia and grabbed her arm.

"I didn't need a paternity test to tell me that baby was ours. She looked just like Creed did as a baby."

Amelia snorted. "She looks just like Creed now."

"Poor kid," a baritone voice broke in.

Amelia dropped a handful of toothpicks. They bounced around her feet as heat seared her ears, cheeks, and neck. There was no slow crawl, just instant, humiliating red. Creed gave her a lopsided grin and knelt to pick up the toothpicks.

Mrs. Williams beamed at Creed when he came close to drop them in the trash. She patted his cheek and said, "Come now, you are just as handsome as ever. Izzie is lucky to look like her Daddy." She picked up the tray of cheese cubes and left the kitchen as quickly as she came.

Creed winked at Amelia. "Did you hear that? I'm just as handsome as ever."

Amelia rolled her eyes. She went back to filling her plate with things she most likely wouldn't eat; she needed to keep her hands busy. Thinking of Creed's kiss alone in the kitchen was one thing. It was nearly impossible to keep the wonder from her expression with him standing next to her. His eyes were on her face, trying to read her mood, she could feel it. She would not look at him. Who knew what would happen if her gaze landed on his lips again?

"I'm fine, Creed," she said, still keeping her hands busy.

"Show off. I'm not," Creed answered.

Amelia looked up at him in surprise. "You're not?"

"No way. All I want to do is sneak you out of here and go get Chinese or something."

"Chinese?" Amelia had to laugh. "Why Chinese?"

Creed grabbed a baby carrot from the veggie tray and crunched it in his teeth. "Well it's probably more appropriate than my other idea," he shrugged.

"And what's that?" Maybe she didn't want to know.

Or, more likely, maybe she really did.

Creed leaned down until his nose almost touched hers. "Oh, I don't know. I was thinking I could sneak you into my mother's pantry for some serious necking."

Amelia pushed against his chest with a snort. "Yeah, dream on, Pal."

His teasing mood calmed her somehow. This was the Creed she knew, and yet it wasn't. This was a Creed that wanted to hold her and kiss her, but could joke with ease, just as he had always done. Isn't this what she had imagined for so long: a romantic relationship anchored in friendship? What she hadn't counted on was the way that Creed seemed to cherish her in that kiss.

A sharp whistle rang out and the chatter in the next room died down. Chad's voice rose above the din. Creed and Amelia stepped into the living room just as he announced that he and Lucy would have a December wedding.

"I know that's kind of soon," Chad laughed, raising his voice to be heard above the surprised murmurs. "But neither of us want a fancy wedding; we want a fancy marriage. So we are going to do something simple and hope that you will all be ready to celebrate with us in six weeks."

Lucy stood to the left of Chad, gazing up at him adoringly. Her right hand was interlaced with his, her left hand held a glass of sparkling cider, her new diamond ring—a symbol of promise—was on full display and glittering proudly. Amelia felt a flutter of joy for her sister. Or maybe it was just Creed's hand on the small of her back. In a move that was in the same breath new and familiar, she leaned back into him, pleased when he cupped her shoulders in his strong hands.

The party thinned out after that. Chad and Lucy left after Amelia's mom had agreed to give her a ride home. They both offered to help clean up and the remaining women worked in happy harmony. Her mom gathered dirty plates and cups. Mrs. Williams stacked dishes in the dishwasher and put away the leftovers. Creed and his dad worked quickly to put away folding chairs and stools that had been brought out.

Izzie conked out on the couch, drool pooling on the pillow beneath her.

Her mom had brought dishes and items to help with the party and Amelia carried them in boxes out to the van, careful not to wake Izzie. On her final trip, she closed the trunk of the van, turning as tires crunched on the driveway. A small two-door truck pulled in bedside the van. A woman drove, but parked in the shadows before Amelia could see her face. The car door squeaked as it flung open and the driver turned to kick it shut, looping a purse over her shoulder and striding toward the house. The light from the porch lit her pinched features and Amelia's heart stammered.

Hailey?

Chapter Thirty

Creed raked his hand back through his hair tugging on the ends in frustration. "I cannot believe you just showed up here," he hissed at Hailey in frustration.

They stood on his parents' lawn, facing off when he told her in no uncertain terms that he would not let her inside to surprise Izzie. He couldn't believe she had suggested it. That she had actually thought this was the way to get what she wanted. They had only exchanged a few short calls in the last week, her asking to see Izzie, him not feeling a peace about it.

Hailey crossed her arms and flattened her mouth. "Well, I was tired of not getting answers from you. I want access to my daughter."

"I told you, I'm still praying through it—"

"And that's not an answer Creed." Her lip curled up in disgust. Her eyes flickered down to his feet and back to his eyes. "And since when are you so spiritual, anyway?" she scoffed.

"Since you dumped your daughter with me and my whole life fell apart."

Hailey's eyes flickered in surprise and a smug expression passed over her face. She reached to adjust her purse strap on her shoulder.

Whoa. Down boy.

That was not what he meant. Izzie was his. His. *He* had raised her. And, yes, his life fell apart. But in the best way. It shattered and came back together stronger. Better. Better than Hailey could ever imagine. He didn't know how to explain that and certainly not when he felt like her could wring her neck.

He thought of his parents waiting inside, ready to stand guard if Hailey tried to force her way in. Amelia and her mom had left right after Amelia slipped inside, face white, eyes haunted, to tell him Hailey was waiting outside. She had locked the door, bless her. She had no idea they had been talking—with all that was going on in her world he hadn't wanted to burden her. But instinctively she had sought to protect Izzie. He adored her for it. But he hated that she had left that evening with he and Hailey facing off on the front lawn.

His life was too ugly, too complicated for someone like Amelia. She deserved so much more. He shook his head. What had he been thinking kissing her? *Not the time to think about that, Buddy.*

"Well, that's interesting, Creed. You think she ruined your life, but you won't let me see my own daughter. I mean who does that? What kind of man won't let a mother and daughter see each other?" she glared at him, challenging.

His blood surged, hot and fierce. "Are you freaking kidding me? What kind of a mother—"

No. Enough. Be still.

He started to open his mouth anyway, his anger blinding. But again, that voice, that prompting of the Spirit cooled the fire in his veins. He clamped his mouth shut, turned and walked a small circle, running his hands down the sides of his face.

One, two, three…

"You know what, Creed? I've given you enough time. I'm done playing nice. Tell your lawyer to expect a call from mine."

He hung his hands on his hips, working a muscle in his jaw as she marched across the grass back to her car. The engine chugged to life and she backed quickly out of the driveway, barely checking to see if traffic was clear. With one last dirty look in his direction, she sped off into the night.

"Well, that went well," he muttered to his parents when he stepped through the front door.

His mother held a still-sleeping Izzie on her lap, concern pinching her features. His Dad sat in the overstuffed chair adjacent to the couch, elbows on his knees, hands clasped together.

Creed sat on the couch next to his mother and smoothed a hand over Izzie's head, taming her wild curls briefly before they bounced back. He leaned back against the couch with a low groan.

"What did she say, Son?" his father asked.

Creed sighed, pinched the bridge of his nose against a dull ache.

"She saw on Facebook—I guess some of our friends from college are still the same and my settings aren't as private as I thought—that we were here celebrating the engagement. She was fed up waiting for me to make a decision about letting her in Izzie's life and thought she could push the issue. I lost my temper—or started to, I guess. Anyway, she's now saying she's going to contact a lawyer." Saying it out loud made the ache in his head grow to a roar.

Lord, I can't lose my daughter.

His father rose to come sit on the other side of Creed. He clapped a strong hand on his shoulder and began to pray in his calm, but firm, voice. Creed felt his emotions swell as his mom's arm slipped around his back. They sat that way, arms around Creed, Izzie snoring softly on his mom's lap, and prayed for God's protection. For them to be kind and loving to Hailey, to show her God's grace while also guarding Izzie.

They thanked God for His care, for His sovereignty.

"And Father," his dad concluded when their hearts had poured themselves out, "we thank you for this opportunity to watch You work. We know You work all things for our good, so we wait and watch, believing that You will do just that. In Your Son's precious name, Amen."

*   *   *

Amelia lay in her bed, long after she had donned her pajamas and crawled beneath the covers, and stared at the ceiling. Her eyes burned with tears.

It was just like last time.

It's nothing like last time. He has a kid, Amelia. Izzie has to come first. And if Hailey wants to be in Izzie's life…

Unfortunately, that was the part where her heart began to ache. What if Hailey and Creed came to some sort of arrangement? Amelia knew that the very best thing for Izzie would be if her mother could be in her life. But, pathetically, she pictured the parents bonding over their daughter, over their intimate history.

Hours ago when Creed held her in his arms and kissed her so tenderly, she felt safe and secure. So certain of them. Though everything else in her life was on shaky ground— her farmhouse was new, the responsibilities of home ownership rattling, the sting of being fired still fresh, the assumptions of people she didn't know, as well as those she did, hurt—but in those moments with Creed, she believed that everything would be fine.

And there she went again, didn't she? Basing everything on a relationship.

Her phone buzzed on her nightstand, the screen lighting up her bedroom.

She rolled up on one elbow, swiped a thumb across the phone.

You up?

Her heart skipped. She shouldn't answer but…**I am now**. No need letting him know she hadn't been able to sleep.

I'm sorry for the way things ended tonight.

I understand. You and Izzie OK?

Three dots rolled in waves on the screen—he was compiling a long text back.

Yeah. Izzie slept the whole time. Hailey never came inside. I don't think it went well. She said she's contacting a lawyer. But I had a good talk with my folks once she left.

Her heart sank. **Oh Creed, no. Is this the first time you've talked to her since she left?**

Uh, no. We've talked a little bit this week.

Amelia blinked at the bright screen. They had? There was no reason to, but she felt like a fool.

Oh, so you knew she was coming?

No, I had no idea. She's asked a few times to see Izzie. I was trying to feel her out over the phone. I never felt a peace about it so I kept saying no.

That makes sense. I'm so sorry, friend. She winced.

Her phone buzzed a full minute later. **Friend, huh?**

Well, yeah…

Hmmm. That was the un-friendliest kiss I've ever had, Amelia.

Let's just forget about it.

A few minutes passed without an answer. She sent another text.

You have Izzie you need to focus on.

Wow, Howard. I never took you for a wuss.

She sat up, shocked. Annoyed. **What is that supposed to mean?**

Nothing I'm just tired. Sorry.

Whatever, Creed.

You know what? I'm not sorry, actually. The way I see it things are getting good between us and you're running. Like last time. Like you have been for years. Hiding from love. From me.

Last time? How could he possibly—she had sent him letters. He had ignored her. And did he really just point out something he *knew* she was so sensitive about? Of all the—

Low blow, Williams. And if I remember correctly you're the one who ran last time.

Nope.

Oh, okay. I'll just pull out all of your responses to the letters that I wrote you…oh wait…

How could she be so dreamy about the man one minute and want to strangle him the next? She waited for two minutes, four, six. The heat in her veins cooled and she began to feel foolish. She was a grown woman fighting through text messages in the middle of the night. She wondered if she should text an apology and just start over tomorrow. She tapped her fingers on the screen.

Look, let's just—

Her phone rang before she could finish compiling the text. She flung it away as if it had burned her. And hadn't it? Hadn't *he*? It fell to the floor with a thud. The ringing persisted. She drew her legs up and wrapped her arms around them, leaning her cheek on the tops of her knees. A tear slipped down, soaking into her pajamas. Finally, the phone went silent. A text came through seconds later. She waited a few minutes before crawling across her bed and leaning over the edge to retrieve it.

I'm sorry, Amelia. I really am.

For ignoring her in college? For leaving? For kissing her tonight and then pointing out her weaknesses in a text message just hours later? She wasn't sure she wanted to know. She took a shuddering breath, struggling for calm. They were going at each other like a couple of high school kids. There were bigger things at stake than her feelings, than some stupid kiss.

I am too. No worries. We were just caught up in the moment. Because of the engagement and all. You just focus on Izzie and let me know if I can help in any way.

She turned off her phone before he could respond and flopped back in bed.

Chapter Thirty-One

Creed lay in the dark, listening to the phone ring, willing her to pick up. Why he had texted her in the first place—when it was so late—he couldn't say, other than he wanted to recapture their moments in the car.

To know that Hailey—his past mistakes—wouldn't ruin everything again.

But then she had thrown in that word—*friend.*

He knew better than to fight with her, to jab low where she was most vulnerable.

But he did it anyway. He acted in emotional desperation like some teenage girl. He felt her slipping away and lashed out, only to be reminded—once again—that he wasn't good enough for someone like her. And it was exactly what he had done before. Only back then, he had kissed her out of desperation…

> Creed had been in a foul mood since the prom.
>
> Where he might have had moments over the years of finding Amelia attractive, he had always been able to overcome them. Until now.
>
> Now he couldn't get her out of his head. Couldn't help but think back on years of platonic hugs, late night movie trips, bike rides, summer nights, winter days…their friendship had gone from saving grace to torture. Especially now that he was on her "team".

Amelia, completely unaware of his feelings, rattled on and on about what she wanted in a husband:

"Smart."

"Funny. He has to have a good sense of humor."

"He has to be serious, though."

"A man after God's own heart. Someone that I can work alongside for God's kingdom. I want us to make a difference together..."

Every new addition to her list proved that he was all wrong for her.

After graduation, Creed found himself avoiding Amelia more and more. She was so focused on her summer job and upcoming move to college that he didn't think she noticed.

He spent the summer torn between the ache of needing to be near her and the pain that sliced through him when he was.

They spent a day at the reservoir the week before Amelia moved away. She had scored a job on campus and would report two weeks before classes started. The thought of her actually leaving weighed heavily, settling like a hot rock in his chest. They parked his truck and strode down the dock, both thankful to have the place to themselves.

Creed averted his eyes when Amelia stripped off her shorts and t-shirt and jumped in the water. For all the times he had appreciated women in bikinis over the years, leaving nothing to the imagination, Creed thought the sight of Amelia's slender form in the modest black and white polka-dot one piece would be his undoing. She drove him crazy. And she had no idea.

She turned to him with some smart challenge, treading water. Creed shook his head, a smile curling his lips. He didn't want to waste another minute moping over Amelia Howard.

He wanted to make the most of his time with her.

He dove in after her, a spark of mischief firing through him.

Resurfacing behind her, Creed popped up just enough to gauge the distance and hear her squeal. He dove under again. Her legs kicked at him. He slid his hand up her ankle, calf, then hip, digging his fingers into her side. Bubbles of laughter released in front of his face as he felt her stomach muscles clench and twist. He let go and burst through the surface, coughing when she shoved a handful of water in his face. Creed swished around her in the water to give her a bear hug from behind. He held her there, his arms wrapped tightly around her middle, and leaned back. She squirmed for a moment, giggling when he dug his chin into where her shoulder met the base of her neck—her secret tickle spot. Finally, spent, she rested her hands on his arms, breathing hard, relaxing into him. Together they kicked toward the shore. When he felt they were only chest deep, Creed lowered his feet and planted them in the sand, easing his grip. She turned to face him, her smile crinkling her eyes into narrow slits.

Their breath came hard and fast from the swim. Water spiked her lashes, dripped down her cheeks. Her hair was smoothed back, but the ends swirled in the water beneath the surface, tickling his arms. Amelia laughed. He didn't remember releasing her arms, didn't know how her wrists were suddenly on his shoulders, her palms on the sides of his neck, her fingers spread into the hair at his nape. Didn't know when the laughter dissolved from her eyes.

Didn't know how long he'd been staring at those lips.

Didn't know how he had ached to hold her in his arms since their dance weeks ago.

He didn't know anything beyond his need to kiss her. To hold her close and kiss all ideas of waiting for some perfect man right out of her pretty head.

And from the look in her eyes, Creed had a feeling Amelia might not refuse such a notion.

He licked his lips and drew closer. His breath broke off at the feel of hers on his cheek. Heat that had nothing to do with the summer day charged between them. His lips hummed as he drew near, within seconds of brushing against hers.

Time stood still for a fraction of a second and then he closed the distance—or was it her? No matter. Their lips met, trembling, careful. Familiar. How was this so stinking familiar? He felt like he had entered a place he had been before hundreds of times in his dreams, only the reality was infinitely better.

Her lips were like coming home. *She* was like coming home. Always would be. This was Amelia. His Amelia.

She broke the kiss softly, pulling her head back, her mouth hanging on as long it could until the distance broke contact. But his own buzzed, unsatisfied. He quickly reclaimed her mouth, cupping the back of her head, his fingers tangling in her wet hair. Amelia leaned into him, giving into the kiss more forcefully. His heart pounded. He soared. He would follow her to—

But then she was reeling back, pulling away, forcing a laugh.

"Whoa, that's not quite on plan, is it?" her voice was high, pinched.

Creed's arms already ached without her in them. His lips were sore, hers swollen. Desperation swept through him and he longed to pull her back, convince her to stay, to forget her stupid oath, to—

But the vulnerable look in her eyes stopped him cold. Creed raked his hands back through his hair in frustration.

"You know, Amelia, you can't plan everything. Especially not this." He wagged two fingers between them.

Her nostrils flared, her chin rose a fraction. "Maybe I don't want some end-of-summer fling, Creed."

"That's not what—"

"Because I've watched it, Williams. I've seen you with plenty of girls and it's always the same. Some quick fling that means nothing to you."

She had him there, but this was different. She had to know—

"Do you have any idea how many girls have come crying to me after a few weeks with Creed Williams? Or Carter Adams or Vince Rodgers for that matter? It's the same story over and over and I'm sorry if I want more than that." Her eyes flashed. "I'm sorry if you've run out of summer romances, Creed, but I have no interest in being the last option at the bottom of your empty barrel."

She turned and swam toward the dock.

Creed stared after her, heart pounding from her words, body still humming from the heated kiss. She was right, of course. Because she had no idea how he felt. Would it make a difference to tell her? And to what end? They were heading to schools in different states. She had her list, her plans...her team. He wondered for the first time who else was on it and how they would advise her where he was concerned. He was pretty sure he knew the answer to that one: run!

Creed watched Amelia towel off and sit on the dock. She pulled her phone from her bag and texted someone. It was as if she could read his thoughts.

His jaw clenched. Someone on her team? Was she telling of her moment of weakness? He should grab the phone and vouch for her. Convince whomever it was that she remained strong, the purity of her convictions intact.

No, Creed couldn't tell her how he felt. Could never tell her. After all, Amelia had her plans and he knew full well he didn't fit into them.

Months later, he had thrown himself completely into the college experience. He dated and kissed a few girls. Nothing compared to those minutes at the reservoir. He went further and further, seeking the same thrill he had felt in her embrace, until...he knew he had blown his chances with Amelia completely.

Wasn't that one of the things at the top of her list? A virgin. She dreamt of a special wedding night where she and her husband shared kisses and embraces that had been saved for each other.

His heart clenched when he received her first letter. He ripped it open drinking in her words hungrily.

"Maybe I was wrong, Creed. Is there any reason you can't be on my team and be the man I'm praying for at the same time?"

Yes, there was a reason. He crumpled the paper, chucked it across the room with a growl. How could he tell her she had been right? He was the same as he always was, chasing women, charging ahead without thought. He could not be that man for her. She deserved more. So much more.

Letters continued to come periodically over the next few years. He always read them hungrily, with a sick sort of ache. She had met someone; they were talking engagement. Then, his sophomore year a letter came telling him of her broken heart, of the nasty things her boyfriend's mother had said to her. He longed to write back or call. But to what end? He found the box of letters he had saved over the years, reread them all before he tucked the latest one away.

His phone buzzed. A text from a pretty coed in his philosophy class. Hailey something.

Hey Creed. Want to get together to study? Or not. Wink, wink. Let me know.

He stared blankly at the screen for a moment before taking a deep breath and tapping out a response.

Sounds fun. What time?

Chapter Thirty-Two

Is it true, Lord, that I have been hiding from relationships? That making decisions for my future husband wasn't about him at all, but about protecting myself? Maybe my disappointment at losing Creed all those years ago affected me more than I realized. Help me to rely on You and You alone. Guide me, please. I want to honor You.

Amelia had risen earlier than usual and spent an hour reading through the Psalms and writing in her journal. It had been a long time since she stopped to dig deep for purposeful soul-searching. She had woken numerous times in the night in a panic, terrified that the kiss—and fight—had ruined her relationship with Creed. She clutched at her covers and drank in deep breaths until her breathing returned to normal. Every time she would remember Creed's hands on her shoulders, the wall of his chest firm and steady behind her while Chad and Lucy thanked their families for their support. It was natural and good.

But then everything seemed to have shattered. Her stomach twisted in disgust. Izzie was what mattered in this scenario, not her feeble emotions. Why was she so afraid?

Because once again, her heart was in his hands and she didn't trust him to be careful.

Once again she let her heart turn from the Lord for fulfillment and to a fallible human being.

The truth hurt.

She had finally given up and ripped the comforter off of her bed, wrapping it around her to ward of the morning chill. She shuffled downstairs into the living room to curl up in her high wingback chair, not bothering to make coffee. A memory of Lucy crying herself to sleep night after night at Amelia's apartment in the days after her husband had left surfaced.

It was followed by the way C.B. had so formally broken things off with her while giving her a list of all the reasons she wouldn't make an acceptable partner.

But most of all, she remembered the despondent way she had gone through the motions her first semester in college. So lost without Creed's friendship, so lonely for what they had been to each other.

For the first-time, Amelia saw with alarming clarity that after college, her years of wanting to be an honorable woman had transformed into a shield; a way in which she could live and protect herself from the sorrow that Lucy experienced.

But it was more than that, of course. Creed's silence when he moved away had rocked her more than she had been willing to admit. She had entered blindly into a relationship with some guy she wasn't very compatible with. It was by the grace of God that C.B. had seen that. Not that it took the sting of rejection away. But that had not compared to what she felt now, on the precipice of losing Creed. Here he was back in her life and she opened herself to him without question. Where she had been guarded with all others, Creed had been the exception. The only exception.

She remembered how Aaron had approached her the night before. How quickly she had backpedaled when he asked her to coffee. Remembered, too the ways other men might have shown interest over the years. In rapid-fire succession the numerous ways that she had given any man who might have shown interest in dating her the impression that she was married came to mind. And it had worked. Her closed responses, refusal to carry conversations that could lead to something more had shut men off immediately. The few that had tried to get to know her had quickly backed off.

Except for Creed.

He already knew her, had seen through her façade, whether he realized it or not. No wonder she was a stuttering mess around him for so long. He had reached into the depths of her seclusion and ripped her right out into the world of the living.

She looked back down at her journal, warmed and alarmed at once. She continued to write, pouring out her heart and asking the Lord to search out all of her fear and confusion so that she could offer it up to Him to be obliterated. After a long while, Amelia set her journal and Bible aside to stretch and finally make breakfast. The sun shone brightly through the windows, brighter than she had expected. The clock on her phone showed Amelia that she was too late to get ready for church.

She was relieved, not at all ready to face Creed.

She made an egg scramble out of veggies she found in her fridge. She only had one egg left and no bread. A peek in the coffee canister reminded her that she was out of that as well. Running out of coffee was not going to fly after her long night.

She finished breakfast and showered quickly, drying her hair, but not bothering to style it. She made a quick run to the grocery store for the basics, remembering when she ran into Creed and raced him through the store.

Amelia treated herself to a coffee from her favorite drive-thru, ordering the same caramel mocha that Creed had brought for her. She inhaled the sweet fragrance, her heart hammering with the memory of his kiss last night. Her lips burned. Was there such a thing as phantom kisses?

No matter how resolved she was, the more awake she felt, the more scenes from the evening before—before Hailey arrived, before they argued—assaulted her senses.

She had just put her groceries away when the phone rang. Had Creed been thinking of her, too?

She found the cell in her purse, but frowned when a number she didn't recognize flashed on the screen.

She swiped the arrow on the screen to "answer."

"Hello?"

"Amelia, this is Dan Laird with Pepperville Elementary."

"Yes?" One of the schools she had applied to. She glanced around for her schedule book.

"I know how odd it is to call on a Sunday. I apologize. I am calling to schedule an interview for next week if you're still available."

She breathed a sigh of relief. "You have no idea how great that sounds. Just name the time." She spotted her planner on the kitchen island and walked across the room to grab it.

A pause. Papers rustled in the background. "How about tomorrow at ten?"

"Perfect," she answered, making a note in the planner.

"I have to say, based on your resume and references we already think you'll be a good fit. The interview is really more of a formality."

"That sounds great, Mr. Laird. I look forward to meeting you."

"Please, call me Dan. And, yes, I'm looking forward to it as well. See you tomorrow."

"Thank you, Bye."

The line went dead and Amelia dropped her hand, still holding the phone on her lap. She sat quietly for a moment, then took a deep breath and tapped out a text:

Can we just go back to the way things were? she typed, hoping deep in her heart that he would say no. That he needed her. Wanted her. That they could figure it out and work through the hurdles that faced them.

Her phone rang almost instantly, startling her. This time she recognized Creed's number.

She took a deep breath. "Hey."

"Hey." She could tell he was smiling. "We didn't see you at church."

"Yeah, I didn't sleep great."

"I'm sorry, Amelia."

"It's okay. And I'm sorry, too. I wonder if we were just caught up, you know?" Hearing his voice, she realized that she would rather have a friendship with Creed than nothing at all.

He didn't answer.

"I mean, watching Chad and Lucy get engaged, and you and I being so comfortable with each other…I just think the air was full of romance and we just…I don't want to ruin this, Creed."

"I don't either, Amelia. It's been amazing to have you in my life again. We won't ruin anything, I—"

Fear roared—old memories snaking through her. She closed her eyes. Romance wouldn't end well for them. "Creed, let's just go back to how it was. You need to focus on all of this with Hailey. I would love to be your friend, Creed. Please let me be."

A heartbeat. "Okay. That works for me, Amelia."

They chatted for a few more minutes. He was excited about her job interview and made her promise to call him when it was over. She promised to pray for wisdom where Hailey was concerned. They hung up with plans to meet up later in the week. She knew she should be relieved, happy.

So why wasn't she?

Chapter Thirty-Three

Principal McClary called to ask that Creed meet him before school the next morning, and Creed agreed, eager to give the man a piece of his mind.

But when he sat across from the principal, Creed stared at the man in confusion.

"What do you mean Izzie is no longer welcome here?"

"Mr. Williams, please. We have a strict moral standard here, which is why after the—uh—publicity you and Miss Howard received I had no choice but to let her go. Unfortunately, that wasn't enough for some parents."

Creed's face flushed. "Look, I know what you think but absolutely nothing inappropriate happened."

"I'm afraid it's no use arguing, Creed. I've made up my mind and I need to ask that you and your daughter leave campus now."

Creed shook his head but stood, irritation making his hands twitch at his sides. "Fine, I'll leave. But not before I make you understand that Miss Howard is innocent of everything that she's been accused of. Unfortunately, she's also very clumsy which is why pictures of us on the ground outside were made public. She tripped and took me down with her. When I saw those pictures, I was horrified that someone had been audacious enough to follow two old friends on a walk in broad daylight. I didn't want Miss Howard to be caught off guard and went to her apartment to warn her. Her phone was turned off preventing me from calling her. I regret that I didn't wait until she turned it back on, but I challenge you to think clearly after seeing pictures of yourself—pictures you didn't know were being taken—on a popular website. I stepped into her apartment for all of seven minutes before she kicked me out. She's innocent, Mr. McClary. She has integrity and class. We had no idea someone was watching—again taking pictures and fabricating stories—but still she asked me to leave so she wouldn't be alone in her apartment with a man."

McClary worked a muscle in his jaw, his eyes blinking slowly. "Well, Mr. Williams, that's all very interesting, but—"

"And then, as if finding out some creep was crouched outside of her apartment in the early hours of the morning wasn't enough; as if finding pictures of herself online suggesting she was improper wasn't enough; as if being thrown into something that has nothing to do with her wasn't enough; as if strangers commenting on her looks and intentions and making assumptions about her when they don't even know her wasn't enough; she was fired from a job she loves and made to feel like scum."

"Look, I don't think—"

"Well you know what? I don't want my daughter in a place like this anyway. I enrolled her in this school because I thought it to be a place of compassion and grace. Where she would learn everything from math to English to science with a Biblical worldview. Unfortunately, I didn't know that the place is run by a pharisaical putz. Good day."

Creed strode from the office before the principal could respond. He knew he would have to apologize later for losing his temper, but not now. He would only go back and give it to him worse. He stopped by Izzie's class where her new teacher had helped her pack her desk. Izzie sat in a chair near the door, face streaked with tears, her overstuffed backpack at her feet.

Her new teacher gave him an apologetic shrug before looping an arm around Izzie's shoulders and guiding her to the door.

"I'm so sorry," she whispered to Creed.

He could only nod, his eyes on Izzie.

"Izzie, we're sure going to miss you," her voice wobbled and she turned abruptly back to the classroom shutting the door behind her softly.

Izzie looked up at Creed, her eyes soulful. "Why do I hafta leave, Daddy?"

Creed took a knee beside her, pulled her into his arms. "You know, Kiddo, bad things just happen sometimes. Things we don't understand. Things we can't control. This is just one of those things. All I can tell you is that we can trust the Lord," he swiped a tear from her cheek with the pad of his thumb, thinking how he might as well be talking to his own heart. "Over and over God has shown me how good He is and how much He cares for us. For now, we just remember that, okay?"

She nodded, squeezing her eyes shut and leaning into him, her small body shuddering with tears. He set his chin on the top of her head and pulled her close.

"I know, baby. I know. We'll just go back to your old school. You liked it there, remember? And hey," he pulled back and caught her eyes in his. "Looks like you have a non-snow snow day. Not many kids get those. What do you say I blow off work and we go get an ice cream sundae?"

She wiped her nose with the cuff of her long sleeved shirt, eyes brightening. "Really? Before lunch?"

He leaned his forehead against hers and grinned. "Absolutely. Come on."

Later there would be phone calls to make. But for that moment all that mattered was that he knew what he told Izzie about the Lord was true—no matter how bleak things appeared. He knew that the Lord was always working for the good of His children.

After their treat, Creed and Izzie went home and decided to change into sweats and veg out with popcorn and Izzie's new favorite: the Beezus and Ramona movie. While she changed, Creed decided to call his lawyer about the way Hailey had shown up that weekend. There had to be some way he could be sure Izzie would be protected from any more surprise appearances.

"Creed, I was just about to call you. Miss Anderson's lawyer called me and requested a mediation meeting. They can do this afternoon which I thought might be okay with you; I assume you want to get this whole mess over with."

"Yes, James, I would. I just need to find a sitter for Izzie," Creed answered. Peabody agreed to wait until he called back with a time to make arrangements. Creed called his mom and arranged for her to come over after lunch then called his lawyer back. Everything in place, he settled on the couch to enjoy a movie with his heartbroken daughter. He would deal with school decisions later.

For today, it was time to settle this with Hailey once and for all.

*   *   *

Amelia's job interview was relaxed and encouraging. Dan was a lanky man with salt and pepper hair and a warm smile. He offered her the job on the spot. After learning about the benefits package and salary—almost double what she was making at the private school—Amelia enthusiastically accepted.

She called Lucy to share her news. Lucy worked in a salon and had Mondays off, so they agreed they should go to lunch to celebrate.

"Maybe after lunch we could look at wedding dresses, too. But only if you are up to it," Lucy added.

"Of course! Let's call Mom to join us."

Over lunch at an Italian restaurant, the sisters and their mother, Stacy, discussed wedding plans.

"My new job won't actually start until after Thanksgiving," Amelia said. "I'm taking over for a woman that is about to have her first baby. She doesn't want to return and is due the beginning of December, so that seemed like a good cut off for her. It will be strange to have so much time off and so little time to get to know my class before Christmas break, but that gives me a lot of freedom to help plan."

"With Lucy getting married in six weeks, we don't have a lot of time. It will be great to have you available to help," Stacy said.

"But we really don't want a big wedding, Mom," Lucy interjected. "I don't think there will be that much to do."

"Well, maybe so, but still, we need to find the dress and flowers and cake."

"Have you decided on a theme?" Amelia asked, savoring a bite of manicotti.

It had been a long time since the three women were able to meet for lunch. The blend of carbs and family time turned out to be just what Amelia needed.

"Well, we're trying to use Christmas to our advantage as much as possible," Lucy answered. "The church has agreed to let us use the facilities for free, as long as we set up their Christmas decorations for them and clean up after ourselves, so maybe you two could be in charge of a clean-up crew. The church already has a couple dozen tubs of Christmas decorations; I guess the gal that normally does it is glad for a break this year because she's had a lot of family junk going on."

"That sounds like a lot of work, Lucy, but also a real bargain," Stacy commented.

"I keep forgetting you haven't seen our church, Mom," Amelia said. "The chapel isn't that big. With the lights and trees, it will be really charming. I'm excited for you, Lucy."

Her sister beamed.

The women finished lunch, and piled into Amelia's car. Lucy sat in the backseat and directed Amelia to a boutique in the heart of downtown.

The cozy atmosphere at lunch stayed with the ladies all day as they shopped for dresses. Lucy told Amelia she was the only person in her wedding party and said she could pick out whatever dress she wanted to wear.

"I just ask that it be Christmassy," Lucy added, rifling through a rack of cream colored dresses.

Stacy fidgeted next to Lucy, glancing around the chic little shop with concern painted on her features. "Honey, are you sure you don't want a true wedding gown?"

Lucy paused, a rare shadow passing over her face. "I already had one once, Mom. Remember? I spent my last wedding so fixated on the details, ignoring all of the red flags. Chad and I have talked about this a lot; we just want to get married and focus more on the pre-marital counseling and the vows. Sure, we want to look nice and make a big deal out of it—it is a big deal. But this time I want to keep it simple. Does that make sense?"

Amelia slung an arm around their mother's shoulders and faced Lucy.

"Of course it does. Doesn't it, Ma?"

Stacy nodded unconvincingly. Feeling mischievous, Amelia reached behind her mother for a dress that caught her eye.

"Hey, Lucy, I think I found my dress," she called out.

Lucy turned from down the row to see Amelia hold up a bright yellow dress with wild, wispy fringes down either side and across the neckline. The way the fringes moved with the slightest breeze reminded Amelia of Big Bird's feathers.

Lucy flattened her eyes and opened her mouth to comment when she caught the sparkle in Amelia's eyes—and the look of horror on their mother's face. With perfectly executed enthusiasm, she grabbed the dress from Amelia and held it up for inspection.

"Oh, I just adore it. It's perfect! See what a great shop this is?" Lucy asked her mom, struggling to keep her laughter at bay.

Stacy blinked rapidly and fingered the red beaded necklace she wore. "Well, now, it's…uh, well, it doesn't exactly go with the Christmas theme, now does it?" She stared worriedly at the dress, wincing slightly. Finally, she caught the look of glee on her daughters' faces and lightly smacked each of them on the shoulder.

"You girls! I ought to take you over my knee," she murmured, raising her nose in the air and going back to perusing the racks.

The sisters laughed uproariously and only teased Stacy a few more times. When Lucy emerged from the dressing room in a simple, but elegant, fitted cream gown, Amelia stepped close to admire her sister.

"It's perfect," she whispered. "Just like you. Chad is going to drool," she winked at her sister. Stacy agreed. Amelia and Stacy also found dresses perfect for the occasion and the women declared the afternoon a rousing success.

When Amelia readied for bed that night, she realized that she hadn't remembered to tell Creed about the successful interview. She texted her news and went about her routine.

She was wired from the excitement of the day. Instead of going to bed, she popped a bowl of popcorn and stayed up late watching a movie on the Hallmark channel.

It wasn't until she crawled into bed well past her normal bedtime that she realized that Creed had never texted back.

Chapter Thirty-Four

Creed and Peabody waited in a conference room at the law office making awkward conversation with the stenographer from a third party company at the law office. Ten minutes past their scheduled time, Hailey and a large man with hair slicked back in a long ponytail finally walked in.

Well, it makes sense her lawyer would be so greasy looking, Creed thought, then quickly chided himself for being so unkind. This was Izzie's mother after all. He rose to shake their hands, very okay when Hailey refused the gesture. She may be his child's mother, but only technically. Creed sat back down, unable to take his eyes off of her.

She had lost weight since she had walked out on Izzie, making her look somewhat ghoulish. Her blond hair had lost its youthful sheen, though she had swept it into a knot at her nape. She wore baggy dress pants and a loose white blouse. Her makeup was slightly smudged and Creed thought she might be drunk, though he didn't smell alcohol. Had she looked this bad the other night? He wasn't sure. But then, it had been dark out, the porch light casting only so much light. Hailey sat back and let her lawyer do most of the talking. As they talked the stenographer tapped away in the background.

"Miss Anderson is seeking full custody of the child, as well as support from Mr. Williams," his gravelly voice and the stale smell he brought with him suggested a heavy smoking habit.

James scoffed. "In what world do you and your client think that this case will fly before a judge? We have proof that Miss Anderson abandoned the child; if anyone is getting support, it should be my client who has solely supported this girl for the last six years."

Creed interjected, "I don't need or want her money."

"According to a recording we recently obtained, it doesn't sound like you really want your child, either," her lawyer sneered.

Creed exchanged confused glances with Peabody. "What are you talking about? I've never said any such thing."

Hailey pulled a small recording device from her purse and set it on the table. Her lawyer set his elbows on the table and steepled his hands beneath his chin as Creed's frustrated voice crackled into the room.

"Since you dumped your daughter with me and my whole life fell apart."

Hailey's face flickered, a passing amusement curled her lips.

Creed's mouth dropped open. She'd recorded him?

"That is not what I meant. Look, she showed up unannounced and I was frustrated. The last time I saw her before that stupid TV show was when she abandoned Izzie with me." Creed felt heat rising beneath his collar making him itchy.

Her lawyer nodded at the device. "And according to that recording, your life would have been better off without Izzie."

Creed rose from his chair. "Now just a minute, that's not at all—"

James set a hand on Creed's shoulder and pulled him back to his seat. His eyes snapped a warning and Creed swallowed the argument.

The stenographer's *tap-tap-tapping* grated on his nerves.

Peabody spoke up, "Like I said, your client abandoned her daughter. It doesn't matter what my client said in a heated moment with no knowledge he was being recorded. If anyone is getting child support, it will be Mr. Williams."

248

Creed clenched his teeth. Over his dead body. "I told you, I don't need anyone's money, and I won't take money from her." His eyes flickered to Hailey, anger coursing through him.

Attorney Grease pulled a stack of papers from the file folder he had carried in under his arm. "Well, no, I guess a man who evades the IRS to keep from paying taxes would have no concern about money," he said as he slid the paper across the table to Peabody.

Creed reeled back in his seat. *What was he talking about?*

"I pay my taxes just like everyone else," he said.

Hailey and her lawyer both stared at him in disdain. Creed leaned forward, pounding the table with his fist.

"Why are you doing all of this, Hailey? You have made no effort whatsoever to see Izzie or contact her for over six years. Why now?"

Hailey curled her lip at him in disgust, but didn't answer.

Creed looked to Peabody who had perched small wire rimmed glasses on his nose to better read the document. Finally, he looked across the table.

"Where did you get this?" he inquired of the lawyer, holding up the papers.

Attorney Grease leaned back smugly in his chair. "I don't reveal my sources," he sneered.

"What is it?" Creed asked.

Peabody removed his glasses. He looked across the table and rose. "I would like a moment with my client."

Hailey and her lawyer exchanged a look of triumph. Hailey crossed her arms.

Creed stood in confusion when his lawyer did, the hair prickled on the back of his neck. He had no idea what they were talking about, but the look on James' face could only mean that he was concerned.

In the hallway, Peabody rubbed his eyes with his pointer finger and thumb, pinching and releasing a few times before he finally looked at Creed.

"Creed, I need you to be very honest with me: have you neglected to pay your taxes?"

"Of course not. I pay them every year just like I'm supposed to," Creed protested, baffled. "And even if I didn't—which I did—what would that have to do with Izzie?"

James sighed and rubbed the back of his neck, handing Creed the stack of papers. "According to this, the IRS is coming after you for tax evasion. And the reason that it affects this meeting right now is because one of the many ways that this thing with your taxes could go down is jail time."

Creed's blood ran cold, sending shivers through him as it drained from his face.

*   *   *

It was all over the news.

Amelia couldn't believe it when she opened her local news app to check the weather. Her eyes were drawn immediately to Creed's face above the headline: *Singing Father Wanted by IRS for Tax Fraud, Could Lose Custody of His Daughter.*

She called Creed immediately. He answered on the third ring, his voice raspy.

"Creed? What is going on?" she asked, realizing too late that just because it was on the news didn't make it her business.

"Oh good, you saw the articles," Creed stated, his voice flat.

She groaned inwardly, broken at the despair in his voice. "Creed."

"Amelia, I don't know what to do. I can't lose Izzie, and I definitely can't lose her to Hailey."

"How can I help you? What can I do?"

"I have no idea, Amelia. I just...there's so much to figure out," he said.

"Okay, well if you need anything..."

When he didn't answer, she whispered goodbye and hung up, not waiting to hear if Creed answered. She sat cross legged on her couch, staring at the pile of empty moving boxes near the front door. She really needed to break them down and take them to the recycling center.

The painful silence was shattered by the shrill ring of her cell phone. Her hopes rose, only to be dashed when she saw it was Lucy.

"Did you see it?" Lucy asked as soon as she answered.

"Yeah. I tried to call Creed, but he wasn't in the mood to talk, I guess," Amelia rolled her eyes toward the ceiling in self disdain. *And no wonder, Amelia, he's worried about his daughter,* she reminded herself, suddenly in full understanding of his abrupt response.

"I know. It's crazy. I was at Chad's last night when he came over. I guess Creed has been doing his taxes through an accountant. He has no idea where this claim is coming from, but the IRS guy he spoke with assures him there is no error. They said it's from an old business he was co-owner of in college, so Creed has plans to meet with his accountant later this week to work it all out. The really crummy thing is how this was presented to him," Lucy went on to explain how Creed had found out about the tax issue from Hailey's lawyer.

"He said the guy was a real slime ball and that Hailey looks terrible," Lucy said, not unkindly. "They implied that since jail time is hanging over his head they are going to push for custody. But then they talked about expecting Creed to pay child support. It doesn't make any sense."

Amelia chewed on her bottom lip, troubled. "You know, Lucy, something just isn't right. I don't know Hailey, but her behavior sure seems erratic, doesn't it?"

"Yes, that's what the Williamses all think. We can't figure it out. In all the times she's insisted on seeing Izzie she hasn't ever asked —not once—to see pictures of Izzie or even talk to her on the phone. Wouldn't you think that would be the first thing she would want if she truly is a broken mother missing her child? Wouldn't you think she'd just want to experience the years she'd lost in any way she could?"

Amelia thought back to her early autumn walk with Creed. She'd been eager to hear all about Izzie's growing up years and she was only her teacher. "Yeah, something isn't right there."

They talked for a few minutes more before they signed off. Amelia read the article, heart aching for Creed. Something that normally could be resolved with a meeting with an IRS employee was being blown out of proportion by the media and a money hungry—

The thought that had begun to dawn in the recesses of Amelia's mind for weeks hit her with sudden clarity.

"Oh my goodness."

She immediately called Lucy back, her hands shaking. She knew her sister would understand.

"Hey, Sis. I have an idea of how to smoke out Hailey's motives and maybe get her out of the picture. But you will have to do most of the work. Are you up for it?"

She explained what she had in mind, her words tumbling over one another. When she was finished, she waited anxiously for Lucy's response.

"You're a genius!" was the enthusiastic reply. "Let's do it."

Chapter Thirty-Five

"Let me get this straight," Creed leaned his head back, bringing both hands up to squeeze the sides of his skull in frustration, "not only did my college roommate lie to me about how much our tutoring business was bringing in, but he also neglected to pay taxes on our income after he listed me as the owner of the company?"

His accountant, a long-time family friend, pointed again to the paper trail he had tracked back through the years that the IRS claimed Creed owed.

"Looks that way, Creed. Robbie must have had you sign something, maybe to make you think you were just a partner in the company. But it looks like after you left the company, he put it all in your name and stopped paying taxes. Before that he must have been, which is why the IRS was alerted to the situation," he explained, his wire rimmed glasses slipping down his nose.

Creed sat up straight again. The chair beneath him groaned from the sudden shift in weight. He pointed to the date at the top of the first paper.

"What I don't understand, Brian, is why it took this long for the IRS to say anything. I mean, most of this is interest, right? I might have been able to afford the original amount owed, but they can't be serious with this interest," Creed picked up the stack of papers and tossed them down again. His chest tightened at the helpless shrug Brian offered.

"The address was a post office box that was closed years ago. And it looks like Robbie had your name spelled wrong and neither of you noticed. Since both this and your current business are under Tax ID numbers and not social security, it took them a long time to track you down. I still don't understand how that lawyer discovered it before you did, though. What a lousy way to find out about this."

Another thought struck Creed, one that frightened him much more than a high interest rate.

"Can they really use this to get Izzie away from me, Brian?"

Brian interlaced his fingers on top of the table and leaned forward, his voice low, "I'm not a lawyer, Creed. I can't help you there. My recommendation would be to find a way to pay this off as fast as you can. You do not want to owe the IRS money or be trapped into monthly payments with them. They will come in and evaluate all of your monthly bills. Then they determine what is necessary and what's not."

Creed snorted. "Fat chance of them being able to squeeze any money out that way; we live on a carefully orchestrated budget."

"Is Izzie in any sports or activities?"

"No, not yet." He had hoped to sign her up for gymnastics after the holidays.

"How much do you spend on groceries?"

Creed's jaw dropped, "They look at that?"

"They look at everything."

"I spend as much as we need for two people to eat."

"They keep an average amount listed out for families of different sizes across the country. They will use that to determine how much they feel you need," Brian answered.

His next question angered Creed. "And do you have a life insurance policy?"

"Of course I do," he answered, lips terse. "I'm a single father."

Brian leaned back, and crossed one leg over the opposite knee. He clicked a pen slowly, considering.

"I've seen them cancel those before. Listen, Creed," he set the pen down. "If you can get a loan, I highly recommend it. You don't want to owe the IRS money. Trust me."

* * *

Hours later, Izzie by his side, Creed knocked on Chad's door. He waited, wishing he could be anywhere else. As the Best Man in the wedding he was joining Chad, Lucy, and Amelia for a dinner to discuss wedding plans.

He hadn't seen Amelia since their kiss, and wasn't in the mood to now. Why he needed to be in on the wedding details was beyond him. Wasn't his job just to be sure the groom didn't toss his cookies right before he said, "I do?"

He didn't stop to remind himself how readily he had agreed to the idea a few nights ago. He had been eager to see Amelia then, wanted to show her just how *friendly* he could be.

Chad opened the door, face beaming, but not fully able to hide the pity in his eyes.

My kid brother pities me, Creed thought. His already bad mood curdled. *Awesome.*

"Well, if it isn't my favorite niece and bro—" Chad, seeing the look in Creed's face, stopped short. He swallowed the jovial greeting and opened the door wider.

"Come on in. Lucy came over earlier to start cooking. She has really outdone herself."

They walked through the small apartment living room and into the dining area next to it. Lucy entered from the kitchen, a tray in her hands, talking over her shoulder. Amelia came into sight behind her, laughing. She stopped in her tracks when she saw Creed. Her eyes flashed with hurt or pity. Or both. He wasn't entirely sure. But the look

256

in her eyes smarted his pride and got his hackles up even more.

It was going to be a long night.

* * *

Longest. Night. Ever.

Amelia took a sip of cranberry ginger ale. Creed's foul mood, and the tension surrounding them, induced a stabbing pain behind her eyes. She focused on Izzie, happy to see her. Lucy had shared that Izzie had started at her old school that week, so she told her about her new job as well.

"I start after Thanksgiving so you'll have to give me tips on how to be the new girl in class, okay?" She smiled into the young girl's eyes.

"Oh, it's easy," Izzie bragged, sipping on the curly straw Lucy had plunked into her glass of milk.

Lucy and Chad had waited until everyone was seated and the prayer had been said to explain the impromptu dinner.

"We know we are asking a lot of you two around the busiest time of year. While our wedding should be simple, there will still be plenty of little details we will need your help with. Before we get caught up in the plans, we wanted to have you over for a thank you dinner in advance," Chad clarified.

Lucy nodded. "We just love you both so much and appreciate how much you are supporting us."

Amelia's throat clenched and she smiled at Lucy, then Chad. "Well, of course. It's my pleasure no matter what time of year it is. I'm really happy for you guys," she said, glancing at Creed.

His eyes were on the table, lost in thought. The lull in conversation should have captured his attention. Izzie stared up at him and gently placed her small hand on his arm. Amelia wondered if this wasn't the first time she'd watched her Dad drift into his thoughts over the last few days. Creed glanced up at her and Chad repeated the reason for the dinner. With a shake of his head, Creed gave a self-deprecating smile.

"Hey, if this charming woman is willing to make you her groom, the least I can do is be around to run interference for your ugly mug," Creed said dryly.

Izzie giggled.

"Gee thanks," Chad deadpanned.

Although the teasing was in Creed's usual tone, the light of his smile was dull, his laughter forced. He pushed his food around distractedly, barely eating the lasagna or garlic bread on his plate. Izzie must have noticed as well; she stared up at her father, her forehead pinched with worry.

Amelia took pity on them both.

"Izzie, what do you say we talk Chad into letting us have dessert in the living room? We can watch that cartoon you wanted to show us." Amelia leaned in and wiggled her eyebrows up and down at her former student.

"Of course!" Lucy answered. "Chad, you don't mind, right?"

"Absolutely not, my beautiful bride-to-be," Chad leaned over to receive a kiss. Lucy brushed her lips against his, serenity painting her pretty face.

In the kitchen, Amelia showed Izzie how to squirt whipped cream from the can onto individual mousse cups in perfect little billows. Together they arranged the cups on a tray. Amelia and Lucy chatted easily with Izzie about her role as flower girl in the wedding. Amelia could hear the men speaking in low voices from the next room.

Before they left the kitchen, Amelia picked Izzie up to sit on the counter and help her measure out coffee grounds into Chad's machine. Izzie pressed "Brew" and Amelia helped her hop down again. They walked hand in hand to the living room.

The men had moved to the couch and Izzie pulled her hand away to sit in between them.

"What movie are we watching this time?" Chad asked with a barely concealed grimace. Apparently Izzie had a reputation for bringing over kid movies.

"A bunch of shorts made by Disney. Rapunzel's wedding is on here; it's my favorite and I thought you could get ideas," Izzie explained.

"That was thoughtful, Izzie," Lucy cooed, carrying in the tray of mousse. She winked at her fiancé.

Amelia handed out the mousse while Lucy held the tray. She gave a cup of the luscious dessert first to Izzie, then held another out to Creed. He stared into her eyes for a heartbeat, saying more with one look than he had all evening.

The chocolate mousse slipped from her fingers and landed upside down in his lap.

Creed leaped off the couch as if he were on fire. He caught the glass cup just before it hit the coffee table, but not before chocolate and whipped cream splattered across the surface.

Everyone stared at them in wide-eyed silence. Amelia's hand covered her mouth, Creed stood frozen.

Izzie giggled. Then Lucy. Chad covered his mouth with one hand and stared at the television. Amelia glared at her sister, then pulled her gaze back to Creed.

"Where's that photographer that caught our last clumsy moment, Howard?"

The unexpected twinkle in his eyes was her undoing. She snatched up the tray from Lucy and marched into the kitchen, her face hot. Once alone in the small space, away from their shocked faces and Creed's handsome grin, she let him have it.

Well, so she let him have it in the safety of her own mind, anyway.

She *might* be acting unreasonably. *Might* be overreacting. *Might* have set the tray down too hard, but honestly? Who did Creed think he was? He had been a jerk all evening. He gave her the best kiss of her life—again—and then disappeared.

Again.

Not that *that* one was exactly his fault. But it most definitely was his fault that he came to a pleasant dinner with a thundercloud over his head and then had the audacity to look at her in that way that reached all the way to her toes.

A shuffling sound in the doorway whirled Amelia around on her heel. Creed held his hands up in surrender, chocolate mousse smattered across his shirt and pants. Amelia grabbed a roll of paper towels from next to the sink and tossed them to him. Her eyes stung and she turned away, mortified.

Good grief, Amelia. Get a grip. Quick!

She busied herself with the coffees, arranging four mugs on the tray. A small mug of hot chocolate was added for Izzie. She found the sugar bowl from a set Lucy had brought over before reaching into the fridge for the matching cream pitcher. The scratchy sound of Creed cleaning off his shirt made her cringe. Without a word Amelia found a washcloth and ran it under warm water at the kitchen sink. She turned to Creed and handed it to him.

"Truce," she whispered.

"I know I've been quiet this week, but do you think you can forgive me, Amelia?" he asked, reaching for the cloth. His fingers brushed hers, but she pulled back before he could affect her more.

"Of course." She lifted a shoulder and puckered her lips to one side, "I'm just trying to crawl down from 'Overreaction Mountain' here with some dignity, Creed."

Creed used the wet cloth to clean up while Amelia poured coffee into the mugs. When she was finished, she glanced over at him where he had leaned against the doorjamb. *I wonder if he knows how utterly attractive it is when he shoves his hands in his front pockets like that?*

Her eyes moved over the giant wet spots all over his clothes and she smirked.

Well, most of the time, anyway.

Creed ignored her smirk and stepped closer. He looked above her head for a moment as if the right words would etch themselves into the cabinets. Finally, he looked back into her eyes. "I owe you an apology. I've been, uh, distracted. But that is not an excuse for coming here in a foul mood." He reached to tuck a curl of hair behind her ear.

Amelia sighed. "Creed, do you think I don't understand your stress? It makes complete sense and you do not owe me any explanation or apology. Would you forgive me for turning into an irrational female back there?"

He snorted. "An irrational female? No, that would only be if you dumped the mousse on me on purpose. I'm sorry I laughed at you and mentioned the photographer. I don't know why I did that," Creed looked down at his feet.

Awkward silence stretched between them.

"Well, it was pretty funny," Amelia conceded, suddenly seeing how ridiculous the entire situation was. Maybe he was trying to get off his own mountain.

Creed glanced up. Amelia picked up the tray.

"Now why don't you go on back out there and have a seat? I'll deliver your coffee right to you," she winked, pretending to be unsteady on her feet.

"Yeah, right to my lap," Creed said dryly, reaching out to take the tray from her.

They stood facing one another, both holding the tray, eyes locked together. The golden flecks in Creed's brown eyes glowed, warming and cooling as a range of emotions played across his face. Amelia felt the heat start from her toes to her stomach and up her neck to bloom on her cheeks.

"Are we ever going to talk about us and that kiss, Amelia? I mean really talk?" his low voice stirred something deep in her belly.

"Guys!" Izzie called from the living room, jolting Amelia back on her heels. The tray rattled as she let go, leaving Creed to catch the weight on his side. He righted the tray just in time.

"Yeah, kiddo?" he called.

"The wedding one is starting," she said. "You need to come get ideas."

Creed set the tray down on the coffee table and sat next to Izzie. He handed out the coffee, turning around to offer one to Amelia. Seeing the couch was full, she pulled up a chair next to it and accepted the mug from Creed, waving him away when he offered her his seat on the couch. The adults humored Izzie as they watched the short cartoon. Rapunzel and Flynn Rider were finally getting married and their animal friends were on a desperate scramble through the village to catch their runaway wedding rings.

Lucy and Amelia noticed little touches on the screen and made comments to Izzie as they watched.

"Look, Sis, you could have those lanterns released afterwards."

"I sure could. And look at that veil. I definitely need one that long."

"Aunt Lucy, do I get to carry the rings?"

"Well are you going to just toss them out for an adventure?" Lucy tossed a wink to Amelia.

Izzie, missing the wink, turned toward the adults with rounded, somber eyes. "No, Aunt Lucy. Never. I would take my job very seriously if I got to carry the rings."

Lucy smiled. "I bet you would, Lucy. My nephew is the ring bearer, though. You get to carry a basket of flowers."

It was clear this news was not what the young girl wanted to hear. She crinkled her nose and sighed loudly as she turned back to the cartoon, flopping back into the cushions.

Amelia bit back a grin and leaned over to pat Izzie on the top of her head. "Well how about this, Sweetie? If I ever get married, I'll let you carry my rings. And that's a big job because mine is a really old, really special one."

"You already have your ring?"

"Can I see it?"

Izzie and Creed both turned to Amelia in surprise. Although the look on Creed's face was less than pleased. Amelia crinkled her brow at him in confusion, but turned to answer Izzie.

"Well, I don't carry it with me. It was my grandma's and I had it resized, because, well…" she faltered, embarrassed suddenly to admit that she had her wedding ring all ready to go.

"Wow, Amelia," Creed murmured with a slow shake of his head. "Did you leave *nothing* for the man to do? Will you cut up his food for him as well?"

It was a low blow. And he knew it. The shocked flash in his eyes told Amelia of his immediate regret, but her shame was too great to bear.

"Um, well, I, uh…" Amelia blinked rapidly. She stood and set down her coffee cup on the kitchen table behind her. She took a deep breath and offered Izzie, Lucy, and Chad a wobbly smile. Lucy and Chad wore matching expressions of pity.

Amelia rolled her bare wrist, feigning a glance at her watch. "Wow, I didn't realize how late it is. I better get going," she whispered past the hot rock that had settled in her throat and pointed over her shoulder toward the door.

She quickly gathered her purse and coat with shaking hands and left the apartment. The hall seemed to stretch for miles until she finally reached the exit. Once outside, Amelia shrugged into her coat and walked swiftly to her car, swiping at the tears that fell from her eyes.

The door opened.

"Amelia!" Creed called.

But she turned the corner, ignoring him.

Chapter Thirty-Six

"What is your problem?" Kate stood on Creed's front step the next morning. He had just returned from walking Izzie to school and had barely begun to filter through his pile of emails. Somehow the news of him owing the IRS money hadn't done much to damage his business. That could have a lot to do with the statement given by his lawyer the day before that the tax evasion was not something Creed had knowingly been a part of and that the truth would soon be revealed. That, and the video of him and Izzie had reached over one million views.

He sighed. "Good morning, Kate. Won't you please come in?" though his tone dripped with sarcasm, he opened the door wider.

"Here, I thought you could use this," Kate handed him a paper coffee cup and brushed past him.

"Thanks," Creed said, shutting the door against the blast of cold from outside. When he turned to his sister, the look on her face spoke of disappointment and disdain. She faced him, arms akimbo, one eyebrow arched high, wrinkling her forehead. So maybe the cold front wasn't coming from outside after all.

"Whoa. Looks who's suddenly Old Man Winter," he said.

Kate squinted her eyes at him. "Excuse me?"

Creed took a sip of the coffee before he gestured to her rigid stance, "You're about as warm and comforting as a porcupine. Let me guess, Chad called you."

"Of course he did. We talk about you all the time." Kate huffed. "What were you thinking? Amelia has been amazingly supportive of you and patient with you. How . could you knock her down like that?"

Creed slumped onto the couch and set the coffee on the side table. He rested his elbows on his knees, hands hanging down between them.

"I know she has, Kate. I wasn't thinking. I certainly never meant to hurt her. I've just—I've been in a funk. I had a long talk with Chad last night and he really did set me straight." He worked a muscle in his jaw, at once both defensive and subdued. He hadn't slept much the night before. Amelia's fallen expression played over and over in his mind. What *was* he thinking?

He'd texted her, but she hadn't answered.

Chad's lecture had been straight and to the point. *"Creed, you know I love you and I know you love the Lord. But you're being a real jerk, dude."*

Although it was hard to hear, Creed knew it was one of those "iron sharpening iron" moments. He realized that although he had told Izzie time and again that they were going to trust the Lord through everything, he had hardly been depending on the Lord himself. He had spent hours in prayer the night before, surrendering the situation to the Lord, repenting of his attitude. It was raw and humbling. But he felt like a weight had lifted from his shoulders that had pressed him down since Hailey walked onto that television set.

"If I were you, I would offer Amelia an apology as soon as possible. But that's not why I'm here," Kate finally relaxed and sat next to him on the couch. She picked up his coffee cup and sampled it.

"You're right. And I will. So why are you here? Other than to bring me coffee only to steal it back again?" he gave her a small smile.

Kate took a deep breath. "I got a call from the producers of *This is You, America.*"

Creed sat up, alert. In the past few days he had done what he could to secure a loan, but had been unable to find a bank willing to loan him such a high amount without a mortgage or car title as collateral. He couldn't bear to ask his parents for the money—not after all they had done for him and Izzie. He would rather take his chances with the IRS. At some point he had stopped praying about it and started putting all of his hope in the contest that got him in this mess in the first place. If he and Izzie won the prize money, all of their problems would be solved. He was convinced of it.

"And?"

Kate averted her eyes. "Creed, they have decided to withdraw your video from the contest."

Creed's heart began to pound. "Why?"

She finally met his gaze. She lifted a shoulder and let it fall again. "They said the news surrounding you and Izzie and Hailey isn't 'family friendly'. They don't want to send the wrong message."

"Kate, one of the competing videos is of some drunk guy singing *Shake it Off* while wearing a tutu," he deadpanned.

"I think for some reason they believe all of your drama will bring down the heart of the show. I'm sorry, Creed. I tried to talk them out of it, but…"

Creed stared blankly ahead and nodded slowly. He swallowed down the panic that bubbled inside him, wondering how much more he could take. Now what was he going to do?

You're going to trust Me…

A calm settled over him. He had read through Ezra seven and eight that morning in his quiet time and underlined every reference to the hand of God being on the prophet.

Six times. He'd almost texted Amelia, wanting to share the encouragement and insight from the Word, but how could he when he had been such a jerk?

"What will you say to Amelia?" Kate wanted to know. Was it that obvious he had been thinking of her?

Creed snorted. "Kate, be serious. How can I say anything to her? What can I offer her? I am a self-employed photographer staring down the barrel of an enormous debt with the IRS because of my own stupidity. I was reckless in college and as a result have the most wonderful daughter. But that still makes me a single dad with an extraordinarily complicated life," Creed raked his hands back through his hair in desperate frustration.

"Amelia, on the other hand," he continued, "has practiced restraint and wisdom. She has carefully laid out her life waiting for her dream husband to step seamlessly into it. She has made every decision for his welfare and I am not worthy to be that man. What could I possibly offer her?"

The clock that hung on the wall ticked loudly over the silence, counting the seconds.

Finally, Kate punched him lightly on the arm. "Creed. You, more than anyone, know that life is full of hiccups and bumps. So Amelia thinks that she has life figured out. Just because she is a master planner and executer of those plans does not mean that all that she has set out to do was from the Lord. Who knows the plans He has for her, but Him? And who's to say you and all that is happening around you right now is not part of that plan? To teach you humility and to teach her to let go of her own ideals? From the time you were kids in high school, I have seen a special spark between you two. You both went your own ways and got lost in them. Looks to me like God is giving you the go ahead to find yourselves in Him and each other. Don't blow it again, Creed."

268

Long after Kate let herself out, Creed sat with his head in his hands, his thoughts chasing each other in reckless circles. Hope and desperation finally collided and he sank to his knees on the ground.

As he had done the night before, Creed called out to the Lord for direction. Over the next few days, instead of acting on impulse, he would stop and pray.

About the changes he and Izzie were facing.

For a heart that was soft toward Hailey.

For wisdom in the IRS situation and custody challenge.

About whether or not he should call Amelia and ask if they could go just back to their easy friendship.

The answer to all time and again was "Wait. Trust."

There was little else he could do.

* * *

"Are you sure you're okay?" Lucy asked at a quaint breakfast cottage days later.

Lucy had dressed for their mission in a smart blazer and dark slacks. She had expertly applied heavy make-up to smolder her blue eyes and neatly styled her blond hair in long, precise curls. She looked like she belonged in Hollywood, which was exactly the idea.

Amelia, on the other hand, wore a baseball cap pulled low over her eyes, a black scarf high on her neck to cover her face, a long sleeved gray t-shirt and skinny jeans tucked into high boots. She brought old textbooks and notebooks from college and arranged them on the table. She looked like a college student cramming for finals, which, again, was exactly the idea.

They had ordered coffee and cinnamon rolls half an hour ago, though Amelia was so amped up she soon realized that caffeine and sugar had been a bad combo. One knee bounced wildly under the table. She tapped her pen in rhythm with her leg on the top of the table. Lucy had finally smacked her own hand on top of Amelia's to stop the wild tempo.

"Yes, I really am," Amelia answered, surprised that it was true. The table shook from the bounce of her leg and she gave a soft laugh. "Well, maybe I am a little nervous."

"I mean are you okay doing this even though Creed hasn't reached out to you at all? With everything going on in your own life, you certainly could back out," Lucy blinked hard and looked up at the ceiling before blinking a few more times.

"Fake lashes bothering you?" Amelia guessed with a slight giggle.

"You have no idea," Lucy blinked her eyes again before she jabbed a finger at Amelia. "Don't change the subject."

"Lucy, Creed is going through a lot right now. And honestly? He's right: I didn't save much of anything for my future husband to do. I built up this idea of what he would want and be like and, truly, I don't think it was realistic at all," Amelia said softly, fidgeting with the pen in her hands.

"Seemed like you and Aaron were having fun Wednesday night at Bible study," Lucy observed.

"Yeah, he's a really nice guy. I don't think either of us felt fireworks so no dates or anything in our future, but we both like hiking and have plans to go next week."

Lucy ducked her chin and looked up through her fake lashes. "Really." Her tone spoke of disbelief.

Amelia laughed. "Honest. He's just a nice guy. It's nice to be friends with a guy again—one that has no complications and doesn't get me all twittery with emotion," she rushed to add. "I'm enjoying the freedom of waiting on the Lord. I think all this time I was burying myself behind these walls of planning and efficiency to hide away from love," she admitted. "But that doesn't mean I'm ready to run after just any male that happens across my path, you know? Besides, I'm having too much fun being a homeowner and planning for my new class and just generally being a normal, twenty-something single gal," she laughed, averting her eyes.

"Why would you hide from love, Amelia? Do you think it's because you were spooked after what happened to me?" Lucy placed a palm to her chest, clearly horrified at the thought.

Drat. Amelia hoped they would skim over that part.

"A couple weeks ago I thought that was the only reason. But Lucy," Amelia leaned forward, afraid to say the words too loudly, lest it make them true. "I think I've loved Creed for all of these years. And once he disappeared from my life for good, I just…hid. I didn't want to fall for anyone else. Even C.B. was just some pathetic distraction. I'm so glad he saw that before we did something stupid like get married. I think I would have been dreaming of Creed while married to someone else and that would have been awful. But back then I was just hurting so badly I was willing to do anything to forget about him," she imitated Lucy's wild blinking to ward off the sudden sting of tears.

"And now?" Lucy asked, her eyes shimmering to match her sister's.

The bell above the front door jingled.

They turned to watch Hailey glance around the restaurant. She was dressed nicer than the last time Amelia saw her and looking slightly more put together. Though she was mostly hidden by a fake Christmas tree, Amelia ducked her head further out of sight, watching through the branches. Hailey spoke with the hostess, who was twenty dollars richer thanks to the Howard sisters, before she was led to a small table in the corner, far away from Amelia's.

"It's go time," Lucy whispered. She pulled out her phone and carefully adjusted a small device into her ear. Hailey would think it was just a Bluetooth device. She should have no idea that their conversation was being recorded. Lucy took a deep breath and released it with a wink at Amelia before she snuck out the door that led through the kitchen and out into the alley.

Minutes later Lucy, carrying a large purse in the crook of her arm, her phone cradled in a delicately manicured hand, swept into the restaurant. She spoke loudly, seemingly to no one, about a deal she had just closed as her gaze swept across the handful of patrons enjoying their coffee and breakfast. She rolled her eyes and strode to the hostess stand, tapping the side a few times to get the young girl's attention.

"Yes, I'm here to meet a Miss Anderson?"

"Ms. McKinley?" Hailey asked tentatively, rising from her chair.

Lucy turned toward Hailey, a slow smile spreading across her face. She brought the phone to her mouth.

"I'll call you after the meeting," she said before she took a seat and set the phone on the table. The women shook hands and Lucy ordered a coffee for herself and encouraged Hailey to order whatever she wanted. They chatted for a few moments, Lucy pretending to be distracted by her phone, Hailey leaning close to see what she was looking at. Once their coffees were delivered, as had been rehearsed earlier, Lucy asked to be left alone with her "client."

Amelia's chair faced them, and with Hailey's back to her, she chewed her thumbnail anxiously. Again, she wished they had found a way for Amelia to hear the exchange. Hailey and Creed were set for their first court appearance the next day; this had to work. But suddenly she wasn't so sure that she wanted it to. Were they doing the right thing? What was best for Izzie and Creed in the end? Of course Amelia knew Izzie's place was with Creed. But would it really be so awful for her to have some contact with her mother?

She watched as Lucy pulled papers from her large bag and spread them on the table before Hailey. Izzie's mother visibly tensed and pushed them away, shaking her head adamantly. Lucy leaned back and crossed her legs, cool as a cucumber. Or, rather, as an executive that could take or leave the potential client in front of her. She gestured to something on her phone and again to the papers. Hailey's knee began to bounce. She looked out the front door, wringing her hands in front of her in panicked frustration. Amelia sat up straighter and folded her own hands to keep from shaking.

Lucy spoke again and crossed her arms with a shrug. She swung her high heeled foot in slow circles, waiting for Hailey to respond. Finally, Hailey pushed the papers across the table hard enough to send a few floating to the floor. She cursed loud enough for everyone in the restaurant to turn in shock. She stood and stormed out into the cold November morning. She passed the wall of windows, air escaping in stormy wisps from her mouth as she muttered something angrily. Amelia's breath caught at the look of pure hatred on her face.

All doubt about what they had done vanished.

Chapter Thirty-Seven

Creed had borrowed one of his Dad's suits, thankful they were the same size. He dressed in cool grey slacks and matching jacket with a crisp white button down shirt and navy blue tie. He had read somewhere that blue signified peace. The bottom of the tie, hidden, though not purposely, behind the buttoned portion of his jacket, was a dove, the symbol of peace. Creed hoped the judge would see him as a man of peace, not of chaos as his life seemed to shout these days. With any luck Hailey would show up looking as disheveled as she had a few weeks ago.

James had warned Creed that most likely the judge would grant a temporary joint custody while they worked out the details. Izzie was kept with Peabody's assistant in a side room, coloring and no doubt being spoiled rotten. Creed had spent the day before explaining to Izzie at last what was happening. He tried to prepare her for what could happen that afternoon. As a result, she had been up most of the night with an upset stomach.

Creed sat in the courtroom next to his lawyer, waiting anxiously for Hailey and her attorney to arrive and change his world. While he was eager to see all that would unfold, his spirit was strangely calm. Yes, his world was crashing in around him. Yes, he might have to release Izzie to this woman he barely knew. Yes, he would have to arrange payments with the IRS and live even more frugally for the next five years.

But.

God was still on the throne. He still had Creed and Izzie and even Hailey in the palm of His hand. Creed saw the goodness of being driven to his knees in complete, helpless surrender. He hoped that even as life rounded out someday that he would always be as dependent on the Lord as he was in that moment.

274

An hour later, just before Hailey and her lawyer were officially declared as a "No Show," one of Mr. Peabody's assistants slipped him a folder. He looked it over, setting it aside when the judge declared that they would reschedule the trial for two weeks later—the day before Thanksgiving. James asked to approach the bench and handed the folder to the judge. They spoke for another moment before he joined Creed at the table.

"Alright, Son, let's go get Izzie. I think I should take you both to lunch," he said, a spring in his step that hadn't been there when they arrived that morning.

Creed placed a hand on his arm. "If you need to tell me anything about the next court date, I prefer you do it now, not in front of Izzie. I am perfectly fine with you buying our lunch, but not if you plan to talk to me about whatever that was," he gestured toward the courtroom they had just exited. A few reporters still trying to keep the story as a trending topic approached, pelting him with questions.

Peabody raised his hands, answering them with, "My client has no comment."

He placed an arm around Creed and led him into a private room.

James closed the door behind them and indicated with the incline of his head that Creed should take a seat. Creed shook his head.

"I'd rather take this standing up, I think," he said, biting the inside of his cheek. He couldn't believe that Hailey had failed to show up for court, and was even more flabbergasted that the judge was giving her one more chance.

"I was able to get some very interesting information about Izzie's mother," he tapped the folder against an open palm.

"Yeah? And what is that?" Creed interlaced his fingers behind his neck and hung his head. Disappointed that they would have to wait even longer to know how the custody of Izzie would play out. Relieved that he had two more weeks guaranteed with Izzie. But what if the judge granted Hailey rights over Izzie just before Thanksgiving? What would that day or even the Christmas season be without his daughter?

"She is addicted to pain pills and will do just about anything to get them," Peabody said.

Creed raised his eyes, hands still clasped behind his neck.

"What did you just say?"

"She's an addict, Creed," his lawyer repeated, tossing the file across the table.

Creed opened the file to find a report with a list of names and numbers. "What am I looking at here?"

"Unofficially, you are looking at a police report. Hailey went to see a doctor last week and complained of back pain. She asked for an exact medication, including the precise dose she wanted. He was suspicious and gave her a prescription for two pills, but refused to give her more. She left in anger and he called to report it to the police. The officer who took the report found dozens of prescriptions at just as many pharmacies that have been filled for the exact amount she asked for just since she'd been in town. He's working to get records from the last year and all of the places she's lived. It explains the erratic behavior, as well as her sudden interest in getting custody. She obviously sees Izzie as her ticket to money."

Creed whistled low, not knowing how he felt about the information being presented to him.

"And the judge is still granting her another chance after seeing this?" Creed asked, baffled.

"It's the law, Creed. She has to be given a fair chance. But rest easy—your little issue with the IRS is nothing. They already said they are willing to work with you. I am confident you will win full custody," Peabody leaned back in his chair, chest puffed out as if he had single-handedly won the case.

"How did you even get this?" Creed held up the folder, not quite ready to celebrate.

"Hailey's lawyer had his sources, I have mine. I have one more thing to play for you that can't be considered real evidence, but might to convince her to drop the case."

"What's that?"

He pulled out his phone and swiped a finger across the surface. "We now know that Hailey saw Izzie as a meal ticket, but it went deeper than we realized."

He pressed a "play" icon and set the phone down. A squiggly white line danced on the black background. Static filled the room, then the staccato of heels on pavement followed by the loud jingle of a bell. The faint sounds of conversation and plates clattering hummed in the background. He furrowed his brow and sat down as a female voice asked for Hailey.

"That voice sounds familiar," Creed said. Mr. Peabody shushed him.

He listened as Hailey introduced herself to someone she referred to as Ms. McKinley. The women made small talk and ordered breakfast. Ms. McKinley asked the waiter to leave them be and he heard the rustling of papers.

"Now, Miss. Anderson, of course you either need to have full custody or have Mr. Williams sign these parental release forms," Ms. McKinley said.

Hailey snorted. "Not a problem. Now how soon after I win custody can we get started? I would like Izzie to get to work right away, of course."

Creed wrinkled his brow. *Work?*

"Well first, Miss—"

"Call me Hailey."

"Of course. Hailey. First we have to arrange for headshots, auditions. You will need to find a place in L.A. and move right away to make things easier. And then there are our fees—"

"Wait, wait, wait. I thought you would take your fees from my, eh, her paychecks. And that you would take care of the rest. Apartment, flights, headshots."

Ms. McKinley chuckled low. Her voice became muffled as if she had shifted back, away from the recorder.

"Hailey, surely you understand the amount you are taking on simply to prepare Izzie for life as a child actor. While we feel she has great talent, we need to work hard to hone it: dance classes, voice lessons, acting coaches. It will cost a small fortune to get her started, but could be well worth it in the end."

"Could be?" Hailey asked, her voice meek.

"Listen, Honey"—the voice was smug—"talented, adorable children are a dime a dozen. I have three more appointments like this one just this week. It's the parents that are ready to put in the hard work and serious cash up front that see their children succeed."

The sounds of the restaurant grew louder for a moment, the women silent.

Finally, Hailey spoke, dejected.

Lucy carried a brown paper bag in each arm and Amelia reached out to relieve her of them. She set them on the counter and rifled through. Bread. Celery. Butter. Sweet potatoes. Pumpkin puree. Cream. Onions. Brown sugar. Satisfied that everything was there, she glanced up.

"Was he mad?"

"I don't think so. I honestly think he's relieved and a little bit sad for Izzie. I mean, she was just a pawn to her own mother," Lucy answered, taking the cream from the bag and placing it in the fridge.

"Mom didn't want to come?" Amelia asked.

"She's out scouting Black Friday deals," Lucy smirked.

They set to work prepping vegetables. The sisters got together every year to make the side dishes and pies for the Thanksgiving meal. It was one of Amelia's favorite traditions. They talked while they chopped. Lucy filled her in on wedding details—RSVPs were rolling in and the caterer had been booked.

"I'm glad you gave in to Mom on that one, Sis," Amelia said, reaching into the fridge for the butter. "That's the best part of weddings—the food."

"Hey, how did that date go with Aaron?" Lucy asked.

"I told you, it wasn't a date," she answered.

"Uh-oh, that doesn't sound too promising." Lucy arched a brow at her.

"Well it's not supposed to be promising, goof. We're just friends. I think we both knew right away that we weren't going to be the next great romance. But," she added, peeling a final sweet potato, "we've texted some. He's actually picking me up tomorrow night to go see that new Will Smith movie."

"Well, that's good, I guess," Lucy commented, going back to the potatoes. They worked in silence for a few moments more before Amelia glanced over at her younger sister. Lucy had a soft smile curling her lips as she sliced the sweet potatoes and tossed them in a pot of water. Amelia elbowed her.

"Dreaming of serving all of this deliciousness to Chad tomorrow?"

Lucy sighed, her smile dreamy. "Maybe," she answered, but didn't comment further. She finished with the potatoes and set the pot on the stove. They worked in contented silence. Nat King Cole's voice crooned from the Pandora station in the living room creating a festive ambiance.

When Amelia was ready to chop the vegetables and bread for the stuffing, she turned to Lucy in confusion.

"Did you mean to buy double the ingredients?" she asked, holding up two loaves of bread in one hand and two bags of celery in the other.

"Um, yeah. About that. We need to make two trays of everything this year," Lucy ducked her face, mashing the now softened sweet potatoes in the mixing bowl.

Amelia scrunched her face in confusion before realization dawned. She set the bags down on the counter and leaned in close to her sister.

"And why is that, Lucy?" she asked through gritted teeth. Her sister wouldn't look at her. Amelia straightened and slapped her hand on the counter.

"Come on! You have got to be kidding! The Williamses? Really?"

"Sorry, Mom and I planned it before you and Creed stopped talking to each other."

"We haven't stopped talking to each other."

Not exactly. There had been a few texts. Apologies made and accepted. A few stilted starts that sputtered before they turned into a real conversation.

She began to attend the singles group to make up for lack of fellowship and had even agreed to help with the youth group on Wednesday nights. *See?* she told herself. *Moving on.*

She hoped that her feelings for Creed would fade into the background. Eventually. She hadn't let herself think about how much she would see him as a result of their siblings marrying one another. But she could do this, right? She could pretend they hadn't kissed. Twice. That she didn't think of it every time she watched a chick flick, snuggled up on her new couch in her cozy living room in front of the hearth.

The house came with a real wood burning fireplace and she had wood delivered the week before. It was stacked and ready to go.

Not that she'd been able to successfully keep a fire going yet, but still...

She realized that her mind had wondered off of Creed and she felt a small squeeze of triumph.

Then she realized she was thinking about Creed again. Sigh. So close.

Right. Sure, you can do this, Amelia. She slanted a look of loathing at her sister.

Lucy at least had the decency to look guilty, although she turned back to her task without comment.

"Lucy, I get that you're marrying this man, but does that mean the rest of us have to see his family all of the time? I mean, Brent and Conner are married and we don't have to spend every holiday with their in-laws," she whined, referring to their brothers. She pulled a cutting board from the shelf above the sink and slammed a bag of celery on top of it.

Lucy jumped slightly. "Their in-laws aren't friends with Mom and Dad the way the Williamses are. You know they all booked a cruise together after the wedding, right?"

Amelia nodded. She thought it was great they were all going on vacation together, but that didn't make her feel any better about spending Thanksgiving with Creed. At least Izzie would be there.

That reminded her. "Hey, whatever happened with the trial? It got pushed back, right?"

Lucy nodded. "Creed's lawyer let them know about the police report and the recording. She agreed to let it go. Creed also called Hailey to tell her he had listened to the recording."

"He did? Did he tell her it was us?"

"No, I don't think so. It sounds like he was trying to let her know what she was up to, but also wanted to offer her grace. Creed's parents watched Izzie earlier this week so he could meet her in person."

"Wow. That's...awesome."

She committed then and there to pray more specifically for Hailey. No matter what, she deserved all the grace Jesus had lavished on Amelia. She was touched by Creed's kindness and forgiveness toward Hailey—and it made her miss him that much more.

Chapter Thirty-Eight

Creed couldn't get Amelia from his mind. Once he heard the recording of Hailey and Lucy, he was sure Amelia had something to do with it. All he wanted to do was storm her house and pull her into his arms to thank her properly.

But he knew the Lord had something in mind for him to do first.

He had asked Hailey to coffee a few days before Thanksgiving and asked for her forgiveness.

"For what?" she'd asked, eyeing him suspiciously. He was surprised she'd even shown up.

"Hailey, when you left Izzie with me I was angry. And, yes, my life—the pointless one I was living—was over. I knew I couldn't make it without the Lord's help. I trusted my life to Him and haven't looked back."

Her eyes had clouded over and she crossed her arms.

"My anger and bitterness toward you since then has not been right. No matter what, you gave birth to Izzie and for that I will always be thankful. I promise to never speak badly of you to Izzie. And while I do not believe it's wise at this time to open a relationship between you two, I would like to keep in touch so that when she is old enough she can contact you if she wants to."

Hailey had blinked, clearly surprised.

She hadn't said much after that, only mumbled a thank you. She promised to withdraw her custody attempts and left as quickly as she came. His breath left in a long rush once she was gone.

It was almost over. Truly over. Izzie was his and always would be. And when the time was right, maybe Hailey would have a chance to see what a great kid she was.

In the meantime, Creed had one more significant problem to deal with. He had left numerous messages for his contact at the IRS, hoping to finalize the payment plan before the court date. Even if Hailey had promised to back out of her custody pursuit, he would feel much better knowing that he had come to an agreement with the IRS and in no way would be facing jail time.

On Wednesday morning, he checked the clock above the stove and called upstairs to Izzie, "Kiddo! Finish up getting ready. Daddy's just going to make a phone call real quick."

"Okay!" she hollered back. Loud stomping overhead made Creed laugh. Izzie being Izzie.

He found the number he'd scribbled on an envelope and dialed once more, praying for an answer.

"Hello, case number please," a bored voice broke through the third ring.

Creed blinked in surprise. "Uh, let's see," he found the number and recited it slowly. She asked the typical security questions and then put him on hold.

Blaring music, broken up by static assaulted him. Why was it that these people always found bad music made worse with a terrible connection? Were they intentionally trying to set people on edge just before they had a stressful meeting about finances and interest rates?

"Yes. For Mr. Williams?" a female voice, slightly softer, but no less bored, clicked on.

"Yes, that's me. Listen, I was on the phone with someone there for hours the other day, and I just need to know how to finalize all of this. I have a meeting with my accountant next week and I—"

"Mr. Williams, that case has been taken care of. All paperwork stamped 'Paid in Full' will be sent to you in seven to ten business days."

Creed pinched his forehead. "Uh, I'm sorry, I think you made a mistake. I didn't make a payment yet, I just wanted to confirm my payment plan."

"Mr. Williams, your balance is paid in full. As of yesterday. Like I said, the paperwork will be sent to you within two weeks," the woman sighed and spoke slowly as if he were dimwitted.

Creed blinked in confusion, stunned speechless.

"Sir?"

"Um, uh, yeah. I'm here. I'm sorry, did you say my balance is paid in full?" he stammered.

Another sigh. "Yes. Your account is paid in full."

"By who?" *Who would do this?*

"I don't see a name, just that the amount was paid. Is there anything else I can do for you today, Mr. Williams?"

"No, I don't—"

"Thank you and have a nice day."

The line went dead before he could respond. Creed sank to his desk chair, staring in bewilderment at the phone in his hands. Was it a mistake?

He called the number again and got another agent, male. Even more precise and impatient.

The answer was the same: someone had paid his debt.

Disbelief swelled in him. It burst forth in rarely shed tears of thankfulness. *Lord, only You could have accomplished this for me. Yet again—in spite of myself—You have given me another chance.*

He felt the Lord's favor the rest of the day, when, as promised, Hailey withdrew her custody documents. Instead, the judge was presented with a letter from her lawyer stating that she wanted Creed to have full custody of Izzie. He truly felt pity for Hailey Anderson. He didn't know how long she had been addicted to pain pills, but it was obvious that her life was an empty shell of what it could be. Only he knew what she had given up when she walked away from the child they had conceived.

Well, he, his family…and Amelia.

When he retrieved Izzie from Peabody's assistant, Creed knelt down to sweep her into an ecstatic hug.

"It's over, baby girl! You're not going anywhere!" he laughed as she squeezed him so tight that that he nearly fell over.

"Does this mean we get to spend Thanksgiving with Miss H and Aunt Lucy?"

Creed grinned, buzzing with excitement. "It sure does, baby."

They drove to his parents' house with a carton of vanilla ice cream to celebrate. Alone in the kitchen with his dad, Creed told him about the baffling call to the IRS. When his father wouldn't meet his gaze, Creed's jaw dropped.

"Dad. You didn't."

No answer.

Creed stepped forward. "Dad?"

His father paused, the ice cream scooper still in his hand. "Listen, Creed. When you called us all those years ago, I was very disappointed. More than I like to admit. But then you came home and I watched you turn yourself inside out to provide a stable life for your daughter. I watched your faith finally become real. I've been so proud of you, Son," his voice wavered.

Creed sniffed and scratched his nose. When his Dad had collected himself he went on, voice slightly gruffer than usual.

"So when all of this garbage happened and still you hung in there, I thought you could use the reminder of what the Lord accomplished for you on the cross. We all need that now and again. He paid our debt, knowing we could never pay it back." He seared Creed with a gaze.

Creed nodded, swallowing past the tightness in his throat, understanding the unspoken message.

"Thanks, Dad."

His father nodded once and Creed knew they would never speak of it again. After the celebration, they drove toward the grocery store, Creed relishing the peace he felt. As he steered through the packed parking lot, he prayed that someday he could accomplish for Izzie what his Dad had for him: a priceless, tangible example of Christ's work on the cross.

"Oh look, Daddy," Izzie cooed when they finally made it out of the busy store. She tugged his hand toward a young couple sitting in lawn chairs in front of the store. They had a box at their feet with FREE KITTENS scribbled on the side.

Izzie leaned into the box and plucked a black and white spotted kitten up and under her chin. The small animal meowed softly and tried to crawl out of Izzie's arms.

"Aren't they cute, Daddy? Can we have one?" She scooped up another—a calico—and gazed up at him.

288

"Aww, Kiddo, I wish I could get you one. But we're not allowed to have pets in our townhouse. I'm sorry." He reached down to pet an all-black kitten curled up in the corner.

"It's okay." Izzie accepted softly. Man, she was a good kid.

Creed brightened with an idea. "You know who I think would want one of these?"

* * *

Amelia considered cancelling with Aaron. But that was rude, wasn't it? What could she say?

"Yeah, so the guy I have feelings for is going to be at dinner tomorrow and I'd like to keep our friendship quiet."

Not happening. She picked up her phone to text that she would just meet him at the theater but she heard tires on the dirt road leading to her house and set her phone down. Olé barked wildly when footsteps and voices sounded outside the door just before someone knocked.

Olé had lost some of his manners since they had moved to the country. She held his collar and inched open the door.

"Surprise!" Izzie yelled.

Amelia laughed and opened the door wider, allowing Olé to sniff her legs. Creed stood behind Izzie with a large box in his hands. Olé sniffed all around the bottom of the box and whined, his bottom shaking wildly.

"Come in, you guys," Amelia said, moving out of the way.

"I hope you don't mind us dropping in, but we have something we needed to give you," Creed said. He smiled shyly.

Amelia returned his smile, feeling warmth spread through her like a cozy hug. "I don't mind at all. But what could you possibly have in that box?"

Izzie danced from one foot to another while Creed set it down and opened the flaps. A black kitten with a white tipped tail and white belly leapt up the side, it's claws scraping the cardboard as it slipped back to the bottom.

Amelia gasped. "You guys brought me a kitten?"

"The kitten was free. We bought the supplies even in the store with all of the crazy people walking around," Izzie said.

Amelia laughed and picked up the little animal. Olé whined and circled her feet, jumping up to set his paws on her waist while she snuggled the kitten close. The cat hissed at Olé and dug her claws into Amelia's shoulder. Creed reached out to help her unhook the claws.

"Here you take her—him—it while I go put Olé in his kennel for now." Amelia handed the kitten over and pulled Olé back to the mud room. She hadn't realized she was shaking until she slipped him a treat. When she came back in the living room, she tried to see her house through their eyes.

The living room and dining room were open to each other. She and Lucy had scored the large farm table and matching benches from a place called Junkyard Chic. When she found the sideboard at the thrift store, she sanded and painted both so they would match.

The living room was cozy and perfectly farmhouse chic with white pillows on the large sectional—a splurge to celebrate the new house. She had painted the brick around the fireplace white after she talked her Dad into mounting the thick piece of recovered barn wood in place of the crumbling shelf that had served as the mantle. A wingback chair recovered with French grain sacks hugged her favorite corner in the house where two windows met at a ninety-degree angle. A small, three-legged table piled with a stack of old books, a small lamp and her Bible kept the chair company.

Izzie and Creed were seated on the sofa when she came back in the room, the kitten curled up on Creed's knees.

"I can't believe you got me a kitten, Izzie," Amelia gushed, her hands on her cheeks. Her words were for Izzie, but her eyes wouldn't leave Creed's face. He shrugged and offered her a lopsided smile.

She knelt on her knees before him and pet the kitten, loving the silk of its fur and the rattle of its tiny purr.

"It's a girl, by the way," Creed said. "I checked." His eyes pierced hers. "I thought it was time for you to have your cat, Amelia."

Her eyes welled with tears and she smiled up at him. "Thank you," she whispered, melting right into the floorboards.

He and Izzie stayed a while longer, helping her to name the kitten—Sassy—and to get the feline and canine properly acquainted. When Creed declared it time to get Izzie home and ready for bed, Amelia reached up on her toes to hug him around the neck.

"Thank you, Creed. I love her." She pulled away slowly, allowing her eyes to study his face. She turned to hug Izzie as well. "And thank you, Miss Izzie. I love the name you picked out."

"You're welcome," Creed said, eyes crinkling in pleasure at her joy.

"See ya tomorrow, Miss Amelia," Izzie called as they walked to their car. Amelia waved and watched while they

"But I spent all of my money paying my uncle to get my case to court. I didn't think it would go this far. I thought her father would just give her back. I never expected him to fight me on this. I barely have money for the court case, let alone to pay for all of this."

Again, papers crackled near the mic. "Well, I'm sorry Miss Anderson, but that's how this business works. I assure you that I represent the best talent agency there is. We have costs just as everyone else does. I have parents drop out all the time; your investment up front shows your commitment to this company."

A loud swish of papers scattering and a spine tingling adjective from Hailey ended the recording. James reached to take his phone from the table and shoved it in his pocket.

"I think your internet fame appealed to Hailey and she thought that she had found a way to keep up with her addiction indefinitely," he said.

Creed, eyes on the table where the phone had been, shook his head in disbelief.

"That woman—Ms. McKinley. She's not a real talent agent is she?"

"I can't reveal my sources, Creed," he answered.

Creed stood. "Then next time tell my soon to be sister-in-law to disguise her voice better," he winked.

* * *

"Well, he knew it was me," Lucy said as soon as Amelia opened the door.

Amelia laughed. "Ah nuts," she said with a snap of her fingers, stepping back to let Lucy in.

drove away. A small smile painted her lips for the rest of the evening.

Chapter Thirty-Nine

Amelia arrived early at her parents' home, ready to help decorate for Christmas as she did every Thanksgiving morning. She knocked and opened the door, letting herself into the wide entry way. Her mom had already pulled out the red and green plastic tubs that they stored all of their decorations in and placed them at the base of the stairs. Amelia stepped around them, her arms full of the pans she and Lucy had prepared the day before.

"Hey, Amelia, my favorite firstborn, come in here," her dad called out from the den. She smiled at his jovial greeting and stepped into the room where he sat in his favorite recliner watching the Thanksgiving Day parade.

"Hey Daddy," she greeted, planting a kiss on his forehead. "Good parade?"

"You know I love parades," her dad muted the television and turned to her, eyes twinkling.

"You know, Dad, one of these days we need to brave the cold and go to the one downtown," she suggested.

"It's not the cold that scares me," he said, glancing behind her to be sure the hallway was empty. "I'm more afraid of telling your mother that we're not spending Thanksgiving decorating the house," he gave an exaggerated shudder at the thought.

"I heard that," her mother called from the kitchen, her tone wry.

Amelia laughed when her dad winked and turned back to the television. She loved the way they spent this day. She would come over early and flit between helping her mom with the cooking and decorations and sneaking glimpses of the parade and handfuls of Chex mix with her dad. It had been their special tradition for years.

She saved the tree in the dining room for last. Her parents still lived in the home she had been raised in, a large, charming two story with a front porch that spread across the front of the house. Across from her dad's den was the dining room, and her mom had a tree for both windows.

"That way we light up each of the front rooms with Christmas cheer," her mother had explained when she first brought home the second tree. Her father had rolled his eyes.

Amelia pulled the tub close to the tall plastic evergreen. She preferred a real tree and would hopefully have one in her home by the next week, but she loved the one her mother had picked out as well. Although Stacy had said it was to light up both windows, Amelia thought maybe the new tree had more to do with the fact that her mother had always wanted a nice, formal tree, but couldn't bear to leave their family ornaments in storage. And thus the junk tree was displayed in Dad's den, and the glamorous one, dressed in red bows and golden ornaments, showed off in the dining room.

Lucy arrived first and took Amelia's place in the kitchen while she finished trimming the trees and strung boughs of holly up the stair railing. Next came Mr. And Mrs. Williams. Then her brothers and their families.

Chad arrived, carrying a big box of wedding decorations. Lucy looped an arm through his and kissed his cheek, before leading him to her room upstairs—also known as wedding headquarters.

Creed and Izzie arrived as Amelia was teetering on the ladder, tying the last red ribbon to the top branch of the dining room tree. Izzie gasped in delight and Amelia looked up in surprise, holding onto the top of the ladder for support. Although it was early afternoon, the sky was overcast, creating a romantic glow from the soft, twinkling tree lights. She hoped they wouldn't emphasize the warmth blooming on her cheeks.

Creed locked eyes with her, standing tall and handsome in a long overcoat sprinkled with snow. Izzie was dressed in a fancy purple dress that looked as if it had been dusted with glitter.

"Hiya Miss Amelia," she called up the ladder.

Amelia smiled down at her, her heart full of love for the girl. Love that went far beyond the previous teacher student relationship.

"Hiya Izzie," she answered. "Sassy wanted me to tell you hello."

She climbed down from the ladder, feeling Creed's eyes on her. Could he see the slight tremble in her knees? She reached Izzie and hugged her close. A cold cheek met her embrace and she pulled back to place her hands on Izzie's face.

"Brrr!" she exclaimed. "Did it start snowing out there?"

"Uh-huh. Daddy said maybe we can play in it after dinner," Izzie beamed.

"Well that sounds fun. But I hope you brought a change of clothes," Amelia looped an arm around Izzie and turned her toward the kitchen. She inched past Creed, barely glancing at him.

"Hi, Creed," she murmured awkwardly as they passed.

"Hi, Amelia," he answered, his eyes seeming to drink her in.

Coward, she scolded herself. *Using Izzie as a shield to sneak past Creed. Seriously, Amelia.*

With a start, she realized that she forgot to tell Aaron that she would meet him at the movies instead of having him pick her up. She couldn't risk hurting Creed, especially after his sweet gesture the night before. She felt doubt rise up. Would he really care?

But did she want to risk it?

She excused herself and slipped into the kitchen to where her phone was plugged in. She tried to call Aaron but it went straight to voicemail.

Drat. He's probably the type that turns off his phone for family dinners. Maybe she could just explain to Creed that they were friends. But her insecurity swallowed that idea. Creed probably wouldn't care.

Or would he?

She groaned inwardly and trudged to the dining room.

* * *

Creed felt like a hero when he showed up at Amelia's with the kitten. Did she see what he was saying? That he would be there for her, supporting her, no matter what?

Of course not, Williams. You have to tell her that yourself, not through some symbol-cat. Still, with the IRS paid off and Hailey out of the picture, he felt free at last to pursue Amelia and show her how good they could be. He followed her toward the kitchen and tried to catch her alone, but his mom called him into the living room before he could.

When dinner was announced, he rushed to slip into the chair next to Amelia's, but she took a seat in between his mother and Chad. Creed captured the chair across from her instead. Throughout the meal, he would smile with assurance whenever Amelia looked up to find his eyes on hers. In response she would fidget in her chair, or with her necklace.

296

Once she dropped her fork, rolling her eyes as it clattered loudly against her plate.

"Well, Amelia, I hear from your mom that you're in the middle of a renovation," Creed's mother suddenly said when they had all been served pie.

A lull in conversation around the table ensured that everyone heard the question and turned to listen to the answer. No one more eagerly than Creed. He had often wondered how it was going—there was so much to catch up on. Things had seemed put together the night before, but they had mostly focused on the kitten and Izzie.

Amelia glanced up, embarrassed to be the center of attention. "Well, I was, sort of. Just the upstairs."

"And how is that going?"

"Dusty," Amelia quipped. Low chuckles sounded around the table. She glanced up at Creed again, tucking a strand of hair behind her ear. "Honestly, though, it's going great. Lucy helped me paint the inside before I moved in. The work upstairs is purely cosmetic so I'm doing most of it myself."

Mrs. Howard spoke up from other side of the table. "Yes this fabulous little home is turning into quite the place. You should see the paint colors she picked out. Her room is extraordinary."

"And have you done anything like this before, Amelia?" his mom asked.

"No, never. Thank goodness for Pinterest and YouTube videos, though. I think I've avoided any major catastrophes. I mostly just sanded down the floors and applied new stain, then painted everything. This week I hope to tear out the vanity in the master bath. I already bought one to replace it. All I have to do is figure out the plumbing. Hopefully it's as easy as the guy on YouTube says." She lifted one shoulder and dropped it again.

Creed leaned back in his chair. Wow.

"That sounds daunting." His mother again.

Amelia swallowed. "It's not bad, really. The couple that sold it to me are really helpful. They also own the large apple orchard next door. I've taken my students there for years"—her eyes bounced off of Creed's—"and we've developed a sweet friendship. This house is on the edge of their property. They took pretty good care of it and their son remodeled the entire downstairs. This summer I'll work on the yard and possibly have a driveway poured. Eventually, I will also have a garage added. Right now I just have a little dirt road and a lot of weeds for my dog and cat to run through."

Her eyes met Creed's again and held them for a moment.

Warmth spread through him and he leaned back, his hand rubbing his sweater where his heart beat wildly.

A knock sounded at the front door and Amelia sprung from her chair like she'd been electrocuted.

"I'll get it," she announced, weaving her way around the table to pull open the door.

Creed watched as she stood talking to someone on the porch for a moment before waving them inside. When she led Aaron into the dining room, something cold and hard settled in his stomach.

Chapter Forty

In her defense, she had planned it before she knew Creed would be there. Before Creed showed up on her porch with a sweet little kitten just because he knew everything behind her reasons for never buying one herself.

But, oh, how awful it felt to drive off with Aaron.

She hadn't been lying when she told Lucy that Aaron had been a saving grace of sorts. For the first time in a decade Amelia was experiencing a healthy relationship with a male. One that had not a wisp of romance involved. She had been honest about that, too. Aaron had felt the same way. In fact, she had helped to set him up with another woman in the singles' group and they were meeting her at the movies that night. They were only a few minutes down the road and she already missed Creed. Why she hadn't thought to invite him?

"Aaron, do you mind if I text Creed and ask if he wants to come?"

"Of course not," he smiled. Aaron was always smiling.

Aaron was a counselor at a rehab center and Amelia was constantly surprised by how cheerful of a disposition he had considering his line of work.

Hey Creed, Aaron and I are meeting a few people at the movies—want to join us?

She waited a few minutes and finally her phone buzzed back.

No, that's okay. Izzie and I have a date after dinner with our Thanksgiving tradition: The Muppets Christmas Carol. But thanks anyway and have a good time.

She tried not to think about how disappointed she was that he couldn't come.

After the movies, Aaron drove her back to her car at her parents and she told him a little about her relationship with Creed. He promised to pray for her and she offered the same for his budding relationship.

It wasn't until she was driving home that it hit her: she and Aaron were both pursuing godly relationships in the normal way. Not with crazy commitments or life-altering plans, but with the promise to keep each other in check. She wanted to text Creed about it, but held back.

What if she had really hurt him? She tried texting him over the next few days, and he always answered. But they were right back to being polite and stilted. Had Aaron picking her up really ruined things so badly?

Principal McClary had called her before Thanksgiving and told her she could come back to school the Monday after the holiday.

"I think everything has died down. The media has moved on and the parents all miss you. I've had more calls asking for you back then I can count," he said.

She had politely declined the offer, but desperately wished she could tell Creed about it. It felt strange to now.

On a hike with Aaron a week after Thanksgiving, Amelia mentioned how sad she felt for Izzie's mother.

"She's really missing out with Izzie. She's a great kid. I hope she reaches out for help one day."

"Just keep praying for her, Amelia. It's all you can do."

She shared with him the strain on her and Creed's relationship. "It's so strange, Aaron. We were in this awkward place and then he showed up with Izzie to gift me a kitten the night before Thanksgiving. I thought we had moved on and regained our friendship. And now it's just as awkward as before. Maybe more so."

Aaron stopped and turned to face her, his mouth hinged open. "The night before Thanksgiving Creed showed up with a kitten—something that's really symbolic for you— and then Thanksgiving night you left with me?"

"Well, yeah. Your phone was off so I couldn't ask you to meet me at the movies and I didn't think Creed would really care—"

"Of course he cares, Amelia," Aaron laughed a little. "And they say men are dense."

She palmed her hips. "Hey!"

"Well, it's true. Creed must think we're together or something. He's probably trying to give you distance."

"Well, what do I do?" Amelia asked as they resumed hiking.

"You know, Amelia, you told me that your friendship, relationship, whatever it is has been kind of up and down, right?"

"Yeah."

"So let him think I'm your boyfriend. Smoke him out. If Creed cares about you the way I think he does, he won't let you go without saying something."

* * *

Three long weeks had passed since Thanksgiving.

Since Aaron had arrived and whisked Amelia away.

Since Creed's heart had pummeled down to his feet and never gotten up again.

Not that anyone would know it. He was a father, needed to put Izzie first. And after spending a month wondering if he would lose her, Creed wasn't going to waste her young life pouting over a lost love.

So when he passed Amelia in the sanctuary at church, he smiled pleasantly and made small talk. When she walked into the same Sunday School room, he nodded cordially and offered to get her a chair. Amelia met his pleasant smile. She raised his cordial nod with a small wave.

He carried the small moments with him throughout the days and once Izzie was in bed, his work done for the night, the house clean, Creed would slump onto the couch and think of nothing but Amelia. Of her smell, her taste. Her deep, throaty laugh, and quick wit. Her kind affection for Izzie. He would stare for hours at the television, having no idea what he'd watched by the time he clicked the remote and went to bed.

When Amelia texted him—obviously feeling obliged to maintain a friendship because of the kitten—he would reply politely, stopping himself from answering as he wanted to. He kept it short and sweet, knowing that anything more would drive her away.

And a casual friendliness with Amelia was better than nothing.

Wasn't it?

When the morning of Chad and Lucy's wedding dawned, Creed vacillated between eagerness to be near Amelia for an entire day and dread.

Late in the afternoon, Creed and Chad stood in the chapel in their suits, posing stiffly for picture after picture, waiting until Lucy was ready to join them. Creed had caught snatches of Amelia as she fast-walked through the halls in baggy black sweats and a button-down flannel shirt, her hair caught up in large curlers, a clipboard in her hands. She was all business an hour before when he handed Izzie over to disappear in a room brimming with tulle and flowers.

Now his heart pounded with anticipation to be near her, even if it was just to pose for pictures.

You're really pathetic, Williams, you know that?

Chad fidgeted, and Creed remembered his role. He clapped a hand on his brother's shoulder.

"You okay, man?"

Chad flashed a shaky smile at him. "I'm just anxious to see my bride."

Movement at the back of the chapel caught Creed's eye. Amelia was waving him over. His chest clenched pleasantly.

"Looks like your wait might be over," Creed answered, pointing to Amelia and hitting Chad lightly on the stomach with the back of his hand as he passed. "Be right back."

Amelia's face softened as Creed approached. She had changed into a silver dress that fit her modestly in all the right places. Her hair was swept back with sparkly clips on each side and hung down her back in rolling waves. His hands itched to run through the long tendrils, remembering the silky texture.

"You look…beautiful."

Was that his husky voice? He was surprised he could even force the words past his dry throat. He hated this awkwardness, longed to talk to Amelia like he always had. Longed for it to be…different, somehow.

But she was dating Aaron now. He saw them talking and laughing together at church, knew that they hiked together often—Aaron was one of those guys that obnoxiously posted pictures on Facebook. Creed would have hidden him weeks ago if not for the chance to see Amelia's smile on the feed. Amelia hiking in her cute knit hat. Amelia smiling in the ski lodge with a cup of hot chocolate cupped between her hands. Okay, so there had only been two pictures, not exactly proof of a romantic relationship. Still.

Amelia blushed, the glow in her eyes breathtaking.

"Thanks. Um," she bit her lip, but a smile escaped, squeezing her eyes into slits. She looked down and pressed two fingers to her temple. After a minute she regained her composure.

"Anyway, can you let the photographer know that Lucy's ready? And then meet me in the hall behind the stage, okay? We'll wait there until they're ready for us."

Her eyes searched his and then she was gone.

Chad and Lucy had chosen to get formal pictures out of the way before the wedding, but wanted their first moments together that day to be special. It had been Amelia's idea to have the photographer capture the look on Chad's face when he saw Lucy for the first time.

Creed couldn't deny the bounce in his step as he delivered the message and found the door behind the stage. It led to a narrow set of stairs curving down from the built-in baptismal. Amelia arrived a moment later, entering from the door at the bottom of the stairs. She left it ajar to offer them some faint light and stepped closer to him. Her fragrance filled the small space and Creed breathed in deep.

"I told them we would wait in here until they call us back," Amelia whispered. "I just wanted to um, well." She cleared her throat. "I just wanted to tell you I'm sorry, Creed. For everything. For overreacting a while ago and being so ridiculous. I've done a lot of praying and growing in the last six weeks and I just wanted you to know how bad I feel about…everything."

"Amelia, there's nothing to forgive. If anyone should apologize it's me. I've been wanting to tell you...Well, I just want to say..." He shrugged. "I miss my friend."

"I miss you too, Creed," she whispered. But something about the way she held herself away from him, and the hesitancy in her voice told him there was more. Maybe she really was getting serious with Aaron.

"Where's Izzie?" Creed thought to ask.

The faint light illuminated her smile. "With my mom. They're having a great time painting their toenails," she answered. "Lucy thought the kids would get bored with pictures, so we'll work them in at the very last. Good thing they have such a small wedding party; this should go pretty quickly."

They waited a moment in awkward silence.

Before he could stop himself Creed said, "Looks like you and Aaron are getting pretty close."

A pause. "He's a nice guy."

Another few minutes ticked by. Amelia shifted to lean against the railing and her arm brushed against his. He willed her to stay put, nearly groaning in protest when she didn't.

You're a special kind of jerk, aren't you, Williams? Wanting to touch and hold another man's woman. She's taken, remember? Because you were too complicated. You kissed her and disappeared. Twice. No kitten is going to erase that. She deserves a guy like Aaron. The admission curdled his insides.

"Amelia—"

"We're all ready for you guys," the photographer poked his head in the stairwell. Amelia left Creed standing alone, wanting. Wishing. Full of regret.

Chapter Forty-One

Why had she implied that she and Aaron were dating?

Um, because you're a wuss? No, because Aaron had told her to let Creed think that. Why did she listen to him?

It had been almost two months since their kiss in his car. Even less time since their fleeting moment of easy banter the night before Thanksgiving.

She'd barely talked to him other than polite "hellos" since he watched her leave her parents' house on Thanksgiving night with Aaron. It was obvious he thought that she had finally moved on. And isn't that what she wanted him to believe? That she was no longer the pathetic woman sitting at home pining and planning for her future husband?

Amelia let the photographer position her next to Lucy, awed at the joy and love on her sister's face. Thirty minutes and four thousand pictures later, Amelia's face began to hurt. Her toes pinched. Stupid heels. She didn't know how much longer she could keep from gazing at Creed, and they had hours left to go before she could call it a night. She chanced another peak at him while the photographer checked the lighting.

Creed looked striking in his black suit and cranberry cummerbund. His hair had been recently cut, the ends mussed with gel. When the photographer instructed Amelia to stand in front of Creed on the step just beneath him, she shivered at the feel of his broad chest against her back. His spicy scent enveloped her and she fought to keep her smile straight.

How she made it through the rest of the pictures and the preparation for the ceremony without fainting was entirely a miracle.

* * *

Within minutes of the family pictures being complete, the guests began to arrive and Amelia whisked Lucy away. Creed gave last minute instructions to Lucy's brothers who were acting as ushers. As he turned away to head back to the front, a couple near the back caught his eye.

Aaron and a woman Creed recognized from church— Melody? Molly?—entered together. Creed's jaw clenched tight. Aaron stood awfully close to her for a man that was supposed to be with Amelia. When Aaron leaned down to brush a tender kiss against the woman's temple, Creed felt cold and hot all over. Seriously? Right here at the wedding of Amelia's sister? Of all the—

Wait.

He knew Aaron. Was in a Bible study with him a few years back. He wasn't that kind of guy. So the only explanation was…

Understanding dawned.

Amelia and Aaron weren't together. The realization struck Creed with blunt force. But why hadn't she corrected him earlier? Why had she stayed away? Questions assaulted him, raced each other around his mind until he was dizzy.

Soft piano music began to play and the lights went soft.

Creed all but growled under his breath. Now was not the time. It was Chad's day and Creed only hoped he could remember that when he stood facing Amelia at the front of the candlelit chapel.

* * *

As Amelia walked down the aisle, she couldn't help but appreciate the twinkle lights wrapped in tulle along the edges of the aisle, the soft runner beneath her feet, the way intermittent candles reflected off the gold and silver ornaments on the evergreen trees that flanked the stage.

307

But when she lifted her eyes to chance a look at Creed, her breath caught in her lungs. He watched her with fixed intensity, his eyes drawing her to him like the pull of the moon on the tide. She barely remembered to veer left when she reached the end of the aisle.

Heat crawled up her neck as she took her place and waited for Lucy, sneaking one more glance Creed's way. His face was turned toward her but the music swelled and Amelia fixed her gaze on her sister. She didn't dare look Creed's way again.

When the ceremony was complete, Amelia met Creed in their practiced spot, looping her arm through his. He leaned close as they neared the end of the aisle, his words for her ears alone.

"Save a dance for me?"

He cupped his free hand over the fingers holding his firm bicep, trapping her in his grip at the end of their walk. Amelia nodded numbly and he squeezed once before letting go.

For the rest of the evening, Amelia managed to avoid him. There was a bride to look after, slight hiccups in the reception to iron out. Her feet were screaming and her head pounded with tension by the time Creed trapped her next to the cake table. She ignored him, nodding politely to an older woman as she handed her a fork.

"I'm here to collect on my dance," Creed murmured in her ear. He settled a hand at her waist.

"I'm needed here, Creed. I'm so sorry," she said, smiling apologetically. Never mind that there was a caterer being paid to take care of it.

Creed eyed the table of already plated pieces of cake and the mason jars full of plastic forks.

"I think the guests are more than capable of picking up a plate and selecting a fork by themselves. Come on," he tugged her gently.

Seeing no way out, Amelia allowed herself to be led to the dance floor. The lights turned down and Lady Antebellum's *Just a Kiss* began to play over the speakers. Amelia's heart stuttered in her chest, threatening to leave her altogether. She licked her lips and set her hands on Creed's shoulders, arms as straight as she could make them without being obvious.

Creed twisted his lips. "Leaving room for the Holy Spirit?"

"Haha…ha," she chuckled nervously.

Creed tightened his hold on her waist. "Or maybe you're afraid Aaron will be jealous?" Creed asked, directing his gaze to someone behind her.

Amelia followed his eyes to Aaron and his new girlfriend, Molly, on the dance floor just beside them. He had tucked his nose into her neck, pressed so close Amelia was certain it would take an earthquake to break them apart. And even then…

Fabulous.

She turned back to Creed.

He waited, one brow cocked.

"Yeah, so…he's just a friend," she said lamely. "That's his girlfriend Molly. She's really great," Amelia added unnecessarily. She cleared her throat. He tilted his head, questioning.

"So…okay. Then, where have you been? I thought you distanced yourself because you and Aaron were…" his voice trailed, thick as molasses. He swallowed. "But, you're not. So why did you disappear, Amelia?"

She stared at his collar. He'd long ago shed his suit coat and cummerbund, unbuttoned the first few buttons of his shirt and rolled up his sleeves. Amelia's hands had slipped slightly from his shoulders down the length of his muscular arms. The hair on his forearms tickled her elbows. He pressed an open palm against the small of her back. She sucked in a breath when he cupped the side of her face with his other hand and tilted her face up to meet his gaze.

She tried for cute, light. "You disappeared first, buddy."

The smile that split his face knocked her knees. "Buddy?"

He was asking, of course, if they could just go back to how things were. And though her heart was fragile—could shatter with just one weak moment—she couldn't say no. Because a friendship with Creed was better than no Creed at all. Even if someday she had to listen while he fell in love with someone else, if he never cared for her in that way, it was worth the risk.

Could he tell that she was holding her breath? "Yeah."

They danced a few more songs, the tension of the last few months slowly evaporating. They gave their best man and maiden of honor speeches before finally sitting down to enjoy the delicious buffet. Amelia kicked off her shoes and vowed to never put heels on again.

"Too bad, Howard," Creed commented, pushing away from the table and reaching for her feet. "Because your legs looked killer in those things." He nodded to the heels as he lifted her feet onto his lap, careful not to tangle the bottom of her calf length dress.

Amelia groaned deep when he knuckled the bottom of her foot. "You're officially my favorite person," she murmured. "And I don't care how my legs look. Heels and I are done. Over. Kaput. No more."

310

Izzie ran up to the table, her Mary Jane shoes clapping noisily on the wood floor.

"Daddy! Miss Amelia! It's snowing!" She had a ring of chocolate around her lips and her curls stuck up more than usual. Amelia gasped in delight and pulled her feet from Creed's lap, hurriedly toeing her swollen feet back into the pumps.

Creed laughed. "I thought you and heels were done," he called after her as she nearly tripped over her dress in her excitement.

"That's before snow was involved!" she shouted back.

Chapter Forty-Two

Christmas came and went. Creed and Amelia rekindled their friendship—mostly through text messages, though they had gone to lunch after church a few times, always with Izzie. Twice Creed had called her after Izzie had gone to bed and they talked for hours about nothing and everything. The day after Christmas she had joined Creed and Izzie on a sledding trip in the mountains. His heart pounded whenever she was near, and he had a hard time concentrating with the cold painting her cheeks a delicious pink, but he kept his feelings to himself. No way was he going to scare her off again. But that didn't mean he wasn't holding out hope that he could eventually bring the subject back around, even if it took years of him showing her that he was sticking around this time.

A few days after the wedding, Creed had looked through his storage and found Amelia's letters. He sat down and read every one, then purposefully answered each and every letter. He said the things he should have been bold enough to say ten years before, then tucked them into an envelope. He didn't know if there would ever be a time he could give them to her, but he prayed often for it.

After the fourth snow storm since Christmas and a third snow day in a row was called after the long holiday break, Kate called to ask if she could have Izzie for the night.

"We're losing our minds over here, but at least my kids have each other to play with. I was thinking I could take them all to that indoor trampoline place and out to lunch tomorrow."

Creed was more than happy to oblige. He could only make so many snow forts in one week. In the weeks since Christmas there had been a record snowfall in their area and the natives were most definitely getting restless. Even

Amelia, who had been staunchly enthusiastic about the back to back snowstorms. Until now.

Being a homeowner officially stinks. What was I thinking? she texted soon after Izzie had left with Kate.

Creed smirked. **I thought you loved your new house.**

That was before snow was involved! she texted back.

Not so fun anymore?

His phone dinged five times in a row. His mouth ticked up. She was feeling chatty. But when he opened the texts he sat up, worried.

My arms are killing me from shoveling. I've never shoveled so much in my life! So far I have only had to shovel a path to my car, but the Forresters' are gone. They've been using farm equipment to keep their road and mine clear. I tried to dig myself out today but it's taking FOREVER. And my car is too low and will definitely get stuck. Oh well. Enough complaining. If I say one negative word about the heat this summer throw something at me, will you?

You're stuck? He shook his head.

Of course she's stuck, stupid. All she has is that little sedan. He had seen numerous cars stuck in the thick snow on side streets, had even helped push a few out. He had never been more thankful for his small SUV as he was that winter. He knew of many people that were stuck at home simply because they couldn't get out of the driveway.

Yes. Very stuck. But it's OK. I have snacks and Gilmore Girls on Netflix and a snuggly pup and cat. I'll survive.

He didn't answer. Just tied up his snow boots, shrugged his coat on, grabbed his keys and the snow shovel he kept in the coat closet, and locked the door behind him. He unlocked the door and ripped the envelope from the top drawer of the desk, and went back out again.

*   *   *

Tiredly trudging up the stairs to her porch, Amelia opened the front door wide for Olé.

"Come on boy, take a break," she said, watching while he trotted off the porch to the side yard. Sassy sat in the window looking down on Olé while he trotted through the snow.

Amelia had been outside shoveling most of the afternoon. She couldn't stand to sit around her house yet another day and was convinced she could dig her way out. But by the time she reached the road her neighbors normally plowed and realized how far the distance was to the main road, she pooped out.

Olé finished his business and trotted back to where she stood eyeing the wood pile. A fire would be good for her sore muscles—not to mention her heating bill—but she suddenly didn't have the energy to lift a single log. Olé leaned into her.

"Spoiled dog," she muttered, ruffling up his ears lovingly. "If you really loved me you would find a way to get me a bbq chicken pizza."

The muted groan of tires trudging through the thick snow pulled her back toward the driveway. She squinted but didn't recognize the car right away. Her eyes widened as Creed's Honda came into view.

She stood numbly on the front porch, waiting while he parked.

"Creed, what on earth—"

She cut off as he exited the car with a large pizza box in his hands. His grin warmed her to her toes. "I heard there was a damsel in distress at this address and I assumed she was in need of pizza."

She laughed as he came closer, bringing the spicy sweet smell of bbq chicken, red onions, and yeast with him.

"My hero," she swooned, titling her head and fanning her lashes at him.

She took the pizza from him and led the way inside. Her eyes swept the room quickly, checking for discarded unmentionables because that is exactly the kind of embarrassing scenario that would play out just then. Her house was pristine, of course. After being holed up for the last few days, she'd spent most of her time deep cleaning.

Amelia set the pizza box on the table and reached into the sideboard for plates and napkins. "You want a soda?" She asked.

Creed turned slowly, looking around her house.

"Creed?"

He faced her. "Your house is so…you, Amelia. I don't know if I told you that the last time I was here. You've done well for yourself."

The pride in his voice embarrassed her. She walked to the kitchen and retrieved two ginger ales and two water bottles, since he hadn't answered her.

"If you keep showing up unannounced with presents, you just might spoil me, Creed."

When she came back he was seated at one of the benches at her table, his coat discarded and draped over the arm of her sectional.

She took the bench opposite of him and opened the pizza box, delighted to see diced tomatoes on their favorite pizza.

"See? You spoil me, Creed."

One corner of his mouth curled up, but he didn't comment. They ate, discussing the crazy weather and record days off of school.

"I was just getting to know my new class. I hope I can reign them back in after all these days off," she said.

Creed asked about school and that led to other topics. When they'd eaten their fill, Creed leaned back with a satisfied smile, and wiped his mouth with a napkin.

"Okay," he said. "I know I invited myself over, and I should do the polite thing and go home now, but honestly, all I can think about is starting a fire."

Amelia perked up. "Really? That would be amazing. My arms were too tired to bring in wood. And I'm going stir crazy our here by myself." She scrunched her nose. "But do you care if I go clean up real quick? I feel like a sweaty mess."

He lifted his chin. "Go. I'll clear the table and get that fire going. Where are your matches?"

"In the vase on the mantle."

"Perfect. Now get out of here."

Amelia grinned. If she weren't so sore, she would have sprinted up the stairs.

Chapter Forty-Three

Creed stacked pieces of wood from the porch on balled up pieces of newspaper he found in a wooden crate next to the hearth. It only took a few matches to get the fire going and he leaned back on the plush rug. Though he wasn't cold, he felt a shiver.

There was a charge in the air. Maybe the cold. Maybe being called her hero. Maybe his impulsive decision to bring the letters with him? Whatever it was, he felt change coming.

And could only pray it wouldn't end in heartache.

The stairs creaked and he turned just as Amelia stepped off the last one. Her hair was piled high on her head in one of those messy buns. His eyes swept her form, appreciating her black leggings and fitted plum t-shirt wrapped in a long grey cardigan.

Just like that his shiver came back.

Amelia came to sit next to him, her lilac and vanilla scent sweeping around him. They sat in contented silence, watching the flames dance and spark.

"I'm surprised they were dry enough for you to start," Amelia commented. "I need to build a wood shed or something this spring. I had to dig those out of the snow this morning. Hear them sizzle?"

Creed could only hear the pounding of his heart at the moment.

"They didn't seem frozen," he finally thought to say.

"I chopped them in smaller pieces to speed up the process," she answered, sitting tall.

"*You* chopped them?"

"Sure did. Who needs the gym?" She curled her arm up to let him feel the flexed muscle.

He wrapped his hand around her offered arm, appreciating the firm cut of her bicep. "Hmmm...I definitely feel muscles. You're a strong woman, Amelia."

She grinned. "Darn right." When he didn't let go, the smile fell from her eyes.

"I mean it, Amelia. You're a strong woman." His lips curled softly. "I'm really proud of you." He slipped his hand from her arm, let it fall into the space between them.

She blushed, though it could have been the firelight. "Thank you."

They leaned back on their hands, legs straight toward the flames. He clenched his jaw. He couldn't think of anything to say. At least nothing platonic. He could think of a dozen things he would tell her if only—

"Creed?" She turned toward him, the fire dancing in shadow and light across her face, accentuating her smooth skin. The window on the wall behind her framed a cotton candy pink sky.

"Hmm?"

"This will work, right? You and me? Just friends?" She drew her legs close to her chest, wrapping her arms around them, nestling her chin on top and refusing to look away from the fire.

Friends. The word hit like a sucker punch. He struggled to answer. To say, "Yes, of course," but he couldn't work the words past his dry throat. He just stared at the flames, chest rising and falling, unable to say anything.

Finally, "Well..." *Well? That's what you got out, you idiot? Well?*

And then, entirely without permission, "Amelia, I know we got off track, but I really do care for you. I don't see why we can't be more."

He chanced a glance at her.

* * *

Her eyes stung and she blinked rapidly, refusing to allow the tears to form.

"To what end, Creed?" she whispered.

He blinked. "What do you mean?"

She gathered her courage from the torn pieces of her heart. "Creed, all I get from anything beyond friendship here is heartache. In high school, the years following…and now."

He swallowed hard, the flames raking over his handsome face, shadows hiding in the hard lines of his jaw and cheekbones. She hated to hurt him, especially when he'd been through so much. But.

"I'm sorry, Creed. I care for you. A lot. Much more than I've cared for anyone in my life." She placed a hand against his cheek, her stomach quavering when he closed his eyes and leaned slightly into her touch. He opened his eyes again, pools of chocolate swirled with caramel.

"But, it hurts too much to be anything more than your friend. I can't."

Tears rolled down her face. Up until now it had been okay. She could still see Creed, dance around the awkwardness between them, pursue their easy banter and fun outings with Izzie all while hoping that maybe…

But he didn't want her. Not really. She was a pleasant distraction, a dance with his past. She couldn't protect her heart from that. It was so much more for her. Always had been.

"I think I've loved you for as long as I've known you. And I think you care about me, are comfortable with me. But you've never felt more for me than maybe a passing attraction," she admitted bravely. "I'm over here falling for Izzie and enjoying the times you two invite me to your little family outings. But I need to be firm now, while I still can, and tell you that I can't play the romance game, okay? I just…can't move forward with our friendship unless we agree on that."

His eyes roamed her face. She closed her own against them and dropped her hand from his cheek.

Probably not getting your point across by caressing the man's face, Amelia.

"I can't be in love alone anymore, Creed."

Embarrassed, she swiped a hand across her face and offered an apologetic smile and shrug. She waved her hand in the air as if she could wipe away the awkwardness.

"Now, how likely am I to talk you into watching *The Never Ending Story* with me?" She rose from the rug and walked across the room to her DVD collection. The sun had set enough that she couldn't see the titles clearly. She sniffed, ignoring Creed's eyes on her and his silence and began to walk across the room to flip on the light. His words stopped her in the middle of the room.

"That's not going to work for me, Howard."

Chapter Forty-Four

He couldn't think straight. Like a pebble thrown into a lake, her words rippled through him, stirring up clouds of memory.

Images of Amelia played through his mind, each taunting, startling in their clarity now: the way she'd always looked at him, always been there. And then she was gone. And then back in his life only to be lost again before he had a chance to show her how he'd changed, how he loved her, too.

The letters.

So, she believed he wouldn't stick around? That was really what this was about. Protecting her heart. And who could blame her? He hadn't been careful with it. And though this time the circumstances had been out of his control, the last two months had ripped open old wounds.

It was time to do what he could to heal them, even if she kicked him out. He wouldn't passively let her slip through his hands again. He stood and began to walk toward her.

"What, the movie choice?" she chuckled nervously as he took a step closer. "We can pick a different one. I just figured you wouldn't want to watch a girly movie and I only have a handful of guy approved films. Let's see, I have—"

"Amelia," he heard the caress in his tone, hoped she did, too.

She turned to him, arms wrapping around her middle as if to ward off an attack. He stopped as close as he dared.

"Sweetie, I can't promise you that. Don't get me wrong; I don't want to risk our friendship. But I…" the words died in his throat when she met his gaze. Her eyes clung to his, searching, hopeful.

Afraid.

"Creed, I refuse to be an idiot any longer."

Idiot. The word stirred something in his mind. He puffed out a laugh and cupped her face in his hands, kissing her soundly on the mouth. She pushed him back.

"Creed, what are you—"

His mouth closed over hers again, hungry; desperate, cutting off her question. He kissed her with a decade worth of pent up hope and piles of regret. He wove his fingers into her hair, feeling her shiver as she gave in to his kiss. Yes, it was impulsive, but she would understand. Just as soon as he could tear himself away from her mouth.

*   *   *

She melted into him, hands clutching the shirt at his waist, desperate to hold on and never let go. She gave in to the moment, accepting all that his lips offered and giving it back in spades.

Amelia, what are you doing? You know how this ends.

She pressed aside the thought, desperate to give in, to throw off hindrances and just be held by Creed, if only for a few moments longer. She had done her best to lay boundaries. What was she to do when a man like Creed pushed right past the barriers she never wanted up in the first place? When he showed up at her door with kittens and pizza?

He was the first to pull back. He slowly drew his lips away and steadied her with a look that made the bottom drop out from beneath her belly. Amelia blinked and stepped back out of his reach, and held a trembling hand to her swollen lips.

"Amelia."

How could he do that? Rouse the butterflies in her stomach with just the whisper of her name on his lips?

"Creed, what are you *doing?*"

"I'll be right back," he said. She blinked at him. What? He was leaving? *Now?*

He set his hands on her shoulders and held her gaze. "Trust me, Amelia. Just trust me." He turned and slipped out the front door.

She shivered despite the warmth of the room. The fire popped loudly behind her, causing her to jump.

She walked a few paces away and reached to click on the lamp on the nearest side table. There was a loud stomping on the front porch before the door groaned behind her. Creed carried in more snow on his shoulders and in his hair; he clutched an envelope in his hand. She folded her arms across her stomach to ward off the pain she instinctively knew must be coming. She walked to the couch and dropped onto the cushions.

Creed watched her sit and followed to kneel before her, his hands resting on her knees.

"Amelia, I'm so sorry," he began.

She closed her eyes. An apology right out of the gate couldn't be good, right?

"Amelia, you have shown me more mercy and grace than any man deserves. You have been my rock, my friend. Even in the years we were apart, your friendship and the things I learned from you shaped me into the man that I am. You have always been my dearest friend." He stuttered over that word and for a moment her words from earlier shattered the moment.

"You said it hurts too much to be my friend, but, Amelia, I want so much more."

She shook her head. "No, you don't. Creed. I've loved you for all of these years, but you've never…" she trailed off when he held up the large envelope.

"No, Amelia. That's not true. You are the best friend that I have ever had. Always encouraging, unflinchingly supportive, funny, loving, tender. You didn't let me get away with anything in high school, and I am convinced that's why I fell apart in college. I was lost without you, my best friend. But God showed me incredible grace. First with my wonderful gift, Izzie, and again that night at the reunion when you ran into me. Literally."

Amelia let out a nervous puff of laughter and shook her head, glancing at her lap in embarrassment. Creed reached to hook a finger under her chin and gently lift her gaze back to him. The lamplight illuminated the flecks of brown in his eyes and golden smattering of freckles across his nose.

"That night, Amelia, you received a letter that changed your life. You set out to be different, convinced that you had somehow wasted your life in the way that you lived it. You see a woman that made choices only for the sake of her future husband. I see a woman that was meant to be a teacher, no matter her original reasons for choosing that profession. I see a woman that God preserved for His good purpose."

His hands trembled slightly as he drew a stack of papers from the envelope and unfolded them. He looked up at her and back to the papers.

"I have letters here that I wrote recently—long overdue responses to the ones you wrote to me."

She rounded her eyes at the papers and back to his warm brown eyes. "Oh Creed…" she breathed.

"But there is another letter in here. One that I wrote ten years ago and was also given the night of the reunion. And although unexpected complications and my own stupidity have derailed me a bit the last couple of months, I want to show you that I also set out from the reunion to be different because of the words I wrote to myself ten years ago."

Amelia wrinkled her forehead and leaned forward slightly, wondering what he was talking about.

"This is what I wrote to myself our senior year, Amelia, and I have never felt it to be more true than I do this moment." He cleared his throat and read aloud, "'If in ten years you are not married to Amelia Howard, you are an idiot.'"

Amelia blinked slowly, letting the words sink in. She took the paper from him and stared in amazement at his neat scrawl. The year of their graduation was scratched in the corner. It was true. He wrote that all those years ago.

"But, the last couple of months—"

"Were the second biggest mistake I've made in my life," he breathed. "The first was letting you go in the first place. I should have fought harder, found a way to have you beside me through all of this instead of tucking tail and running."

Amelia's mind buzzed. Creed loved her. Had loved her as long as she had loved him. And he wanted her. Was kneeling here before her with such a glow of adoration in his eyes her breath caught at the wonder of it.

"So what do you say, Amelia?" Creed whispered to her. "You willing to marry me and recue me from my idiot status?"

She closed her eyes, a smile spreading from her heart to her lips. Yes! Her heart soared. How many years had she dreamt of this moment—of a man to love her and ask her to be his alone?

But not just any man would have done. It was Creed she had dreamt of all those years; his face in her mind as she wrote letters to him and made plans for their future. And then he came back into her life and the Lord wrecked all of her deliberate, ridiculous plans.

He showed her that He was her hope, her only joy.

And because He loved her, he also led her back to Creed. Her one true love. And to his daughter, a little girl she loved and longed to claim as her own. What a wonder it all was. And how foolish she had been to hide from it.

She leaned forward slightly, suddenly sure she couldn't go another minute without his lips on hers, without his arms wrapped around her. One corner of his mouth ticked up, reading her look, relishing it. He slowly met her lips. She savored his taste, shivered from the pleasure of his unspoken promises.

He pulled back. "Is that a yes?"

A bubble of laughter escaped and she kissed Creed again and again. "Yes, Creed. But on one condition: you let Izzie be our ring bearer. I made her a promise, after all." She leaned back and arched a coy brow at him.

His grin stretched and he shook his head, eyes clouded in wonder.

"I love you Howard. And I can't wait to start a new life with you and make you a Williams."

"Oh, Creed," she whispered, leaning to touch her forehead to his. "Yes. Let's make a life here. Let's seek the Lord's will for you and Izzie and me for the rest of our lives."

As her arms came around his neck, Creed stood and lifted her from the couch, hugging her tight around the middle, his lips never leaving hers. Sassy meowed and wrapped

326

herself around Amelia's leg, purring. Amelia smiled against Creed's kisses thinking of the verse she had underlined in her Bible that morning:

"For I know the plans I have for you,' declares the LORD, 'plans for welfare and not for calamity to give you a future and a hope.'" Jeremiah 29:11

Acknowledgments

My Lord and my God. Once again You have let me write a story and been with me for every twist and turn. Thank You for Your love and generosity with your people.

My handsome lumberjack hubby, there is no one else I want to do this crazy, messy, beautiful life with. Your unyielding support of me is astounding. Long live the red beard!

My wonderful daughters, thank you for letting Mommy write…and being (mostly) okay that you can't read it. We'll talk when you're allowed to date—so when you're forty.

Mom and Dad Brown, your support has carried me through so many years. Thank you for reading this, for the technical support as well as emotional, and for encouraging me always. And Dad, let's pretend you didn't read the kissing scenes, okay?

Katie Brown, my favorite roommate, long-time friend, and now wise and wonderful editor. Thank you, thank you, thank you. Your suggestions made the book exceptionally better—I'm so glad I finally got brave enough to let you read it.

Lisa, Lynn, Jeni, Angie, and Amanda. Thank you for reading this. For your tips and your encouragement. I am filthy rich with friends like you

Mike and Debbie Sloane, thank you for answering so many questions about the publishing process. Can't wait to work with you and the rest of the NCC Publishing team soon.

Author's Notes

Thank you for reading *Trending*. I hope you enjoyed Amelia and Creed as much as I did when they first introduced themselves to me.

I honestly can't tell you where this story came from. I only know that I was the girl in high school underlining, dog-earing, and making notes in dating books just like the ones Amelia read. I definitely didn't go to the extremes that Amelia did, but I have had my moments of planning my life out only to look around and see that God has taken me completely off that path.

And I can say with full assurance that His path is always better. I hope as you go through your days you will fully rely on Him and follow His lead. I imagine He just can't wait until we meet Him at the curve and we finally see all that He has been planning.

If you have time, a review on Amazon goes a long way for authors and I always appreciate feedback. My other books, *The Earth is Full* and *The Heavens are Telling*, are published under B.D. Riehl and also available on Amazon.

Thank you ☺

54099756R00207

Made in the USA
San Bernardino, CA
07 October 2017